I, WALTER

By Mike Hartner

– I, Walter –

Copyright © 2013

Eternity4Popsicle Publishing

Vancouver, BC

Library and Archives Canada Cataloguing in Publication

Hartner, Mike, 1965-
    I, Walter [electronic resource] / Mike Hartner.

Electronic monograph.
Issued also in eBook and audio versions.
ISBN 978-0-9733561-5-1 (Print)
ISBN 978-0-9733561-3-7 (eBook)
ISBN 978-0-9733561-4-4 (Audio)

    I. Title.

PS8565. A6686I83 2013 C813'. 6 C2013-901061-0

This is a work of fiction. Names, characters, businesses, places, events and incidents are either the products of the author's imagination or used in a fictitious manner. Any resemblance to actual persons, living or dead, or actual events is purely coincidental.

– Mike Hartner –

Chapter 1

"I, Walter Crofter, being of sound mind. . . ." Bah, this is garbage! I tossed my quill on the parchment sitting in front of me. People may question my sanity, but they should hear the whole story before judging me. I'm sitting here, now, at the age of 67, trying to write this down and figure out how to tell everything. I don't know if I'll ever get it right, though. Too many secrets to go around. However, this is my last chance to offer the truth before I die. The doctors say it's malaria, yet I'll be fine. Perhaps. But if the malaria doesn't kill me, my guilt indeed will. Maybe if people know the facts surrounding my life, everyone will have a better understanding.

I dipped the tip in the inkwell again, and wrote:

I was born September 2, 1588, and named Walter. I didn't belong in this Crofter family, who were storekeepers in London and not farmers as our surname might indicate to those who study this sort of thing. My parents were courteous and even obsequious to our patrons. Yet they received little or no respect. The ladies came to us to buy their groceries or the fabric for their dresses, but as seemly as they comported themselves, and some even called my father 'friend,' it was not out of regard for him. I was forced to run. Well, "forced" might put too harsh a point on it, like that of a sword, but others can judge for themselves.

By the time I reached the age of 12, I'd found another family that was more "me". They weren't rich, but they were comfortable. The parents had several children, including a girl my age who was named Anna. Within two years, we had come to know each other quite well, and were getting to know each other even better. Her father caught us getting too close to knowing each other better yet, and showed up at my parents' house with a musket in his hand, telling them if I ever came near his daughter again, he'd use it on me--and then on them.

I paused to dip the pen and wipe my brow. Even though I was wearing a light cotton shirt, it was bloody hot in early August in Cadaques. My wife, Maria, entered the room and looked at my perspiring face and what I had just written. Between fits of laughter, she smiled at me with wide lips and said, "You can't possibly write this. You're not the only boy a doting father ever had to chase away. Nobody cares about this sort of thing."

"It will at least give a pulse to this writing," I replied. "It's too boring to say I left because I was mismatched with my own family, so much so that I was positive someone had switched me at birth. Or that I thought I was ready for more in life than what I could find at home. Nobody would read that, not even me."

"I agree, so tell the story that really means something. All of it." She sighed softly and placed the parchment she had been reading on the desk in front of me and kissed my cheek. The gleam in her eyes shed 20 years off her age and reminded me of a much gentler time. God, how much I love her.

I said, "Before I met you, I spent my life like a square peg trying to fit in a round hole. I'm just trying to make my story more interesting."

"I've heard the accounts of your life before you met me. Or I should say found me. It was anything but boring. So, if you insist on including in the story lines like those you just wrote, make sure they're the only ones. If you don't, I'll consider adding my own material." She winked. "You know I've had good sources."

She turned and walked away, laughing loudly as I called after her, "Yes, dear."

I dipped the quill and put it to parchment again.

In my earliest days, I remember my father, Geoff, being a bit forceful with other people. I also recall my brother Gerald, nearly five years my senior, and myself being happy. Or at least as contented as two boys could be who were growing up in the late 1500s in England, and working every day since their seventh birthdays. It was a time when boys were earning coin as soon as they could lift or carry things. The money could never be for themselves, however, but for the parents to help pay the bills.

Father lived as a crofter should. He was an upright man and sold vegetables off a cart like his grandfather did, and he also dabbled in selling fine fabric for the ladies of status.

One afternoon, when I was eight years old, my brother came home and got into a heated debate with my father about something. When I ran to see what was the matter, they hushed around me, so I never got the full gist of the argument. But whatever it was about, it was serious, and the bickering continued behind my back for five straight days. When I awoke on the morning of the sixth day, Gerald was no longer at home. And he never came back.

Soon afterwards, my father lost enthusiasm for his business and became generally passive. I assumed this was because of Gerald's leaving, and only on occasion would I see flashes of my dad's former self.

At the start of my tenth year, our family moved closer to London. We rented the bottom floor of a three-story building in which several families lived in the upper floors. My father said we relocated because he needed to be closer to more business opportunities. But my mom didn't believe he'd made the right decision, since he was now selling food out of a cart and not inside a storefront. One night, she greeted him at the door when he came home. She was wearing a frown and a dress that had seen better days.

"Did you bring in any decent money?" she asked him before he had time to take off his coat.

"I told you, it will take some time. It's not easy to make good money these days."

"Especially when you let the ladies walk all over you."

"I know, I know. But what am I to do when they aren't running up to me to buy what I'm selling?"

– I, Walter –

"You at least bring home some food for us?" My father had carried in a bag under his arm.

"It's not much, a few carrots and some celery." He handed her the bag.

"What about meat?"

"We're not ready for meat yet."

"That's true enough," my mother said. "But you should at least try to feed your family. Walter's growing, and so are our other children."

"Leave me be, woman. I'm doing the best I can for now." He sat in his chair, leaned his head against the wall, and fell asleep.

That same debate played out between my parents for the next two years. Except for the summer months, when food was plentiful; then the arguments subsided. But for the rest of the year, especially during the winter, the same discussions about money continued on a daily basis, and they were often quite heated. I lost two younger siblings during those two years. One during my tenth winter and the other during my eleventh winter. Neither of the children was older than six months. I always suspected hunger as the primary cause of their deaths.

Just before my twelfth birthday, my father started taking me with him when he went to work. My closest living sibling was nearly six and not feeling well most of the time, and the family needed the money I could bring in by helping my father, who was bland and wishy-washy, particularly when selling fabrics. I had no idea what he was like before, but in my mind his lethargy explained why our family was barely making ends meet. Our lives had become much harder since Gerald left, and part of me blamed him. I'm going to thrash him if I ever see him again and teach him a lesson about family responsibility.

It took me less than a week to realize that the people my father was dealing with, as with those in Bristol, had no respect for him. They regularly talked down to him. Rather than asking the price, they regularly paid what they wanted to pay. And he took it without a quibble. And when he tried to curry favor, he would never get it. His customers looked upon him as a whipping board, at least that's how it seemed to me.

I remember when we got home in the dark after a long day of work in late November, and my mother started in on Dad.

"Well? Have you got the money for me to buy food tomorrow?"

"A little. Here." He fished a guinea from his pocket.

"A guinea? That's it? That won't feed us for a day. You've got to start working harder. With what you earn and what I bring in sewing clothes, we can barely pay the rent, and there is nothing left over to heat this place. And it's going to get colder, Geoff."

"I know, Mildred, I know. I'm trying as hard as I can."

"You haven't worked hard since Sir Walter Raleigh left favor. You can't wait for him forever."

"He'll get favor back. And when he does, I'll be right there helping him. You'll see, we'll be fine again."

She groaned. I was aware that this was not the first time my mother had heard this from my father. It's great talk from a man trying to get ahead. But after several years of the same song, it loses its credibility. She had enjoyed respectability in the early days when my father grabbed the coattails of the then revered Sir Walter Raleigh, and it was hard not having this luxury now. She hadn't planned to be satisfied with being a shopkeeper's wife, and she wasn't even that, at present. She changed the subject, not her tone.

"I overheard the ladies gossiping on the street today. They were talking about seeing Gerald's likeness on a 'Wanted' poster. A 'Wanted' poster, Geoff. There's a warrant out for our son's arrest. What are we going to do? What can we do?"

My father stared at the wall. "Nothing. He's an adult. He'll have to work it out for himself."

I watched quietly as my mother cried herself to sleep, her head on my father's shoulder. No matter how bad things got, they loved each other and wanted their lives to be better, the way I was often told they were before my birth. Maybe this is why I wanted to get away from them as soon as I could.

I didn't usually watch my parents fall asleep. But, that night I did. And, after they were sound asleep, I left. I had no plans. I didn't know where I was going. I just left in middle of what was a dark, chilly night.

I could hear the dogs barking around me as I scurried along the roadside. It felt as if they were yelping at me and coming towards me. I began running, faster than I'd ever sprinted in my life, my speed assisted by my sense of fear. Every time I heard a dog, or an owl, or any other animal, or even my own heavy breathing, my pace increased until I was exhausted and had to stop. This continued throughout the night until the sky started to lighten and I found a grove of overhanging bushes and crawled inside for some sleep.

I scavenged for food during the day and swiped a few pieces of fruit from merchants along the way. This became my means of subsistence. I left a coin when I could, as I'd pick up an occasional odd job, but I was always out of money. I also tried begging, and while I did survive on the street, I found life difficult. Yet for nearly two years I stayed with this vagabond existence before deciding to make my way to the sea. Too bad my internal compass wasn't any good. Turns out I was moving more to the west than to the south. But before long I was on the shores of Bristol. And my life changed forever.

Chapter 2

"Aye, boy, get over here."

I looked around but could see no one. I kept on until I eyed a big man on the ramp to a large ship with many masts. I stared at him. His face, though rugged, showed a lot of integrity, and his blue eyes instantly shone honesty to me.

His arms were the size of large branches, with massive biceps and muscles seemingly coming from other muscles. His chest was broad and sturdy, and while he looked to be only 30 or so years old, I could also see that age was starting to take its toll on him, as he was losing the battle with gravity.

"Aye, boy," he hollered again. "I said get over here."

I went to him.

"Grab that box and take it inside to the captain's quarters."

I did as I was told, not knowing who the captain was or where to go. One of the men on board saw me and showed me where to take the box as he yelled down to the big man, "A little young and scrawny, eh, Bart?"

"At least he's working, ya' old salt!"

I grunted and moaned, hauling boxes all day. They were quite heavy, and while I'd done considerable manual labor in my young life, it hadn't been close to this hard. Later, I started rolling large round barrels filled with salted meats. While I and another eight or nine men were bringing in supplies, an equal number were polishing the brass fittings on the ship. And I watched a half-

– I, Walter –

dozen men doing wood repairs or sewing what I came to know as mainsayles.

At the end of the day, I was told to sit for dinner. While we were waiting for the food, the man named Bart came over to me, laid a paper on the table in front of me, and said, "Sign," as he shoved a quill in my hand.

I did as I was told, and wrote my name "Walter Crofter." He shook my hand as he read my signature and said, "Congratulations, Walter Crofter, ye are now a member of the Royal Marine Merchant Navy. Tomorrow, I take ye to get clothes, and ye real education begins."

It wasn't difficult to sleep that night. But I was roused at an ungodly early hour.

"Get a move on!" came the command from a man I learned was named Coon and called a midshipman. He was yelling and shaking me at the same time. I rose slowly, but dressed quickly and followed him to the galley. We ate a breakfast of hardtack and grog.

Putting the quill down, this memory made me shudder. Grog is a term I will forever use for it, since it was basically everything wet thrown together, and most often it was disgusting. It often contained raw eggs with lemon or orange juice and was spiked with spices. I tasted cinnamon when we were in the Caribbean, and olive juice or oyl in the Mediterranean. I'm pretty sure that the cook spent most of his previous evening gathering all the leftover dinner juices and trying to figure out what else he could put with them to properly torture the stomachs and taste buds of the crew the following morning. Yet, as revolting as it generally was to eat, somehow we all managed to survive it.

Picking the quill up, I dipped it once more into the inkwell.

After the breakfast of hardtack and grog, Bart took me on deck. The skies were gray and overcast, and the breeze was heavy at times, making it seem much colder than it really was. He told me about the ship. Our vessel had three main masts, one in the fore, one in the mid, and one in the aft. Each of them had the riggings for at least five sayles, and they would be large sayles, too. I didn't see the sayles hoisted while I was with him this morning, but I found them later being cleaned and sewed. Coon told me that was one of the things we'd do when we came to port, we would fix the sayles. The sun started to peek out, and it was strangely warm and beautiful. Blue skies were something I had such little experience with, I appreciated it every chance I saw them.

Bart taught me a number of knots and how to tye the various sayles down. He also showed me, with the help of a pair of ensigns named Frog and Cat, how to climb to the crow's nest, and how to walk along the mast branches to tye sayles and let them out properly without falling. Since even the captain on this ship, who I hadn't met yet, didn't want anybody falling, the men rigged a few extra lines as clip supports. A good thing it was, too, since I needed them in the early days. But truth be told, as time passed, sometimes I slipped just for the sheer joy of swinging down on that line.

Bart got me to a shoppe and I was fitted with the right clothes to work in, and before my first full week was over I could walk the mast and get up to the crow's nest with ease. The knots for the sayles were no challenge to tye. Holding one end of the string or rope, the other gets looped once or twice, pushed through the eye either over or under, and cinched. Big deal. Three-year-olds could tye these knots, and would do it without learning what the names were, either.

On the last day of my first week, we got up early with the tide and pulled in the ropes that had been holding the ship fast to the dock. Then, the crew was told to stand shoulder to shoulder in formation. Even these many years later, I still laugh at what I saw. A bunch of greasers from India took up the back row. Many of them wore turbans, and the cook was no different. I learned later that the cook was Christian and from Goa. This allowed him to serve food that was edible without going against his religion. Why he never managed to make said food taste reasonable continues to confound me.

The second line was made up mostly of Asians who appeared to be Chinese. I would later find out that the only Chinaman was the carpenter's assistant. His nickname on board ship was Chippy.

The rest were deck crew, and they propped themselves up with mops and the like. The third row included a man who was called Doc, even though his only credentials were having hands steady enough to sew. Bart was also in that line, as well as the old sycophant he was yelling at when I came on board my first day. I was also in that group. I was told that I was there because it was my first time aboard the ship, and I'd be expected to learn from the senior officers.

A grizzled old man of at least 40 years stood in front of us. His face looked as if he'd been hit many times with a blunt object, and he had a red welt running down his right cheek. One of his legs was wooden; one of his hands was gone. He was dressed in a white shirt, with blue seaman's jacket open at the neck. His belly was well over his belt, the boot that he wore on his good leg was black and matched his felt hat. The only thing, frankly, he was missing was the parrot, and I wouldn't have been surprised to see it either. His coat had a brass plaque with the name "Captain Thomas" on it. In a gravelly voice, he said, "We leave today to trade for the Crown. We'll be stoppin' along the coast of Spain and Italy, but be careful and look out for the French flags. Those ships will have it out for us. Now, me hearties, let's get this ship moving. Hoist them sayles!"

He turned and left as we all scrambled to get the boat in a good wind. I could hear his wooden leg clopping as he entered the stairs to the captain's room. The air was filled with excitement, as was I, since it would be my first time at sea.

***

My first voyage will always remain with me, if only because it was so very different from anything I'd experienced previously in any other aspect of my life. The protected waters of Bristol took a while to sayle clear of. On this morning the clouds were their customary gray, and when we finally made it to more open water, the wind started gusting, making it very cold. The pea jacket I was given, the cost of which I was told would be taken from my pay, offered little buffer from what at times was a gale.

While I worked, I stole constant glimpses of the shoreline, which was lined with stately old trees. I didn't know their names, but I knew they provided ample shade and cover, since I'd slept under their like many times. In the late afternoon, I spotted a castle that was mostly hidden by the same sort of trees. The sky began clearing for the first time that day just as the sun was setting and we were sayling south by southwest and turning into the English Channel.

Two hours of stargazing followed, as I was given lessons by Coon on how to locate Polaris and other stars that would help us guide the boat at night. With that first session out of the way, I ventured off to sleep. This ship was now my place of work as well as my residence. Yet I could never call it 'home,' because something was missing from it.

In the morro, the water was dark, almost as gray as the sky, as if trying to hide its treasures underneath. I knew that there was plenty of life below the veil, but I couldn't confirm or deny it by looking down at the water. I only know that the temperature was a little warmer as we turned into the ocean. Once we left the land, we also left the majority of clouds, which I found odd. Oh, sure, there would be clouds when squalls were coming toward us. But otherwise, the skies would be clear.

The memories were vivid now, as they all kept coming back to me. There were no regrets, just nagging questions. I dipped my quill in the ink again.

Once we were on the open sea, Bart sat me down in front of a table next to the wheelhouse. He showed me the ship's compass and how to use it. Then he brought out something he said was new, called a Davis Quadrant, and explained its function. During the remainder of the voyage, whenever there were spare moments, he'd insist on teaching me more about the use the quadrant, and he provided large maps from the captain's table to work with.

The quadrant was a very interesting device, with a long, straight piece of brass down the middle, and two movable pieces that provided a 90-degree angle, which Bart told me was the reason for its name. The challenge wasn't sighting the ship, it was fixing the stars above it. Approximating the angle wasn't easy either, and when this was determined to the best of my ability, I was still far from finished.

I needed to apply that angle to the map to find our location. Then I had to factor in the time of day, the season of the year, and fifteen other variables. So if looking into the sky on a rolling ship and trying to pinpoint a star and figure out the angle between it and another star wasn't daunting enough, there were so many error factors to consider, it was no wonder the quadrant's effectiveness was far from absolute. And if our true location varied by even a small degree, the ship could be several days off course.

As I was working with the quadrant one evening, Bart was talking with an ensign named Pepper, who was in charge of the cannons and saltpeter, a combination of duties I never understood the reason for to this day. I distinctly heard Bart say, "Aye, and be prepared for pirate attacks." I shuddered at the thought, and wondered whether pirates attacked during the night. Regardless, from that point forward, I was determined to sleep with one eye open.

Chapter 3

I read the last paragraph aloud, smiled, and returned to my writing.

I never really did find any real calm in my life at sea, since there was nary a chance. It didn't help that Bart was more privateer than saylor, and so was the rest of the crew.

On the first trip out, riding a stiff wind, we turned the corner on France, heading due south. Unknown to me until much later, that night we passed across the wake of a schooner flying the French flag that was carrying a declaration of truce with England. Oh, well, it didn't negate what was about to happen. We were sayling along smoothly the next day, when Gimp, one of our midshipmen, approached me. His back was rounded, and one of his legs was shorter than the other; hence, he limped, which accounted for his handle. By his gait and posture, I'd have sworn he was in his forties. His face, however, showed him to be barely beyond his teens.

"Oy, boyo, now that you're a shipmate, there's some other things ye need to learn."

"Like what, sir?"

"Like how ta use a knife, and throw it."

And so, when we got the time in the eve's when I wasn't working with the quadrant, he'd teach me how to hold and throw knives. He also taught me how to flick my wrist and position the hilt for more accurate tosses. Once I understood his instruction, I developed a level of proficiency that surprised Gimp as much as it did me, since before I started working with him, I'd never picked up a knife except to peel an apple.

***

The map said we were about halfway down the French coast when, just after grog and tack, the morning sun helped Crow spot a commercial trader carrying the French flag. This two-masted ship was considerably smaller than ours. Its flag was flying crooked and the sayles were in poor shape, and Crow reckoned it was a crew of local pirates, trading in stolen goods from Spain and Portugal in a boat not meant to ply hard or long trips.

My first adventure at sea turned out to be rather uneventful. We captured the ship with very little effort, as the crew didn't put up much of a fight. The reason that they weren't capable of defending themselves any better was that they'd been on the ocean several weeks longer than planned. And they'd been stuck in calm seas much of that time and had needed to ration food and water for the past seven days.

After feeding the starving crew, we placed the men in our hold and lashed the ships together so we could control both vessels while we sayled. Bart decided we would head for Northern Spain, which was nearly three weeks away. Releasing the crew of pirates to the authorities would earn us a reward, and whatever goods were on board would get us even more money. Bart told me to search the captured craft thoroughly and bring him a list of the inventory.

A chest of money was in the captain's room, but it didn't hold much coin. A logbook sat on a desk, but I ignored it for now and went below to the midship level. Clothes were strewn under the boards used for beds, but I didn't find anything of real value. Whoever this crew was, they hadn't done a very good job of trading, at least for anything worthwhile.

Toward aft, I found some larger boxes and some kegs. A few of these cartons contained very sparse foodstuffs, but most were empty or held cheap cloth. Some more boxes and kegs were stowed on the lower level: More cloth, of better quality this time, with bolts of linen of various dimensions, a few empty wine casks, a store of muskets and ammunition, and one small box with a pittance of coin in it that likely belonged to one of the crew.

Box by box, cask by cask, I moved slowly through the hold. A few hours later, deep in the bow of the boat, I heard a light snuffling noise. My first instinct told me it was a rat. I kept moving, knowing that ships had rats, and I hated the filthy vermin. But I heard the sound again, and this time I didn't think it was made by a rat. So I investigated further, and hiding behind some boxes and shivering uncontrollably, was a girl about my age. This little thing was in tattered clothes, her long brown hair all over her face, and she looked considerably thinner than any of the starved crew. However, behind that tangle of hair and the dirt and ragged garb, I saw great beauty, and as I looked into her deep brown eyes, my heart skipped a beat.

I took off my pea coat and offered it to her. It took a few minutes while she fought against my help, but I was finally able to drape it over her shoulders. I hoped it would help her to stop shivering. It didn't take me long to realize she wasn't cold, she was terrified. I had to hold her tightly to prevent her from running off.

I asked her who she was and where she was going. She said something, but I couldn't understand her. She began crying, and I put a finger to her lips to quiet her.

She started to fight me again. Even in her frail condition, it required quite a bit of effort to control her, since the harder I pulled the harder she resisted me. She didn't want to come from her hiding place, and it was obvious that something or someone had scared her, and quite badly.

To remove her from behind the boxes, I had to pick her up and carry her like a sack of potatoes. She wasn't heavy, but I had to stop several times as she was kicking at me with all her strength while flailing away and biting and scratching me at the same time. Thank goodness I'd given her my pea coat, for *my* protection. When we reached the top deck, I held her tight and stared deeply into her eyes. I don't know why, but she relaxed and stopped fighting me. I clasped her hand in mine and slowly walked her across the plank to our boat.

– I, Walter –

I was wrong. There was something of considerable value on that ship.

I carefully moved her along the deck of our ship, and the crew was more than a little surprised to see a girl with me. I stopped at Bart's door. She jerked her hand away from mine and smoothed down a part of her dress that the wind had blown up. When I brought her in to Bart, the look on his face was one of shock.

"She was hiding in the back of some boxes down in the hold," I told him. "It was a fight to get her here, but I believe it'll be better than leaving her on that ship. She doesn't speak English, so I couldn't even get her name."

"What were you doing on that ship?" Bart asked her in a gentle voice.

She started speaking very fast, but I still couldn't understand a word of what she was saying.

Bart said, "Sounds Spanish or Portuguese. We can find someone in San Sebastian who can interpret what she's sayin'. I planned on docking there anyhow." He smiled at her in a fatherly way. "Let me try and get her name."

"How you going to do that?" I asked.

Bart pointed to himself and slowly said, "Bart." He pointed at me and said, "Walter." He pointed at her and asked, "Señorita?" and raised his eyebrows and opened his hand to her as a sign of friendship.

"Maria Castabel," she said after a pause, but that was all she offered, at least that either of us could understand.

"Aye, now at least we know her name," Bart said.

"Can I get her some food from Cookie? From here on out, until we find where she belongs, I'll take responsibility for her."

He waved us both off and out of his room. But as we were leaving, he asked me to tell two ensigns I knew to report to his office. One man was called Crab by the crew because he moved across the deck like a crab sidling from point to point. The other ensign was three inches taller than me and the spitting image of a willow tree, so tall and thin that I swear if he turned to his side he'd be invisible to most people who weren't looking straight at him. We called him Fatboy just for the irony.

I hollered to them, "Hey, Crab, Bart wants to see you. You, too, Fatboy."

They would be stationed on the captured ship until we made port.

Towing the boat made the journey a bit slower.

I took the girl to the galley for some food. "Eating for two are we now, Walter?" Cookie asked me, a smirk crossing his face.

"I found the poor thing starving. We've got to feed her and get her back to her normal health."

One of the crewmen I'd seen only a few times but had never spoken to pointed to the girl and asked, "Aye, is that our dinner?"

He never saw the right cross coming that laid him out. As I connected with his jaw, I said, "Next time, mind your manners. That's no way to speak about a young girl."

Stunned, he got up, apologized, and we ate a meal of "surprise stew," which was called that for two reasons. The first was because the meat was unidentifiable the way Cookie prepared it; the second because it was a genuine surprise that anyone would call a dish this watered down "stew."

Following the meal, we went up to the midship area, where the large sleeping room was located. I showed her to a windowsill wide enough that she could easily fit on it. I also fashioned a makeshift hammock that I attached to the top beams next to the sill. An extra piece of sayle was all it was, but it worked quite well.

I motioned for her to climb onto the sill. When she did, I indicated to her to curl up and lie down to sleep. That night, and for the rest of the trip, I slept next to her. The first two nights, I remained in the hammock. But by the third night, I was restless and not getting a good night's rest. I moved behind her on the sill. She said nothing and fell asleep easily, as did I.

Neither of us could understand the other's language, but gestures worked. The quarters were cramped, yet she was protected and there was not a chance of anyone's attacking her without going through me. In truth, the odds of that were slim, since I learned later that Bart had put out a warning for the crew not to touch her.

– I, Walter –

By the end of the first week, the two of us were getting to the stage of incidental body contact during our sleep. We were always fully clothed when we went to sleep, so it didn't seem to bother her, and I enjoyed being close to her. I slept better in those few weeks than ever before.

After an early, pre-dawn breakfast--two days into my third week at sea--we docked in San Sebastian, the northernmost port in Spain. As the crew raced to market, Bart and I took the girl to the sheriff, who I prayed spoke English.

I heard the sheriff's gasp when he saw her face.

I asked if he knew of her father and where she lived. He said in English, "Yes, her father is the Don of this whole area. He is patron to all of northern Spain, and he lives only two hours from here."

I asked if he could find me some horses so I could see she got home safely. Bart nodded to him, and he took care of it immediately, his deputy saddling up three of the most beautiful horses I'd ever seen. When I asked about them, he called them quarter horses.

The sheriff volunteered to guide me to what he called a hacienda. I followed him, with Maria seated on a horse next to me. We rode through the rolling green hills of this section of northern Spain. For the first half hour, there was grass everywhere. However, for the next hour and a half, the grass gradually surrendered territory, eventually losing out altogether to scrub.

We were two hours into the trip when we came across a man of considerable stature sitting on a horse. He held up a musket and signaled for us to halt. He then motioned to us to come toward him. As we got closer, he saw the sheriff's badge or recognized Maria, I didn't know which, and gestured wildly for us to pass. Maria grabbed the reins from me and kicked her horse in the ribs. It galloped in front of the sheriff and me, and she soon reached her father's hacienda just as he appeared at the door. She jumped off the horse and embraced him, as the sheriff and I followed her into the yard, but at a respectful distance.

The sheriff and I heard her chattering rapidly to her father as we dismounted. While the father was taking a good hard look at me, the sheriff said, "Maria is telling the Don that the ship he originally sent to bring her from the British islands was attacked and captured by pirates, who took her prisoner and stole the merchant goods on the other ship. They'd stayed out in the ocean to avoid capture by ships along the coast, but then the winds stopped and the ship couldn't move, and when the food started to run out, they were forced to come closer to shore. But it was too late; their food had been gone for about a week when your ship captured theirs. The pirates were too weak to fight, and *you* alone were responsible for saving her.

Her father is now telling her that one of the crew from the original boat Maria was on had sent a letter to him saying that everyone on that voyage save him was dead, including Maria. The Don is telling her he never gave up hope, not wanting to believe she was dead. Now, as you see, he is weeping, and so is Maria."

After several minutes, the father and daughter gained their composure and approached the sheriff and me. The Don was a few inches taller than I was at the time, and he walked with an air of authority and confidence. He talked to the sheriff for quite a while and then turned to me. He spoke in broken English that the sheriff helped him with.

"My name is Juan Carlos Manuel Rivera Castabel. My family has lived on this land for several hundred years. I'm prepared to give it *all* to you, because of your heroics in bringing my daughter safely home to me. She is worth more than all of my land and everything else I own combined."

I put down the quill and wiped my brow. Unless a person has been in a similar situation, it's impossible to understand the emotion associated with a statement such as that. Such emotion, such love, such caring.

I dipped the quill once more, and remembered.

I looked at the man and then at the sheriff and said, "Please tell Mr. Castabel that I'm honored and touched by his offer. But taking responsibility for his daughter was the very least I could do. And returning her safely to him has been an honor. I do not want or need his money, because doing the right thing is its own reward." I wondered where all that came from, and bowed.

Don Castabel bowed to me in kind and came forward to shake my hand. He gripped it tightly, and then hugged me and kept repeating the word "Gracias." Even I understood its meaning, and at that moment it was I who was close to crying. I was able to fight off the emotion, but it wasn't easy.

He bade us all inside. His hacienda was a one-story construction, generous in length and considerable in width. The dining room was huge, bounded by the kitchen on one side, three glass windows on another, a hall to the servant's quarters on a third side, and a wide opening to the main living area. The quality of the furnishings and the tableware only further confirmed that Juan was an aristocrat, and that if I ever wanted to be worthy of his daughter, I would need to work very hard.

We ate a hearty lunch with him before I announced it was time for me to return to my ship. Maria gave me a long hug and brief kiss and said, "Gracias." The moisture in her eyes and her soft lips made me believe that she might feel something for me. I knew I felt something grand for her. She turned to the sheriff and he translated, "Please come to see us again as soon as you can, and you must let us show you our thanks for what you have done."

The Don watched with a wry smile. He insisted that I carry a pouch and a letter back with me. How was I supposed to refuse this man? I waited for him to write the letter, then bowed and shook his hand, and with the sheriff translating, I said, "I promise to come back as soon as I possibly can."

The sheriff laughed as he translated Don Castabel's reply. "You'd better. For both me *and* Maria."

On our way back into town, it seemed that we were racing the sunset. Fortunately, we arrived just before dusk turned to dark.

As I was about to head to the ship, the sheriff told me, "Don Castabel has insisted, no matter where you stay in this town, or where you eat, I'm to inform the merchant to put the charges on his bill. He has instructed me to tell you that you're to be given a great deal more money than what is in that pouch. You obviously aren't aware of how much you have affected him by doing the honorable thing."

I returned to the boat and helped load on another week's worth of fruit before nightfall halted the crew's labors. Before I went to my bed, I stopped at Bart's office.

"Aye, Walter." He paused, obviously expecting me to say something. When I didn't, he asked, "Well, how did it go?"

"The girl's father offered me all of his land and more for bringing his girl back to him."

Bart's eyes widened at my remark.

"I said no, of course. How could I take anything from him for bringing his daughter safely back to him? Isn't that the right thing to do? And isn't it enough of a reward to see them reunited? He shook my hand and thanked me, and Maria kissed my cheek. What more could I ask for? But then, when I was ready to return, he gave me this pouch and letter, which I guess I'm to give to you."

I turned my back to leave, but Bart said, "Stay while I open 'em."

From the bag, he poured gold coin out onto the table. When we counted, there were 50 of them. He placed them back in the pouch. Fifty gold pieces would buy a home or business. Even a large house in Devon wouldn't cost more than 90 gold pieces.

He then turned to the letter and broke the seal. He found that it was written in Spanish, so he spent some time deciphering it.

"How can you read Spanish, yet you couldn't understand Maria?" I asked.

"I can read some a the words 'cause it's close enough to Latin, and that I can read."

He added, "This here is a letter of commendation. Thanking people for... Walter, and his bravery... in bringing my daughter home ... safely from pirates." He put the letter down to adjust the candlelight before coming back to Don Castabel's message. "Nar the end, there's a passage committin' large amounts of land and money to you if ye ever want to return."

I was thrilled, but I knew that coming back wouldn't assure me Maria's hand. I'd have to earn that in other ways.

We discussed what had been said between Maria and her father, and what both of them had told me through the sheriff. Bart said, "These gold pieces are yers. Keep them for yer own, and don't let the others steal them from ye."

I saw Bart return the letter to its envelope and put his key in his command safe. Things wouldn't "get lost" in there. I asked him if he wouldn't mind placing my gold coins in there too. He agreed, and I left his stateroom a rich and happy young man.

Chapter 4

I closed my eyes and focused on the images that were running through my head. I tried very hard to come back to the point of leaving Spain, but alas, it just didn't want to happen. I vaguely remembered setting sayle early the following morning. The captain stood as Bart called roll and then explained that we were to head around Gibraltar and aim for Sicily. The crew was left to its duties, which mostly involved ship's maintenance. I, however, continued to study the maps and the navigation instruments under Bart's tutelage.

As memories of the departure from Spain faded even further, I wet my quill again and proceeded to write.

We left San Sebastian, and it was a long journey westward, hugging the coastline of Spain, before we arrived at the edge of the country and turned south. A fog that had been dogging us lifted long enough for us to see a large display of Portuguese flags, since we were skirting Portugal. Continuing south, we finally turned east and stopped to trade for food in Portimao. From there, we turned the boat slightly to the southeast, and kept a tight watch until we saw land in front of us.

I was on deck a few days later, watching the sunrise. In all its reds and storied pinks and yellows, it drove the last vestiges of the night away. It also illuminated a great wall in front of me that appeared just below the horizon. I turned the ocular from left to right and spied a very small opening in the middle.

– I, Walter –

I asked Bart about it when he came topside, and he told me this was the Strait of Gibraltar. When we sayled up to its mouth, the land separating Spain and Africa was so close, I could easily conceive that one day there would be a bridge between the two.

I was enjoying watching a lot of sea life, and initially startled by huge black and white fish that Bart later told me were whales, and not called fish, and surprised by the playful behavior of what he referred to as dolphins. The entire experience with the giant rocks and the creatures in the sea left me amazed.

After passing through the Strait of Gibraltar, I was scanning the horizon with the eyeglass and came across two images. In the distance, in front of us, was an English ship, and it was taking cannon fire from *The Royal Pain,* which was flying the skull and crossbones along with a Tunisian flag. Bart reckoned that we should be able to save the English vessel, or at least her cargo, but that we'd need to act fast before the pirates realized we were on the way to aid the English vessel.

We approached the pirate craft wide from the backside of where the fighting was occurring, and rapidly closed on both ships. Apparently no one on the pirate ship saw us coming up from behind, because not one cannon flash came in our direction. Upon reaching the right distance, we put a dozen large balls into the ship, and her crew sank along with her.

The British merchant vessel was listing quite badly. Only two of its crew were still alive. But with their help, I and a few of our men were able to recover most of its cargo. We went into the hold and retrieved leather and linens, crates filled with salted meats, and rounds of cheeses. We also offloaded barrels of olives, olive oyl, vinegar, and several cases of Italian wine. Behind the stores of foodstuffs were three footlockers that contained shoe leather, and two more filled with gold and silver coin.

For the next week we made repairs to the damaged English boat so it was seaworthy enough that we could tow it to port and a much-needed extended stay at dry dock. A month later, we literally drifted into Sicily, slowed by the extra ship and the lack of a steady, stiff wind.

Late in the afternoon of our first day in the harbor, we were able to tie to a pier in preparation for unloading our cargo the next morning. I finally had a chance to relax and take in everything that had happened. Who would have thought that a boatload of experienced pirates would not have had someone watching their backsides while on attack? Yet, this is what had taken place.

It required until noon to remove all of our cargo, and I was part of the crew that hauled our merchandise to market. But while the others sold our wares, I spent my free time looking for something special for Maria.

The market was filled with a variety of smells, many that were new to me. The fishmongers were enjoying a bustling trade, and their section was redolent with the odors of squid and cuttlefish. The combination of brine and the fish was indeed intense at times. The olive market was farther down the street. Olives of every kind were sold, including some with pimientos, and these too carried their own unique odor. Then came the cheeses. Feta and Parmesan were the prominent brands, although provolone, Asiago, and Romano were offered as well. Fresh vegetables were displayed along another street, and across from them were the spices from every part of the world. Saffron and paprika from the Spanish mainland; nutmeg and cinnamon from the Spice Islands; fresh basil and oregano from the local fields, and even mustard seed from the north of Italy.

On the way back to the ship, I found a few stands that were filled with candy. After sampling them, I bought two boxes of a Turkish variety. Later that evening, in a tavern called The Drinking Fish, Bart and I met another saylor who said his ship would be trading in San Sebastian. I left the boxes of candy with him, addressed to Maria, with a note inside one that also contained a silver chain with a cross on it that I'd bought in a local shoppe, and asked him to give everything to the sheriff.

We left Sicily after storing what seemed like way too much food aboard ship, that is until the crew was assembled and told by Captain Thomas we were headed for the island of Hispaniola in the Caribbean, which meant I'd be going *across* the entire Atlantic Ocean.

– I, Walter –

The best part for me occurred in an earlier stage of the voyage, when I got to see Gibraltar for the second time. Even now, so many years later, I still marvel at the Straits and the land on both sides. But once we entered the ocean, there was water, water, and more water. Most of the trip across the Atlantic was boring, except I was provided with an inordinate amount of time to think about Maria. I often found myself consumed with thoughts about her, and now I fully understood why Cookie laced all of our meals with saltpeter.

This voyage took us on a west-by-southwest heading. The waters of the Atlantic were dark, but the ocean lightened substantially as we sayled southward. Some days we had the wind and currents working with us, and it felt as if we made a lot of distance with all sayles full. Other days, the winds were nonexistent and the sea calm. To hinder our progress even more, twice we encountered huge storms, and each time we'd been tossed backwards and lost a day or two.

Even with all the food we'd brought aboard, we were starting to run low, but we met another ship that was heading back to England, and we were assured by its captain that Hispaniola was no more than a day away. Sure enough, the following morning, Crow signaled that he'd spotted a shoreline in the distance. Was I ever relieved!

One really good thing about that long trip stands out, though. I learned to "read" the skies and waters and tell right away when rainsqualls and the trouble they always brought with them were headed our way. The seaman's ancient poem about pink skies was accurate:

Pink sky in the morning, saylors take warning,
Pink sky at night, saylor's delight.

We dropped anchor and were given a few days off before doing any serious trading. During that time, Bart showed me the sugarcane fields. When I sampled sugar for the first time, a burst of sweetness overpowered my senses. The locals made various candies with it, and also some sugar sticks for coffee and tea. I bought a large supply of the sticks to take with us on the voyage home.

"Why aren't there boatloads of this stuff going to England?" I asked Bart, thinking it could be a real moneymaker.

"I guess nobody has thought of it yet, or they didn't think we English folks would put it in our tea." He laughed.

I didn't, and let that thought linger.

On what turned out to be our last night in the islands, I went to a tavern with Bart for a good dinner before what might be months of Cookie's awful excuse for food. The Sandy Crab looked much the same as any English pub, which it should, since we were told it was built by a man from Liverpool. The main room was wide open, with benches and tables, and a few smaller corner tables that abutted the walls. The only real difference from a pub in England was the walls, which were of the open-air variety, as the weather was a welcome aspect of daily life here. Truthfully, if I'd stayed on the island I would've become an immediate regular.

Soon after we sat down and ordered our meal, I heard behind us a trader from another ship talking loud and slurring his words with enthusiasm. He was sitting by himself and telling those around him about his schedule for sayling to and from England.

"I the cap'n. Wiffin seven months, I be sayling every trip to Europe. I will trick them pirates, too, you'll see. I got, got me flags of ever pa…place, and I'll fly them, too. Keeps them pa. . . privateers and pirates away, yes siree. They come close then, I'll put me cannons into 'em. Then, boom!" He continued to ramble with one drunken outburst after another, and he was now so loud that I and everyone else in the tavern had no choice but to listen to him.

I couldn't help but notice some of the men in the bar bending over and talking in hushed tones to the people they were sitting with. I distinctly read one unsavory guy's lips as he said, "He looks like easy pickin's," and, "When 'e leaves here, we slit his throat and steal his ship and kill his crew. We done it before, we can do it agin."

I'd finished the last of two large mugs of warm beer when I asked Bart, "You think we might give this drunk sea cap'n a lesson in stayin' alive?"

"Drinks gettin' to ye?"

– I, Walter –

"No." I lied.

"What's your idea?"

"We can get him to pay you to protect him so he gets back to England with his cargo and his head on his shoulders."

We finished our meal, paid the bill, and went over to the man, who was now about to fall off his chair. He looked to be about 35. I could see salt in his hair and embedded in his scalp. This gave him an odd glow, it did. And by the deep creases on his leathery face, it was obvious he'd been sayling all his adult life and them some.

He was dressed in a pair of frayed short pants with legs that looked worn off, not hemmed. He wore a white shirt that had thin red strips down both sides, lending the appearance that a tailor had run out of white and used red to marry the two pieces of fabric. He was a little taller than me, and his rotund belly made him appear almost as wide as he was tall. One thing about this boisterous captain, he'd missed nary a meal.

Just as I was about to speak to the old captain the two admitted murderers stepped in front of us. Bart tapped on the shoulder the fellow who'd been doing all the talking. I did the same with his partner. When they turned to us, we hit them with right crosses and they went down. A third fellow sprang to their aid but was tripped by Frog, one of our ensigns who had gotten up when he saw what was going on. The guy hit his head on a table and Frog kicked him unconscious with one blow to his jaw as he was trying to right himself.

The tavern owner and two other men threw the three pirates out in the street.

Without an invitation, Bart and I sat down with the captain. With all the commotion right in front of him, the round mound of a man was alert. "So, you think you can keep the privateers and the pirates away from your ship, eh?" I asked him.

I paused and watched the braggart's head as he tried to clear the cobwebs and understand what I was really implying. When he stared hard at me and wouldn't turn away, Bart hit his fist hard on the table and got his attention.

"What happens if we take it from ye right now?" Bart asked.

"Who are you?" the captain asked in return.

In a low voice, Bart said, "We're two of the privateers ye been calling out all over the bar. Everyone heard ye say ye'd keep us away. Those two guys were going to kill ye. Now, ye've got a target on ye back and they'll be a gaggle just like 'em ready to go after ye at every turn."

He seemed to study the room, and as he saw people watching him, his face colored until his cheeks were nearly the same hue as his nose. He sputtered something, but I stopped him before he could say anything more and pointed to Bart.

"Tis a good thing for you this here privateer is a commander of honor for his King's country."

We pulled him up and moved to a table the farthest from any other in the room.

"What's your name?" Bart asked him.

"Me name's Marek."

Bart told him who we were and said, "It'll cost ye a third of your profits. Our ship will lead yours, and we'll make sure ye're looked after. And don't think about getting out of the price in England. We have many ways of making people pay." Marek scanned the room, and as he did I noticed men at several tables continuing to look our way. The captain gave one more glance around, gulped deeply several times, and nodded his head to Bart and me.

We agreed that after we arrived in England and Marek's boat and ours were offloaded, we would meet in a Portsmouth pub named The Drenched Seaman.

***

I celebrated my fifteenth birthday at sea. There were festivities all around as the saylors got their chance to tease me about being so young--and a whole lot more I won't discuss. I lucked out with the quality of the crew that I had been thrown in with. Bart gave me the bumps, and in his stateroom offered me a glass of a very dry, very good French wine called brandy.

Two weeks after that, I celebrated the completion of my first year at sea. It had been an amazing, busy year, and when I looked back at everything, it was the best move I had ever made--except for rescuing Maria, of course.

– I, Walter –

Just before we arrived in England, I had a conversation with Bart. I said, "Should be interesting to see if the cap'n shows up at the tavern."

"You keep the money if he does."

"You really mean that?"

"Your idea, wasn't it? I just went along because I thought you might've had too much to drink and got carried away."

I gave him a wary look. "But then you thought it was a bloody good idea."

"Can't argue that, lad." He paused, and the vein protruded that showed in his forehead whenever he was deep in thought. "I don't want the money, regardless. It was your idea and you deserve the spoils, if we can tell 'em that."

"Are you serious?"

"Yes, I am."

"Then I'd like put the money with what Don Castabel gave me and see if we can't get him to bring sugar to England."

"Now I'm going to ask you, are *you* serious?"

"And I'm giving you the same answer, yes, *I* am."

"Good luck," was all Bart added to the conversation, and I left his stateroom wondering if I'd made a good decision, because if I lost the gold coins from Maria's father, I'd certainly stand no chance of ever amassing enough money to win her hand.

We arrived in Portsmouth a half-day after Marek's ship. At midmorning we tied down and began unloading our cargo. Early afternoon the next day, I noticed the sayles on Marek's vessel had been hoisted, an obvious indication he was preparing to leave the harbor. Bart and I rushed to his ship. The first mate knew who we were and led us up the gangplank and to the captain's office. Without knocking, I pushed on the door and it opened.

"What the hell are you doing here?" Marek yelled as he got up from behind his desk.

I yelled back at him, "I saw your sayles flying, and it looked like you were trying to skip out on us."

"That would not be a good choice," Bart interjected. "I can guarantee ye don't know how much trouble that would cause ye."

He stared at us for a while, then said, "I don't have the money on the ship. It's in a bank."

"Then let's meet at the tavern, like we'd agreed to in the first place," Bart said. "Tonight, at the dinner hour. We'll be leaving now, and I don't expect ye'll disappoint us, will ye?"

Marek stood in silence, then groaned and said, "I'll be there."

Just as we were finishing our meal at The Drenched Seaman, Marek walked in and threw us a bag of coin. He walked away, saying, "There's ye third ya' scallywags. Clear sayling all the way, and ya' still wanted me money."

Bart jumped up and ran after him and grabbed him by the shoulder. "Ye need to sit with us a minute or two longer. We're not done with ye."

"I'm not givin' ya' no more coin."

"We don't want any more a yer money. Now I want ye to sit with us an' listen what young Walter has to say."

"What more does he want with me?"

"He wouldn't say, just that he wants ye to listen to him." I nodded and stood behind Marek so he couldn't leave without stepping over me.

We paid the bill and went to our favorite table, which was away from the crowd. We ordered a round of ale, and I watched Marek intently, trying hard to figure out whether I'd judged him properly. If so, then what I was about to do would be warranted. If not, I'd be broke and lose any chance at Maria forever. I took a long drink of my ale before clearing my throat, which didn't need it.

I told him, "I think you know you got very lucky getting across the Atlantic this time. But that's not what I want to talk to you about." I opened the bag he'd given us and scanned the coin inside, then I reached into my pea jacket and pulled out the pouch with the gold pieces I'd received from Maria's father. "It seems each of these bags contains roughly the same amount of money. I'm handing both over to you on the condition that you use them as an investment in a new product you'll be bringing into England. This particular line should be very lucrative for both of us, and we'll split the profits equally. You'll have full control, but every year you'll have to provide me with a report."

"Depends on what I be carryin' and sellin'. I won't do nothin' that'll get me swinging in front of Newcastle. Ye hear what I'm saying?"

"It's nothing illegal," I said. "It's called sugar. And if we do it right, we can corner the supply of all the sugar that's grown on the island of Hispaniola."

"You're mad, lad. I know what sugar is. It won't sell at all."

"The way I see it, it could be put into tea or used to cut bitter tastes. Or it can be eaten as candy. I brought a bunch of sugar sticks with me, and the crew had them all eaten before we were out a week. Sugar might even make some of the swill we drink more bearable. And don't the islands use it to make spirits? But ye might be right, and I could lose everything. But if *I'm* right, we could both make a lot of money. So I'm asking ye to give it a try."

Marek said nothing to my request. Instead, he ordered another round of ale, then another. His last mug now empty, he slowly raised his eyes up to mine and let out a loud sigh. "I think you're crazy, boy, but I'll do it." We shook on it, agreed to communicate through this tavern, since Marek and Bart knew the pub owner for one reason or another, and I handed over both bags of money and left the bar. As we parted ways, I really hoped he hadn't heard my heart pounding. If this worked, I could make enough money to keep Maria in a life to which she was accustomed. But if I was wrong.... Well, I didn't want to think about it.

Chapter 5

The next morning, we woke to the gray skies that were typical of Plymouth and much of the rest of the country. I observed Marek leaving port and watched the sayles open fully as his ship rolled across the waves. With him went my hopes and prayers for good fortune.

Now came the waiting. Other than my meager wages as an apprentice crewman, I was back to being poor again, so I went to the boat, where there were always chores that had to be done by someone. I polished brass fittings and thought about Maria and wondered if packages with my message got to her. I wondered about the fastest way to get a letter to her.

Bart wasn't aboard, he was in London on business. And after five days of relative inactivity, everyone on the ship had gotten antsy, including me. We wanted to be on the sea again, and we needed to know when this was going to happen and where we would be heading. The longer the wait, the rougher things got with the crew.

Just before supper, I was out on deck and heard two voices being raised. As I turned towards the mizzenmast, I could see Gimp jabbing his mop at one of the midshipmen, who grabbed it and pulled it from his hands. Gimp was able to connect with one punch, but that was it. After that he was hit in the stomach by the mop handle, and then it was used to sweep his legs. The midshipman jumped on Gimp, and I ran over to pull him off. Before I could get a grip on one of his arms, the midshipman elbowed me in the right eye. After considerable effort, I was able to pull the two of them apart. To my surprise, instead of going back at it or threatening each other, they shook hands and began laughing. It seemed that the only person who'd gotten hurt was me, as my eye was throbbing.

Bart returned the next day with men from town carrying food and supplies, as well as a list of new goods to trade. Bart asked me about the shiner I'd developed, and I told him that I'd tried to break up a minor fight between two members of the crew. I wouldn't give their names out, though. He didn't say anything.

We spent the next two days loading everything aboard. In the evening, just before we finished, several distinguished-looking men came up the gangplank, asking for Bart. He met them on deck and called to me, "Walter, we're headed to the captain's quarters. We need ye to join us in a while. I'll have someone come get ye when we're ready."

Gimp teased me, "Sure ya should run to the master's room na, sir? Might not be good." He followed this with a laugh that was unsettling.

Gimp himself was the saylor who told me a half-hour later that it was time for the meeting. When I entered, except for Bart, the men were sitting down. All three stared at me, making me uncomfortable. The table was lit by candles, and so were the torches on the walls, making the room unusually bright.

"These men are here to test yer skills," Bart said to me as he pointed to where I was to sit. "They'll be going over things that ye learned on our last voyage."

I turned to Bart and asked, "Are you referring to how to swear like a saylor? Or how to walk like I'm drunk, even on land?"

I heard a snicker from one of the gentlemen and Bart chuckled. He cuffed me and said, "Cheeky lad. No, I'm referrin' to knots and sayles and mappin'."

It got all serious and they showed me blueprints of the ship, and then using a pointer they'd brought with them, one man asked me, "Where is this?"

"Midship, sir, about underneath mizzenmast."

"And this?" he asked, moving the pointer.

"That's the kitchen, sir. Nothing good ever comes from it."

Bart laughed again and left the room.
"And this?" Again, the pointer moved.
"That, sir, is the cannon area."
"What do we call this sayl?"
"The mizzen top gallant staysayl, sir."
"And this one?"
"Foresayl, sir."
"Where did you go on the last trip?" another man asked
"I'm afraid, sir, that I'm not at liberty to say."
The only man who had not spoken yet became indignant. "You're not at liberty to say?"
"No, sir."
"Why not? We're asking you questions on behalf of the government. Why can't you tell us these things?"
"Because, sir, it's not my place. Ask Bart if you truly want to know. I do not have the authority to tell you."
"Thank you, Walter." His tone was more reserved, and he brought up the map of southern England. "Can you show me on the map where we are right now?"
I quickly found Portsmouth and showed him our location.
He pulled a diagram from a pouch. "What is this?"
"That, sir, is rigging. It helps support the sayles, and the seamen who regularly try to maintain them."
He threw me a small piece of rope and said, "Tye me a knot for securing a sayle."
I did and handed it back to him.
The questioning went on for another hour.
Bart pushed open the door and entered the room.
"Gentlemen, yer time is up."
Each of the men stood and shook my hand, and they left without making any comments. I asked Bart what that was all about.
He said, "Walter, go get some rest. Tomorrow comes quickly, and there's a lot a work still needs to be done before we can shove off."
While I was swabbing the deck the next morning, a messenger arrived with a note for Bart. I saw him open it as I continued to mop the smooth wood.

– I, Walter –

"Walter!" He yelled from the far side of the wheel.

I hurried over to him.

"This is a note from those men, who are called proctors. Ye passed all of the tests with high marks, and they recommended ye for promotion to Able Seaman. The final step is that ye promotion must wait for the colors to fly in approval. That means that one of the admirals must see fit to approve the increase in rank. Don't get too excited, though; some people wait several years for their promotions."

Bart told me that the goods we'd be trading during the voyage would be arriving soon. I wondered how long it would be before we'd return to land again and I could go to Maria. Then, would she even want me, no matter how well Marek's trading might do for me? As my eyes scanned the horizon, I saw an older man leaning against a small craft. He was tall and thin and wearing a hat down over his face, as if trying to avoid anyone's getting a good look at him. He had his arms folded, as if waiting for someone or something. I quit looking at him and went to my sleeping area.

The next afternoon, Bart called me to his office. When I entered, he poured two shots of French brandy with a fancy name. He handed me one and said, "This is a little late, but happy birthday, Walter." I smiled. He'd remembered my birthday, even though it had already passed.

He drank the whole thing quickly and I followed his lead. The burn in my throat caused me to cough several times. But in a few minutes I found myself realizing that it tasted good. Bart gave me my pay packet. When I looked, the money was substantially more than I'd ever received before. Bart said, "The approval came through this morning. Ye have been promoted, lad."

My head was a little light from the strong drink, and I needed a moment to let everything sink in. "I thought you said it could take years."

"Usually does. Someone must like ye." He winked. "Ye are goin' to need to get new clothes to match your new position on this ship. There's a tailor by The Drenched Seaman. Go there first thing in the mornin' and tell him I said to get the clothes finished for ye by the afternoon, 'cause we'll be on the water the next day by first light. By the way, Walter, I was given orders to take dock in San Sebastian. We need to see a few local captains about Portuguese raiders who are attackin' them. Goin' there won't bother ye, will it?"

The moment I head the words "northern Spain," my heart seemed to want to jump from my chest. I was so excited I was speechless.

"Off ye go, then," Bart said, clearly seeing the effect his news was having on me.

I mustered, "Thank ye sir," and left for what was sure to be a restless sleep.

– I, Walter –

Chapter 6

I remember this trip more than any other, and almost more than anything else in my life except for Maria. But I never breathed a word of it to anyone, and now, even Bart is gone. Telling the truth isn't going to damage anyone now. I survived, but I didn't see myself as a hero. I'd have to say I've been very lucky on so many counts, so I'm going to keep writing.

We left from Portsmouth at first light and crossed the Strait before sayling down the coast, heading for that corner of northern Spain that abutted both France and Portugal. All went well until we were about midway down the French coast.

Crow yelled from his perch atop the tallest mast, "Ahoy, Bart! A Portuguese Man o' War is heading towards us, and she ain't looking too friendly."

Bart looked through his glass and immediately altered course, but the approaching ship mirrored our every movement. And however we maneuvered our vessel, the more she countered and yet closed. This cat-and-mouse game lasted until we were too close to use the cannons, and three of their saylors swung off the riggings from their boat and onto our deck. Gimp, me, and a few of the others drew our cutlasses and started defending our ship. Soon more of our crew was engaged as several more of their men swung across our bow. In a short while, almost everyone on our ship was fighting, including Bart.

In addition to helping me learn to throw a knife, Gimp had also taught me how to handle a sword. But I never thought I'd have to use one. My first opponent matched up with me well. We parried and thrust across much of the deck for five minutes, until I was able to corner him near the edge of the bow. He stepped away, and when he bent backwards to avoid my thrust, he fell overboard.

I quickly was engaged by a second pirate. We sparred our way back and forth across the deck several times, and had reached the stern when he stumbled against a set of ropes that was behind him. He fell forward, and I took advantage of his misstep to push my sword into his chest. Another of his crew attacked me as I was pulling my sword from his chest. This battle took a little longer, and the crucial point came middeck when one of my mates knocked his head into my foe's when he ran into him.

I ran my cutlass into his side. I finished him off and took a look around, my heart racing too fast to even realize I'd just killed two people, and maybe a third had drowned because of me. I spotted Bart having a hard fight with a pirate much bigger than him, and I saw a pirate run his cutlass through Gimp's good leg, forcing him to the deck and rendering him useless to fight any longer. That man was now heading towards Bart, from behind his back.

I took stock of the dead bodies around me and found a knife in one of the pirates close by. I lunged over the body and pulled out the knife. Flipping it so that I held the hilt, I stood and threw it as hard as I could. The point hit the man approaching Bart in the eye and the blade buried itself in his skull. He dropped to the deck less than an arm's length from Bart, who was too occupied to see what had happened.

I turned and saw clear passage onto the pirate ship. I grabbed a few knives and another cutlass and worked my way toward the vessel. Barely visible through the netting in the ship's crow's nest, I made out one of the crew slumped over with a knife sticking out of his chest. The only other person I saw aboard the ship was its captain, dressed in a fancy uniform. He hadn't spotted me, and I was expecting to see more of the crew. I quickly sneaked behind him and ordered his surrender with my cutlass point in his back.

– I, Walter –

When he said something I didn't understand, I moved him with the cutlass over to the edge of the ship. I kicked him overboard and watched as he hit the water.

Looking back across to our ship, I noticed that Bart had finally vanquished his foe at the end of his cutlass, and that there were now three of our crew attending to the last of the pirates. I later learned that we'd lost three crew, and that several men such as Gimp required major medical attention. But we were lucky.

Bart shouted across to me, "Where's the captain?"

I pointed to him treading water between our ships.

"Yer doin'?"

I nodded.

I noticed one of the pirates had been playing possum and now decided to attack. With his cutlass drawn, he got behind Bart. I grabbed a knife I had with me and hurled it. This one left me with all the prayers that I could muster. It missed Bart by an inch, and I saw him move away in shock and confusion as it passed him. He turned just fast enough to follow its path, and I saw his face go pale when he realized just how close the man was to him. He watched as the knife buried itself in the face of the attacker, and this time he fell to the deck for real.

Bart wiped his forehead with his hand, and I saluted him. Under my breath I whispered, "Thank you, God, for that."

We pulled the captain from the water, as well as the first pirate I'd shoved overboard. Both men had survived, and we tied them up in the hold, along with several other pirates who were alive although wounded, some badly. I calculated it would be another six weeks before we reached northern Spain at the slow speed we'd have to travel with the other craft tethered to ours. The good news, if there was any: Gimp would likely recover from his leg wound, leaving him even more of a gimp than he was in the past. He laughed about his prospects, but I could only imagine how difficult his walking aboard ship would be once he was up and about.

That night, and for several more to come, I couldn't sleep. Every ounce of my body recognized that what we'd done was in self-defense. But it didn't make it any easier for me when I realized I'd actually killed people. I had never thought of myself as a killer. And even though I had no choice, those men were someone's father or son or brother or cousin or uncle or nephew.

Although I had no physical wounds, the anguish of taking another life dwelled heavily in my heart, and I wasn't sure if I'd recover from what had transpired. Every time I tried to sleep, I found myself reliving the battles. Or when I did sleep, I dreamed about killing pirates. Soon, I was no longer dreaming of killing pirates, I was killing normal people.

One day after a particularly hard night, I went to check on Gimp, who said to me, "Aye, you look pretty rough, almost like that was the first time ya' killed a man." He turned my head away. "So that's it, aye?" He reached up from his cot and tousled my hair. "The whole crew knows how well ya fought. If you hadn't killed them, ya think they wouldna killed you?"

"That's what I don't know." I was almost in tears. "I'm not sure. I. . . I…don't know."

"You think that pirate if 'e had ya' would a stopped his sword in mid-flight and thought, oye, maybe I should only take him as a prisoner. Let's me stop tryin' to kill 'im now?"

"Well, no."

"No is right. They want the ship, the cargo, an' the money. An' won't stop till they get it all, and if that means killin' you and me and ever'one else, that's fine with them too."

I wiped my eyes. "You're probably right--"

"Ain't no prob'ly to it. Ya' not done what ya done, you'd be dead. Me and some a the others too. A lot of us owes ya."

"None of you owe me anything."

"Aye, I'm sure you'll do more honorable things in your life than all a them pirates combined. Just remember ya acted in self-defense. Me, I thank God for what ya did."

That night, I was able to sleep without the bad dreams. I clung to what Gimp had told me until we got closer to northern Spain and my thoughts swung around to Maria. I was happy again, but nervous about what seeing her after almost two years would be like. Then something awful crept into my mind. What if she'd forgotten about me and was married to someone else by now?

– I, Walter –

Chapter 7

The pirate ship's hold was loaded with money and stolen booty that was someone else's treasure, but also with readily saleable goods including linens and leather. When we finally arrived in San Sebastian, our ship was much easier to dock than the captured pirate ship.

As soon as both craft were tied down, Bart and I headed for the sheriff's office, along with the ship's captain and the two pirates who'd survived the trip while in our hold, now guarded by four of our saylors. I held the door as Bart entered the office. A deputy asked him in Spanish, "Como estas, Señor?"

Before he could answer, the sheriff burst through the door."Hola, Señor Bart," he said as he shook his hand firmly. He then looked at me and said, "Hola, Walter."

Bart told him about the pirates, and the sheriff called to several of his deputies to take the thieves into custody. Bart said, "I believe it's the same pirate ship that's been targetin' ye merchant vessels for some time. The ship is in dock, and it's yers if you want it."

The sheriff said something in Spanish to one of his men, and they talked for several minutes.

"I think I might want that," the sheriff said. "For now, though, please accept my thanks for bringing in these banditos."

Bart noticed me nervously looking out the window and said to the sheriff. "Ye will have plenty a time to decide about the ship, since we're goin' to be here a few days. I wonder if ye can lend Walter a horse so he can ride out to the Don Castabel hacienda?"

The sheriff issued a command in Spanish a deputy, and the man motioned me to follow him. I wanted to ask if anyone knew anything about Maria, but everything had happened so fast, I was taken to a horse that was already saddled and on my way without even saying goodbye to Bart. All I could do was salute the deputy and give the horse a gentle kick in the ribs.

By the time I made it to the edge of town, I was willing the horse to go faster and faster, even though we were already at full speed. It took much less time to get to the ranch than I remembered oh so long ago, but it was still too long for my heart. I slowed when I saw the same big, burly guard on his horse whom I recognized from before. This meant I was less than five minutes from the house. He must've remembered me, too, because he smiled and let me pass.

When I arrived at the ranch, Don Castabel was standing in the yard holding a musket. He set his gun aside and gave a wide smile when I dismounted.

"Bienvenido, Walter Crofter," he said, grabbing me and hugging me hard.

"Gracias," I replied.

Maria ran to me, and my spirits rose. I bowed to her father and turned to her.

"Hola, mi amor," I said.

She laughed and hugged me as tight as her father had, and she said, "No, no, it's mi amigo, not mi amor. Mi amigo is my friend. Mi amor is my love."

I stared into her eyes and lost myself in those beautiful pools of dark brown emotion. "I was right the first time."

She laughed, blushed, and swatted me lightly with her hand.

"Maria, you've learned English."

"A little bit." She laughed again. "I wanted to be able to talk to you."

Nothing she could have said would have made me feel any better. After all I'd been through, I felt truly at peace. Holding my hand in one of hers and my horse's reins in the other, she walked me to a road she told me was used to bring horses and carriages inside the hacienda. From there, it was a short distance to the stables.

As we walked, she'd pointed out different places and things and started naming them in Spanish and then English. She started with, "El camino is road," and pointed to the road we were walking on. "Patio is yard," she said as her hand spanned all of the area around us. "Jardin is garden," and she gestured to the back yard and some vines. She laughed as she pointed out the chickens, "El gallina," and the pigs, "El cerdo," and the horses she called "El caballos." I kept repeating the words and getting smiles. Finally we came to "Cercado," as she called it, which was the corral, and for me, not a moment too soon.

Once inside the confines of the building I put my arms around her and went to kiss her softly, hoping I wouldn't offend or scare her. When I tried to move my lips away from hers, she grabbed the back of my neck and pulled me toward her and kissed me for so long and hard that it took my breath away. I had no idea a kiss could be like that, or that it could have such an affect on a person. I never wanted to leave that moment. She kissed me again, but not as enthusiastically, yet she made it clear that if I was patient, more of the other variety might be in the offing. I promised my patience.

Don Castabel had a magnificent dinner prepared for me, and invited me to spend as much time at the hacienda as I wanted. I couldn't accept his gracious offer fast enough, but was just as quick to tell him that I had to be back at the ship by the following evening.

After eating the finest meal I had ever eaten, I was put up in a guest room. I didn't think I'd see Maria until morning, but she came by and kissed me goodnight. A kiss every bit as good as the first one. Cookie's saltpeter would have come in handy, and I was happy she left when she did.

At breakfast, Don Castabel had many questions, and I answered every one as honestly and accurately as I could. When we finished, Maria and I went for another walk. Thrilled that she could understand me, I told her how lost I was, constantly thinking about her when I was at sea, and how lonely I felt.

We stopped and I fastened a necklace around her neck. She was wearing the necklace with the cross I'd sent her. She told me she'd never taken it off from the moment she received it. Overwhelmed by everything else, I hadn't thought to ask if she'd gotten my packages. But now I knew.

The necklace I was giving her now was made of small, beautiful seashells, intricately strung together on a strand of silver. As I put it around her neck and fastened the clasp, I tried to find words to express my feelings, but I stumbled with the words. She gave me another one of her fantastic kisses, and I didn't care how stupid my words of affection might've sounded.

She darted away and returned with her horse and the one I had ridden, both saddled. We rode off, exploring the hills that led toward a mountain range. We arrived at a spot with a grassy meadow containing wildflowers of all colors. Cutting across the middle of it was a long, winding river, with some trees along its shores. In front of us I could now clearly see majestic snow-capped mountains.

We spurred the horses to a gallop and raced toward the river. At the edge, we let the horses drink before tying them to a tree. As she was looping my horse's reins around a branch, I slipped my hand around her waist and held her tightly. She turned and embraced me. We held that position for several minutes. Holding her was very special. My whole body tingled from touching hers and my face felt on fire. As we separated, I wondered just how much longer she would've let me hold her like that. There had to be a limit, and I wasn't going to press my luck.

We walked along the river, hand-in-hand, and she taught me some more Spanish. I was not grasping her language as quickly as I would have liked, because her command of English, which she told me she was learning from a new priest in the area, was already as good as that of most of the saylors on our ship--and not too far from mine.

She made a wide circle and outlined the land below the horizon where we were standing with her arms and said, "All this is ours."

I assume she was referring to her and her father. Yet my heart hoped it meant hers and mine. If my heart is right, I wondered how I could ever have enough money to be worthy of her hand or her father Don Castabel's approval.

After a lovely day and several more intimate moments that I knew would remain with me for however long I'd be away from her this time, I stayed for dinner and left to get back to town and the ship before the sun set. Judging from Maria's tears, my departure was indeed tough on her, but it was difficult for me as well, and for a reason that went beyond pure emotion. I wanted to be worthy of her, and I had my work cut out for me before I would return.

As I looked upon my shelf of books, I pulled out Don Castabel's diary. After his death many years ago, I inherited his writings. Most of them were about the maintenance of the grapes and the land, but every once in a while I'd find him interjecting his feelings about things that were happening around him. I searched for the writings about my meetings with Maria and found them. Here are his own words:

"I have watched him with Maria now more than once. I do not know what his background is. Is he a farmer or a merchant or merely a well-behaved pirate? Frankly, right now I don't care. What I do know is that this young man has brought my daughter home safely and away from grave and unspeakable danger, and that the last time he left, he took her heart with him.

She has tried very hard to ignore her feelings, but the evidence was shown to me just minutes ago when he arrived for the second time. One look at him, and her face broke out in a smile that blinded the sun.

I hope very much that whatever they end up doing, it makes them happy. It is so good to see my daughter like this.

I know Bart from his many years of trading in my country. He has always dealt with my subjects in fairness. He's an honorable man, and the fact that this boy Walter sayles with him is all the recommendation I need.

He is the first young man I've seen to have such chivalry and character. I wonder if he'd be any good at doing things on the land."

– I, Walter –

Chapter 8

The moment I set foot on deck after returning from Maria and Don Castabel's hacienda, Bart called me into his office.

He pointed towards a large chest, and asked me to open it. Inside, there was nothing but gold coins. While gawking at this horde of gold, I barely registered hearing him say, "This is the money from the capture of the pirate ship and its cargo. Another chest the same size is in the captain's office."

I couldn't imagine this much money in one place, let alone another amount just like it.

"What you're looking at is the reward for capturing the ship and getting what was left of the crew to the authorities. Since it was ye who subdued the captain, this chest of gold is yours, lad. It be a lot of money, so be careful how ye spend it."

I stammered before gathering enough composure to ask, "With the three crewmen we lost, this leaves us with fifteen men, including you and me but not Cap'n Thomas, right?"

"Aye."

"Cap'n gets the one chest for himself, right?" Bart nodded. "Let's split the rest evenly among the crew. This is theirs as much as mine."

"Ye be givin' away a fortune. Ye really want to do this?"

"How many pieces of gold are in that chest?"

Bart stroked his beard. "Don't know exactly."

We set the coins on Bart's desk in stacks of ten, and when we finished there were forty-seven with ten and with one five.

After dividing the 475 coins by 15, each pile had 31 pieces of gold in it, with 10 left over.

Bart said, "Ye give this much to each saylor on this ship and the men will mutiny and make you captain."

"No, they won't. I'll split the ten left o'er with you, if that's agreeable?"

"I can't take any of your money, lad." He gave me a searching look that puzzled me.

I took five coins from a half stack, added it to a full one, and swept the money toward him, some coin falling on his lap. "Take it. Ye told me about your wife and family many times. Buy something for them to make their lives better."

"Ye are a better man than I. I know of nobody else who would divide the spoils like that."

"The way I see it, this way everyone on the crew is happy."

"Aye, you're a good man, Walt. Go on, now."

If I didn't know better, I'd say I saw a tear in Bart's eye. I grinned as I left him.

Unable to sleep, I thought about 475 gold coins well into the night. They might've been enough to win Maria's hand, but even with how much I loved her, one thing was undeniable. If our crew hadn't fought off the pirates, I wouldn't be alive to love anybody. At that moment, my ship meant more to me than even the person I loved more than life itself. I fell asleep knowing it had to be this way.

***

Early the next morning, instead of sayling as planned, I was awakened and summonsed on deck. All of the crew was there, even the captain, who called us to attention. Something didn't seem quite right, when it dawned me, this was the first time since I'd joined this crew that I'd seen the captain smiling.

Bart called me forward and sat me down on a table next to him. The chest from his office was to my right. He addressed the crew, who still stood at attention, "We sayle tomorrow at first light, so everyone needs to be on board by nightfall, and no later. Before I let ye all go ashore, however, there is a detail to attend to." He drew his hand over the chest. "This contains the money

– I, Walter –

from the spoils of the pirate ship. I offered it to Walter, but he wants to split it with all of ye." A cheer went up amongst the crew that I thought would never cease. Bart patiently waited for them to settle down before continuing. "Each man will receive the same amount. It comes to 31 pieces of gold." The crew went wild again, this time even for longer than before.

Bart had to hold up his hand to quiet them. "Be careful with it. That's enough to buy a good house or a share in a ship. And don't forget where it comes from. Now, I want ye to form a line in front of this here table." The men did so and nearly all of the hands shot out at once. But, Bart was systematic. He went through the roster and made sure that each saylor signed for or made his style of "X" for his share.

Bart handed them the money, and each man tried to shake my hand off as they thanked me. Some pounded my back for so long and hard that it became so sore that I couldn't wait for this to be over with.

When the last man had his coin, Bart said, "We will delay a day and sayle tomorrow in the morn, so be back early tonight. And don't lose all ye money to some señorita. If ye want, I can keep ye coin in the safe." A few of the crew took him up on his offer, but most went on their way with the money jammed in their pea coats.

I wanted to ride back to Maria and see her again before we left, but it would be too hard on both of us, so I lolled away the day on the windowsill, my thoughts with her. I wanted to spend the rest of my life with Maria, but I'd convinced myself that even a fortune of 475 gold coins would not have been enough to win Don Castabel's approval. I daydreamed of treating her like the princess she was, and of us going many places and doing many things. And when I fell asleep, I dreamed of the two of us growing old together.

Chapter 9

Six months passed before we rounded Gibraltar on a return voyage from Sicily and later Cairo, and I was almost a year older. I was more in love than ever with Maria, and even though she wasn't with me, she was present in all my thoughts. I had picked up numerous gifts for her in both the Sicilian and Egyptian markets, and couldn't wait to give them to her when we docked in northern Spain. When I asked Bart about docking so I could see Maria, Bart had already made an excuse for me, saying he had to meet with the sheriff anyhow to discuss the final disposition of the pirate ship, since this hadn't been resolved before we'd departed. He was certain this would take several days.

Our trading during this trip had involved the usual ferrying of cargo from place to place, but the commerce was lighter than normal. Yet much of our time in port took longer than the transfer of goods to and from market. Bart was always the culprit. Even the captain was getting tired of waiting for his often quite tardy returns. It was during Bart's return to ship from when we stopped in a port in southern Spain that I learned the worst news I could possibly hear.

We had to return to England immediately, and we wouldn't be able to dock in northern Spain for even a minute. I barely had enough time to get some of the gifts for Maria to a local sheriff, who said he'd try to see they got to her. I took a chance that he might know of Don Castabel, and he did. All I could do was hope,

– I, Walter –

and I scribbled a letter to Maria with such haste that I didn't even remember what I'd written.

Two weeks later, I agonized when we sayled right by the dock in northern Spain where we'd tied down twice before, so much so that I imagined Maria waving to me.

***

When we arrived in Portsmouth, Bart rushed from the ship the moment it docked, carrying a ream of parchment so large it required both hands to keep him from dropping it. Several distinguished-looking men met Bart with a carriage, and I saw him smile and wave at the captain as he entered it. I saw the answering scowl on the captain's face as he acknowledged Bart's leaving the ship again. It occurred to me that the captain was acting like a courier, and Bart was not the messenger but the goods. But it wasn't my position to question either the captain's or Bart's actions, so I shrugged off my silliness.

Turning my gaze back to the dock, I saw that the coach Bart entered had a shield on it. This confirmed something I'd believed for some time, which was that Bart held some distinction.

Although Bart left, the crew couldn't depart yet, as plenty of work needed to be done before any of us could set foot on dry land. For two days, we took everything from the hold, including bringing all the foodstuffs up to the top level, and then we worked with tar and sap to repair the small leaks that had opened up in the hull. The crewman who served as ship's carpenter added a few blocks to make the cannons more level, while I spent what little spare time I had polishing brass.

On the third day in port, just before I was to get off the ship, Bart returned in the late afternoon. He sat me down in the stateroom, and I found myself facing the same proctors I'd seen many moons earlier. I wanted to get off the boat, but if this meant I might earn another promotion, I determined to stick it out. I shrugged my shoulders and steeled myself for what I was certain would be a brutal battery of questions and tests. The man who was the sternest of the three the first time started in on me.

"Walter, can you tell us who is in command of the ship?"

"Please ye, sir, the cap'n is in command of the ship."

"And who does all his bidding?"

"Everyone, sir. But mostly his second in command. He gives the crew the cap'n's orders."

"Who's the second on your ship?"

"Bart, sir. We all answer to him, since we don't see the cap'n nearly that much. He mostly comes out when we're in formation, but Bart still gives the orders."

"And after Bart?"

"I reckon that'd be the ensigns, sir. They seem to be cap'ns in training, sir, since they're the brown-nosers."

"Brown-nosers?" one man asked and snickered.

"That's what the rest of the crew calls 'em, sir, since their noses are so far up the cap'n's ass, they don't know anything but how to obey." I was trying to lighten the mood in the room, but none of the men gave me so much as a faint smile.

The man who'd begun the questioning leaned toward me. "Are you a brown-noser, Walter?"

"Not really, sir. I at least ask when I don't understand something."

"And if you were told to do something you didn't want to do?"

"If it was dangerous, sir, I believe I'd need some explanation."

"Bart says you threw knives with great skill the last time your boat was attacked. Where did you learn this?"

"One of our crewmen, Gimp, taught me, sir, but mostly I started praying when I threw them at the pirates, sir."

"Prayer made your throws accurate?"

"Must have, sir, it was the first time I'd thrown them in a battle."

"Then you were very lucky?"

"Very sir, and so was Bart."

"You've been to Spain several times. Do you like it there?"

"The land's fair enough."

"You have a young woman there you're fond of?"

While this question bothered me, of equal concern was who had told him about Maria. Bart? "Yes, sir, she's quite nice."

"Do you listen to her?"

– I, Walter –

I didn't understand what he was asking me, but said, "Yes, sir, I do."

"If she told you to go against Bart, would you?"

Questioning my loyalty was making my blood boil. But before I could even answer, another proctor asked, "If she told you to go against the captain, would you do it?"

Before I could utter a word, the third man interrupted, as the other man had, what I was about to say. "Or against England if it involved Spain? Would you listen to her then?"

I stood up. My whole body felt flushed, but I forced control. "Gentlemen, what you're asking me is if I'd commit treason." I was so mad I was having trouble continuing, but I did. "My loyalties are with my England, my cap'n, and Bart, who's become my best friend. Maria and her father would never ask me to go against my own country."

"Maria is the woman's name?" the lead proctor asked.

"Sir, I believe you full well know her name." He was now going to try and twist someone who was so beautiful into something ugly. I wouldn't, couldn't let him dishonor her. "You leave Maria out of this. She's young and beautiful and pure. She'd never ask me to go against my country. Or against Bart and the cap'n. Leave her out of this." I hadn't realized I was now yelling until I sat back in my chair and felt my throat tighten.

"So that's where your loyalties lie, with Maria?"

"Sir," I said with as much disgust as I could muster, "whatever your opinion of me happens to be, it doesn't matter. I have fought alongside Bart and for my cap'n for over three years. My loyalty is not worthy of questioning. I'm loyal the Crown, to the cap'n, and to Bart."

"But perhaps more so to Maria."

"Don't ever…don't ever bring her into this conversation again. You can question my loyalties till you're blue in the face, but leave her out of it. She'd never ask those questions." I gave up any thought of a promotion and stood. "Who the hell do you think you are to question my loyalty? I'm a British subject. My loyalty is to the King. I am proud to be saylor for the Crown. My loyalty is to it, to my cap'n, and to Bart."

"You don't need to yell," the man said. "Calm down and please take your seat."

"Why should I? What right do you have to question my loyalties? I've never given anyone any reason to doubt me."

"Take your seat and let's go on in a different direction. Who commands the boat?"

While the question was juvenile, it made more sense than the recent ones, so I sat. I took a deep breath and said, "The cap'n."

"Who has the right to know where you're heading when you're on the sea?"

"The cap'n first, since he's in charge of getting us there. Then his commanding officer. On our ship that's Bart, since he takes care of the details, like charting our route." I thought a moment. "That would be about it."

"Who does the second officer command?"

"Everyone on the ship, except the cap'n, of course."

"And if a saylor on the ship was saying he wanted the crew to go against Bart or the cap'n--"

"That's treason, sir."

"Aye, and well it is. Would you report it?"

"I'd make sure it was what he was really saying, sir. No need to make anything out of empty grumbling."

"But if it wasn't?"

"Sure as I'm here, I'd report it, sir."

"To whom?"

"I'd go to Bart."

"What if Bart was the one calling against the captain?"

"Then I'd reckon he'd have a pretty good reason, sir."

"Would you report him to the captain?"

"Only if I knew he was serious and without valid reason. Otherwise, no."

"So your loyalties lie with Bart?"

"In the order you described first, sir, yes."

"So you'd be loyal to Bart over the captain?"

"If the reason was valid, sir."

"So you'd go against the captain if you thought Bart wanted it?"

– I, Walter –

"You're twisting my words. Like I said, my loyalties lie with the King, the cap'n and Bart, in that order. If the cap'n wanted to go against the King, then Bart would relieve him. But I know Bart well enough that he'd consider his actions long and hard before doing anything like that. And I'd support him, as long as I knew what and why, and it was in the interest of the King."

"So, we've established you'd go against the captain if there was a reason you agreed with."

I clenched my teeth and fists. "You're trying to twist my words again. I'm loyal to my King, my captain, and my commander. You have no right to question my loyalty to any of these people any more than asking me about Maria." I arose from my chair and started yelling about the nature of their questions. I was about turn my back on them and leave when Bart opened the door.

He pointed at the proctor who'd been badgering me with such passion. "There is no reason to question Walter's loyalty. Go on to something else or I'm going to ask all of you all to leave."

The man looked at Walter as if he was expecting this response. For the first time in the interview, he smiled. "We're done here. We'll send you our answer in the morning." They stood, and as they were leaving, the lead proctor squared up with me and said, "Believe me, Mr. Crofter, everything we asked you was necessary. And while some of it was highly personal, it had to be."

I'd never been called "mister" by anyone before, so it took some of the sting out of what had occurred. After the last man left and Bart shut the door behind him, he said, "It's late, lad, and nearly everyone has had a meal. Ask Cookie to get you some leftovers, then if you're goin' ashore, stop by the ship tomorrow about this time.

I needed to check on any messages from Marek, but I was so tired that I decided to stay on the ship, eat one of Cookie's horrible meals, and go by The Drenched Seaman in the morning.

***

After a hearty breakfast at an inn near the tavern, I waited for the pub to open. Unfortunately for me, the owner was out and his help didn't know anything about a sea captain named Marek or any messages left for a man named Crofter. I didn't remember seeing the young man cleaning the mugs and sweeping the floor from the last times I was in, so he was likely telling me the truth. He did tell me that the tavern owner was expected back by nightfall.

I stopped by a store and bought materials so I could write a letter to Maria. Since my last letter was so rushed, I spent several hours writing out exactly what I wanted to say, sparing nothing. When I was finished, it was a small book. I put it in my pocket to give to Bart later, as I was sure he'd know a way to send it so it would have its best chance of getting to Maria.

The position of the sun told me it was time to return to the boat. I went to my sleeping area and tossed off my pea coat and became melancholy thinking about Maria. My doldrums were interrupted when I heard Gimp shuffling across the wooden floor. He'd made an extraordinary recovery from the wound to his good leg, and in truth he appeared to be walking better now than before he was injured. After Bart, he was my next best friend on the ship, and I always welcomed his presence. He came up to me. "Sir, ye best be gettin' to Bart's office."

He knew how much I hated being called "sir," and he always exaggerated the word when he addressed me. I found this especially nettlesome, since we were the same rank. I made up my mind to get back at him at the first opportunity for this latest abuse.

Other than Gimp, only a few of the crew remained on the ship, but I bade my good wishes to those I saw and made my way to Bart's cabin. He welcomed me and said, "Lad, you'll be wantin' to head to that tailor again. You'll be needing a real suit this time, and another pair of ship's clothes, with the proper insignia of course. I've taken the liberty to warn him you'll be in. I gave him a list of what you'll need. And tomorrow I'm going to take you to a bank to deposit your money so it's in a really safe place."

What proper insignia? Did that mean that I'd proctored okay? Bart read my mind.

"You've been promoted again. So come on, Walt, let's go to The Drenched Seaman."

I told Bart that the owner was supposed to be gone all day. He said he'd stopped by himself, and was told the same thing. But this had nothing to do with a good meal and a little celebration.

Upon entering The Seaman, we saw the owner behind the bar. We exchanged pleasantries and he handed me a letter. We found a table in a quiet area, and I read the letter aloud for Bart. Marek wasn't much for "particulars," but he said that things were well, whatever that meant, and if I'd be in England in September, that's when he planned to be back in the country. He left a postscript: "I'll have everything when we meet."

Money, a boatload of sugar he couldn't sell, notification he was going out of business? I could only be heartened by reading that things were well from Marek's point of view, even if I didn't have a clue about his meaning.

I ate the best meal I'd had since Don Castabel fed me last, and how long ago was that? I kept asking myself. I'd had one too many pints of ale, but as Bart and I were leaving the tavern, I once again saw the tall, thin man with a hat pulled down over one eye. For all the thousands of people I'd seen in the past few years in dozens of countries, his appearance was such that one look made him impossible to forget. On our way back to the ship, I kept asking myself, was he looking at me this last time? It certainly seemed to be the case. My head was spinning from too much alcohol, but I had all sorts of strange thoughts about this man's identity, even the absurd notion that he might be following me.

***

Maria entered the room, and gave me a long hug. She looked at me, almost with a tear in her eye, and said, "Querido, why, even after all this time, won't you tell me and everyone else how you got your scar, and what happened on that trip around the Cape?"

"Because it's one of those life-defining moments that every one of us has, and this one was very painful and disturbing."

"Now you've piqued my interest even more."

"Bart took the secret of that trip to his grave. To my knowledge, the only time he ever spoke about it or wrote about it was in the letter he sent to me just before he passed away. I'll give it to you someday to read. Then you'll understand."

"What's stopping you from giving it to me now?"

"I'm not even sure I know where to find it anymore." I wiped my brow. "Please don't press me on this."

She turned to leave the room but swung around and stomped her foot. "Walter Crofter, you are a terrible liar and always have been. You know where you've hidden scraps of paper that you haven't seen in twenty years, and you're trying to convince me that you don't know where you've placed a crucial letter from your best friend? Have your delusions, fine. But don't insult me by lying to me. I love you and always will, but I hope one day you'll feel close enough to share what went on during that voyage with me."

I looked at her very sheepishly and said, "It has nothing to do with being close to you, so that's ridiculous."

"Then what is it?"

I couldn't come up with what I wanted to say, so I offered, "I promise I will, when the time is right."

Maria stuck her nose up in the air and slammed the door on her way out. I can't say I blamed her. I shuddered. I knew I had to get that story out, but it was oh, so difficult to rekindle those memories, and I was confident they were mine alone, as I think I would have known had Bart told anyone, especially his cousin.

– I, Walter –

Chapter 10

When I returned to the boat after picking up my new clothes, even though I was to receive a promotion, I was depressed. I'd missed meeting with Marek, and I didn't have any idea about what was happening with the sugar. I'd asked Bart if he had any way to find out if Marek had sold any of the sweetener, and he said he'd need time to get an answer. He was afraid we'd be at sea before he'd get a response. So, all I could do was wait and worry, something I was getting pretty good at of late.

An ensign interrupted my aggravation to tell me that Bart was ready for me. I had to wait a minute until he finished with another crewman before he sat me down in the chair across from his desk and handed me my pay packet. "Lad, here's ye pay for the last trip. I've taken the charges for the clothes already. By the way, I heard ye not speakin' too highly of ensigns before, but now that you're one of 'em, ye better watch the way ye talk about yourself."

I was certain I was blushing. I looked inside the pay packet and found a note that told me my new wage would be almost double. This helped my disposition immensely, and I excused myself to get to the bank before it closed so I could deposit my money in the account Bart had helped me open. I made it just in time and hustled back the to ship. The captain held a rare after-dinner meeting and told us to prepare for a predawn departure. "We're goin' on a longer voyage this time. We'll be saylin' to Sicily and Greece, with plenty of stops in-between, and on to Turkey and then to Cairo. So sleep hardy, and get ready."

On a trip with this extensive an itinerary, there would be zero chance of any dillydallying in northern Spain, even if we docked there, that I could be sure of. I always wondered what the sheriff or the people above him had done with the pirate ship, but I never found out or thought to ever ask Bart what had happened to it. Maybe he never knew either, or didn't care.

Although I was now an ensign, I passed the days working my regular job, which involved the quadrant and plotting the ship's course under Bart's direction. However, I managed to learn some complicated knots from Gimp, and how to steer the ship into high waves from another saylor I didn't know very well but whom the crew called Hambone because he had shoulders like a hog. He was one of the replacements for the crewmen we'd lost, and I'd watched him fight. Nobody after went after him a second time, and soon no one wanted any part of him except to salute or say hello.

I spent most of my time thinking grandiose things about Maria. I'd use all of my money to buy her things that she'd love. The first would be a home on the coast and a boat of our own. We would teach our children to sayle. Children. Oh, yes, I could see us having many, but not a lot like was common in England. The thought of a couple of boys and at least one girl etched a permanent smile on my face. The boys would be strong and able to do many things. And they would know honor through their mother. And between Maria and me, we would make sure that they wanted for nothing. We'd make sure that they didn't need to work at the age of seven to find their own food. And the girl would be a princess, just like Maria.

Children and Maria and me. What great food for my thoughts and dreams. But I was at an age when I wanted a lot more than thoughts and dreams, and I began to wonder if Maria really would wait for me. She was no longer a girl, and I could tell when we were together that she wanted to be a woman.

The first leg of the journey was without any untoward incident, other than covering many miles at sea with few stops. We didn't dock in northern Spain, and when we sayled by San Sebastian, more than once I wanted to jump ship and swim to shore and go to Maria. If the proctors had known how hard it was not to, they never would have worried about my loyalty. The bastards, all of them.

We arrived in Sicily without fanfare, with the crew just wanting to get off the boat and onto dry land. The captain brought us all to order. We were confined to quarters for the evening, and the next day we would begin unloading our cargo. Hardly what anyone wanted to hear, the staying on board part, that is. But Hambone of all people gave a few stern looks and everyone calmed down.

Very early the next morning, to my surprise, Bart woke me. I was to put on my suit, not my saylor's clothes.

The moment my feet touched the dock, my body started swaying. I felt I was the image of the drunken saylor, but I hadn't had the first drop.

We walked from the harbor to the market, absorbing the sounds of merchants haggling with suppliers for fish and spices, then getting their purchases placed in their tents. Even though I'd experienced this many times before in Sicily, it was still something to behold.

I smelled the aromas of baked goods and spices and olives, and my stomach grumbled as I passed through the market on this early morning in Sicily. We found our way into the business district, where we sat on a bench, listening to the natives' almost hypnotic speech as they passed by.

In the distance, I noticed a man who seemed to be coming directly toward us. He was using a closed umbrella as a walking stick and occasionally swinging it in an exaggerated arc as he closed in on us. He was tall and dressed in a suit with a vest.

A chain dangled from a button hole, implying that he carried a pocket watch, which only a few of the richest people owned, and most of these were European.

He walked closer to us, and I confirmed the British in him immediately, as his gait was too stiff to be Italian. It surprised me when Bart didn't flinch as the man came up to us.

The man reached inside his coat and Bart immediately did the same. I was thinking the worst; instead, they swapped envelopes. Bart's was a bit thicker than the one he'd handed the man. I never understood why I had to dress up in my new uniform for this, and since Bart didn't say one word about what had transpired as we went about the rest of the day, I didn't ask. But it was at this point that I realized our "trading" involved a lot more than the common swapping of goods.

We returned to the ship just before sunset. Our next stop was Venice, and we made port in a day; what had occurred with the man in Sicily happened again, except this time we piloted a gondola, which was my first experience with a tiny, cumbersome craft such as this, and Bart met his contact under a bridge. Late in the day, we parked the gondola and found a carriage that would take us on a two-day adventure that included Verona and Parma. Each of our stops had similar assignations to the events in Sicily and Venice. On this trip, however, everything was more relaxed, and I had time to savor the true beauty of the region and sample the wonderful food. Fresh, real Parmesan of the Reggiano variety and Parma ham are real treats for the traveler. And we had plenty of both. Bart told me that the food was the real reason he liked coming to this region. But he volunteered nothing more, and I was smart enough not to ask.

I put down my quill. Before anyone thinks that everything on this trip was ordinary, please understand that I had never known Bart was a courier or emissary or whatever his title. All of this was new to me, and I wasn't close to knowing what to make of it.

From Italy, we sayled on to Greece and Turkey. Our last stop before we headed back to England was Cairo. We stayed three days in the bustling city. Whenever Bart and I left the ship, he always insisted I wear my dress uniform.

When his mission or whatever he called it was completed, the two of us spent our time in the market district, where he traded for food and supplies. I was able to make many contacts. I'd decided that merchant trading was probably in my future, and that I would need outlets for whatever I was selling or buying. After three days that provided me with a lifetime of learning I had never absorbed in England, we returned to the ship and readied it to sayle home.

On the second day of the second week out, we were at high sayle in the middle of the Mediterranean. Bart and I were using scopes from different positions. He was at the wheel, and for one of the few times since I'd been a saylor, I was in the nest. Crow seldom relinquished his spot high atop the ship, as he relished his solitude.

After a lazy morning, I focused my glass. I sprang alert. To our northeast, I made out a pirate ship with its Jolly Roger whipping in the wind. I'd been at sea long enough to know if we sayled with the sun behind us, it would difficult for anyone on the other ship to spot us.

Bart deftly maneuvered our ship, and we rapidly closed on the pirate vessel. My contention proved correct, no one saw us approaching. The cannons were readied, and when we were within striking distance, all of our portside guns were fired at the same time. One shot hit the wheel, another the mainmast, and one ball smashed the mizzen to pieces. A cannonball also hit halfway down the hull, leaving a good-size but repairable hole.

I was swinging down on a rope when I saw a flash from the pirate ship and heard the report. I watched a ball coming straight for the wheel. Already halfway to the deck, I swung the rope and jumped, landing close enough to Bart to shove him out of the way. Both of us tumbled on our backs, and the cannonball landed a few feet from us and cracked the deck in front of the wheel.

Shaken, I staggered to my feet and extended my hand to help Bart stand. He dusted himself off and said, "That's twice now that I owe ye me life."

I said, "What are friends for?"

We had no time to rejoice. Our cannons loaded, we fired again. This time we disabled the enemy craft, and its crew raised the white flag of surrender. We boarded the ship and began questioning the pirates before locking them in their own hold. I was interrogating one man, who spoke broken English, when I heard Gimp shout something indecipherable, which wasn't uncommon for my friend. He was hugging one of the crew from the other boat, someone I at least thought was a pirate.

Gimp brought this man over and introduced him to Bart and me. "This is Ian Dixon, but I always knowed him as Git. 'E's a

Scot, and 'is family and mine was next-door neighbors when we was growing up. 'E left home about a year before I did, and I 'aven't seen him since." Ian shook hands with both of us.

I asked, "Why do they call you Git?"

"I'm not sure if it's cause I'm gittin' into so much trouble, or if it's just 'cause I like to play pranks on people." He smiled, showing a wide dimple.

Git explained that he'd been shanghaied while returning from a trip to Africa on a ship on which he was first mate. After a rather lengthy explanation of what had occurred when he was kidnapped in a village near the Horn, and how he'd been forced to work on the pirate's ship as a slave, he pulled a small pouch from his coat pocket and handed it to me. I could smell its contents before opening the bag. I peeked inside and gave it to Bart.

Git said, "This here came from the area near the African horn. They grow it there, and a ways up Africa, too, on the east coast side. When I was captured, they took my entire store of tobacco, it's what this is called. To keep me happy, they'd give me a pouch e'ry once in a while."

Bart stared inside the bag and put it up to his nose. "Aye, supposed to be good to chew. I e'en heard about some Frenchmen supposed to be rolling the leaves together and smokin' it." Bart took a large bite. I followed suit, took three chews, and spit it out. Later, Bart broke up some of it, rolled it together in a pile, and lighted it. We inhaled as much of the smoke as we could--and promptly went into coughing fits. Bart told me my face had turned green. I didn't tell him his had as well.

I would've given it up forever if Git hadn't shown me, along with Bart, a way to roll a small portion of it tightly together, light one end, and take the equivalent of a hard pull from the other. The smoke settled in my mouth, and the smoothness of taste was there once it settled in my lungs. It still made me cough most every time I inhaled, but I could see how others might enjoy it, as the experience, other than the gagging, relaxed me.

Splitting the labor between our ship and theirs, it took us two months to reach port, this time in Devon, where we handed over the pirates so they could be hung.

Before we tied down, Bart and I had a dram in honor of my nineteenth birthday. He offered to take me to a house of prostitution, but I refused, saying that I'd found the only woman I ever wanted to be with. I felt somewhat embarrassed by my candor, but how can I deny what was so true? And Bart never said a word to try to dissuade me, as I'm certain he knew it would be futile.

When we arrived in Portsmouth ten days later, I had again missed Marek. Two years was a bit too long to wait to get news. I'd have to figure out a better means of communication. However, the tavern owner at The Drenched Seaman did have a letter and some papers for me from Marek. In part, the message was: "Check the balance on this ledger sheet, then go to Portsmouth Mercantile Bank and ask for this account, which I opened in your name." He'd left a bank account number, but the money the account showed made no sense, as it had to be error. As I left the pub for the bank, I once again saw the thin man with the hat pulled down over his face. I wondered why he kept showing up, then I decided he was simply a regular at the tavern and I was making something out of nothing. Still, each time I spotted him, I got the feeling he was looking at me and had just turned away.

When I introduced myself at the bank, none other than the manager came up to me. He shook my hand and offered to help me with anything I wanted. What I wanted was to find out how much I really had in the account Marek had set up. He verified the sum on the ledger, and I had to sit down. My account had the equivalent of 1,000 gold coins in it. I was officially on my way to having enough money to win Don Castabel's good graces--and Maria.

Immediately, I wanted to write a letter to her. I told the banker about Don Castabel. He said he was quite familiar with the Castabel name, and if I gave him the letter he would personally place it on the next ship bound for northern Spain. He said his bank insured many of England's shipping companies, and he had a list of itineraries and departures.

I had a month in England, so I went to see my parents. While shocked to see me, and to learn what I'd done with my life, they were consumed with their financial woes. Sir Walter never got back into favor as my father had hoped, and his life was much the same as when I'd left. I expected as much, and I'd brought some money with me. Not a lot, but enough to tide them over, and even provide a few luxuries, until I'd see them again. I promised them it wouldn't be another five years.

The visit was upbeat until we were saying our goodbyes. My mother broke into tears, not because I was leaving, but as a result of the constant reports she was receiving about Gerald. And not from the neighbors; from "Wanted" posters. Gerald had become one of England's most notorious outlaws.

***

A month after docking, we sayled. But before we debarked, I'd given the banker two more letters for Maria, along with several small packages that contained items I'd assembled for her from the past voyage. In one, I included a ring with small diamonds around the band that I purchased in London. Its meaning didn't require explanation.

This time, we were headed on our most adventurous journey yet, around he Horn of Africa and farther east, and then up to central Africa on the Pacific Ocean side.

A few days out of Portsmouth, we encountered a cloud cover that hampered our navigation, especially at night, but it cleared up and we had clear sayling all the way to Gibraltar. Once again, as we glided by the port of San Sebastian that would allow me to be with Maria in two hours, I wanted to jump ship. But I held to my principles and kept my feet planted on deck.

By the time we passed Gibraltar, the temperature had warmed enough that most of the crew went shirtless. The men were constantly grumbling about the heat, but they got used to it.

Every two or three weeks we anchored and then rowed our small boats to shore to restock our food supply or fish or hunt for our meals. Frankly, the fresh fish and occasional game was the best food Cookie had ever made. We were also able to stop several times along the western African coastline to trade. I was amazed at the amount of goods we were able to get for even a small amount of salt. I soon learned that south of the African bulge, salt was a sacred scarcity. I'd begun keeping a diary, and I made a note of this, along with anything else I thought might help me as a trader.

The bulge also meant even warmer temperatures. While England was cool and wet during the fall and winter months, all the areas around the equator were just coming into their hot season. I loved the heat but some of the crew hated it.

***

By the time we got to South Africa, the sayles hadn't felt a good wind since crossing the equator, and this had slowed our progress substantially. The slow speed of the ship and the constant heat caused tempers to easily flare amongst the crew. Add to this the rationing of drinking water, and things were a mite tense as we sayled into a port at the Cape.

However, a three-day hiatus on land did wonders for the crew, and the new varieties of food seemed to put the men in better spirits as much as anything. A very attractive native population of the female persuasion didn't seem to hurt either. After seeing some of these women walking around almost naked, and not approaching any of them, I realized just how much I must love Maria.

Rested and happy, we left the Cape and sayled on a north-by-northeast heading.

After a few days of nothing but blue water, Fatboy, who was spelling Crow, hollered, "Land ho!"

Bart and I shared looks through a mounted ocular he'd bought during our last dockage in Portsmouth, and there was indeed a land mass ahead of us. But I was confused, since none of our maps had shown it.

Bart said, "That must be the island called Madagascar. I'm goin' to ask the captain. Aye, there've been several sightings over the past 20 years, especially by Portuguese saylors, but nobody's confirmed it for the mapmakers yet."

He left and came back with a map I'd never seen before. He laid it on deck. "Captain says he's heard that this island is long and thin. He thinks it's roughly here." Bart pointed and then ran his finger in an oblong circle. "Captain says to stay away. Avoid the savages."

We couldn't change course fast enough and gave the island wide berth.

A week later, with Crow now back in his familiar haunt, we heard him bellow, "Land ho!"

This time it was a smallish island, and we determined it to be Santa Apolonia, claimed by the Portuguese. We anchored well offshore and stayed less than a day. The only reason for going there was to replenish our fresh water and see if we could kill any game and catch some fish. Plenty of fresh water, but no animals, and the island didn't have any settlers. We did, however, catch a bountiful supply of fish.

After Santa Apolonia and its lack of human population, during the next month we anchored off a number of island communities with vibrant native populations, including the Seychelles and then the Maldives and its Island of Male. Trading was always friendly, lively, and brisk, and we filled our hold with food until it was bulging.

After all my travels, I can look back and say that the Indian Ocean just beyond these groups of islands was the most dangerous stretch of water I'd ever sayled. And while the native populations were small and there wasn't much to trade for, there was fresh water and plenty of fruit and meat for which we could barter.

We braved storms, devilish currents, and high seas on the Indian Ocean for three weeks before dropping anchor off Goa. The trading wasn't special in any way, and I couldn't understand why Captain Thomas wanted to spend all the time and effort to get here. But my job wasn't to ask questions, and after spending a few days to rest and rejuvenate our bodies, we were back on the sea and passing through the islands in reverse order, with this section of the Indian Ocean on the return trip no less treacherous.

I put down my quill and wiped my brow. All of the others were gone now. All my friends; the men who had made my life what it was as I myself became a man. I knew that Bart was aware of *all* the details, but was thankful he had never forsaken me. I forced myself to drink some water, and prayed that the delirium I was now experiencing would hold off long enough for me to commit this, what had to be written, to the parchment in front of me. Yes, Maria was right. The time had come.

I dipped my quill into the inkwell once more, and with a trembling hand and a heavy sigh, returned to the writing.

Upon leaving Goa, we were blown off course more than once. The Indian Ocean is dotted with small reefs and islands Bart referred to as atolls. We had to steer clear of them, and some were barely larger than a sandbar. Luckily for us, the shallow water around them was light and clear on calm days, which made them easier to spot.

We managed to avoid becoming shipwrecked on any of these "shallows," because gale winds blew us into deep seas where the Indian and Arabian oceans met. Along the way we encountered six horseshoe-shaped reefs, and running into any one of them would've spelled instant doom. Sayling at night was especially dangerous, and I used prayer more than the stars to help guide us. I don't know how we did it, but we made it back to the Seychelles unscathed, except for our nerves. Once anchored, after a day of rest we restocked our supplies and headed out to sea.

The next morning, just after tack and grog, we all heard Crow yell, "Ship Ho!"

I stood next to Bart as he looked through the ocular mounted near the wheel. Just as he was raising it to his eye, we both heard Crow again: "She's carryin' the Jolly Roger flag, and she's flyin' toward us."

Chapter 11

Bart handed the ocular to me as he ran to ready the crew. The cannons on the approaching ship were larger than ours, and the firing began before we could get in range to return the favor. Several shots came up just short before one hit the hull and cracked it. Three cannon balls later, the crack was now a hole. But the pirate ship was now within our range, and we fired our own cannons.

The gods must have liked our company, since they gave our guns accuracy, and our opening fusillade of 20 cannon shot took down both their foremast and mizzenmast, as well as blasting the deck, which was on fire. Three gaping holes appeared in the hull, and the vessel was taking on a lot of water. But we hadn't hit the knockout blow.

Our ships crashed together, and several of their crew jumped to our deck. Their plank was thrown across, which they secured, and the rest of the pirates raced aboard.

All hands were on deck to battle the pirates. Captain Thomas even came out and joined the fight. Braced behind the wheel, he leveled a musket with his one good hand. Hambone had brought powder and ammunition for the captain, as well as several other muskets he'd already loaded. He then entered the fray with a musket of his own and several knives. He was also wearing a sword with a fancy hilt.

Hambone and two of our crew ran headlong into the main field of pirates. Each of our saylors carried a musket and fired and

– I, Walter –

then drew their swords. Two of the pirates went down, and then I heard another shot and a third pirate fell. The captain was the shooter, and a moment later he fired another musket and hit his mark again.

A pirate swung from his ship's crow's nest and battled Fatboy while another engaged Crab. Each of our men fought honorably and spent many minutes in the parry and thrust stage. Fatboy's foe couldn't get a good run at him because he was so agile. On one of the man's missed thrusts, Fatboy stabbed him in the heart. I don't know how Crab did it, he was so awkward, but he cornered his man and skewered him.

I heard a click and an explosion. The musket the captain fired this time had blown up, and he was dead before his torso hit the deck. Lucky for him in a way, as there was nothing left of his face.

The skirmish lasted until the pirate crew had lost twelve men and was down to the five who were continuing to attack us on deck. Within ten minutes, they too were dead and we were in the process of getting our wounds looked at. I ordered Git and a few other saylors who had escaped the battle unscathed to go with me to scavenge the other ship.

Maria was standing over my shoulder and reading as I was writing. "That's it? That's all you're going to tell about what happened?"

"What more do you want?"

"That does nothing to explain either your injuries or why you never went back on the water after returning home."

With excruciating reluctance, I reached into a drawer and pulled out an envelope. "I've never wanted to relive this again. But if you are so interested in the full account, then read what Bart wrote." I passed the envelope across my desk. Her hands were shaking as she picked it up.

"Dios, Walter, it's addressed to me." She gave me a glare I seldom saw from her. "And you read it and never gave it to me?"

"Maria, read the letter. You'll understand why."

With fire in her eyes, she stood over me and began reading.

"Dear Maria,

Walter will likely never tell you what really took place on our last voyage together, so here is the story. I'll be gone within six months, and I've not breathed any word of this to anyone, but you should know the events of that trip."

She pulled a chair next to me and sat down and continued reading:

"We were attacked by pirates in the Indian Ocean, and a furious fight took place on our ship. A pirate came running forward and lunged at Walter just as another went for me. I dispatched my foe and went to help Walter, who was having trouble with his adversary's speed even though it was obvious the man didn't know how to wield a saber. But Walter managed to slice his neck and he went down, mortally wounded. When he fell to the deck, the scarf came off that he was wearing to cover his head. Knowing Walt as I did, he was hoping the pirate had found peace, wherever it would take him.

I watched Walter stagger, staring at the man he'd just had to kill, and thought he was wounded. I ran over to him and saw the face of the dead pirate, who was no man but a boy no more than ten or eleven.

Before either of us could say a word, another boy just as young rushed at Walter with his sword raised. He dragged the blade down Walter's leg and give him a long and deep cut. Walter reacted on instinct and didn't give the boy a second chance to harm him. He aimed his sword low and cut him up the middle, eviscerating the child.

Again, with no time to think, another set of pirates were on us. The one who attacked Walter was again a boy, a little older than the others this time, and he displayed skill as a fighter. Like Fatboy, he was tall and lean, and hard to make contact with. I was able to watch them fight because I tripped over a dead pirate and had to slash the knees of the man who attacked me, who was Walter's age.

He went to the deck, and I got on top of him and finished him off with my knife while Walter and the boy dueled. Just as I stood, Walter's sword pierced the child's throat and came out the other side of his head. Soon, the remaining pirates aboard our ship were either killed, wounded, or too weak to fight."

Maria's face was ashen as she turned from the letter, which I could see was only half read. "Now, I'm understanding. But I don't want to read any more of Bart's words. Will you please tell me the rest?"

I sighed heavily. How do I explain to my wife what I felt about killing children who were forced to fight against grown men? I didn't want the pain this would bring me, but now she had the letter with the whole story in her hands, so I decided to spare her reading it. Frankly, I'd much rather have continued to understate the affair, and say that Bart and I were injured and decided to get off the water. But, Maria wouldn't stop at that, so I had no choice but to lay it out for her, replete with all my anguish.

I took the letter from her and placed it on my desk, face down, and wiped my brow. I fanned myself and fumbled with a cup of tea she'd brought me. I closed my eyes and saw a little boy holding up a white handkerchief to surrender. I cleared my throat and went on with my narrative.

"From that day forward, I've wanted to forget everything about that battle. But the horror of killing boys is fresh in my mind to this day. These children-- they should have been in the streets of London, or Cairo, or wherever, playing with others their own ages, or working with their parents. But they were pirates. And even if they were sold into slavery to help their families, they were intent on killing people, swinging swords and sabers too large for them to hold comfortably, while running at breakneck speeds like kids that age are wont to do, and thrusting their weapons in broken angles because each movement was too difficult and hurt their wrists. I didn't want to kill children. I even paused when the last one came at me. Long enough that he was able to injure my leg seriously. And I killed him. I know it was self-defense, but it still hurts me terribly to think about it. Perhaps the hardest part of killing those children was seeing myself at their ages."

I paused as I let out tears and sobs for the souls of those children. I had said prayers for them upon their deaths, and I still hoped that their afterlives were better than their first ones. Maria came up to me and held my shoulders as I leaned closer to her and began speaking again.

"I remember the sun was high now, and it was hot. Once we'd tossed the dead overboard and rounded up the few marauders who were still alive, I walked the plank to their ship, the faces of the dead children I'd killed as fresh in my mind as if they were standing right in front of me. I still have no idea what possessed me to step aboard that vessel and not take some of the crew with me.

Without paying any attention to my safety, with only my sword drawn, I charged into the rooms on the other ship, searching for pirates or stowaways. I know now that I wasn't looking hard enough, but then again hindsight is perfect, isn't it?

I burst into what I expected to be the cap'n's office, and then that of the first mate. The rooms were a mess, as it appeared the crew had robbed its own ship, since in another room I found two large coin trunks thrown open and containing gold and silver, and a book in one of them detailing pay and paymaster.

I was scanning the numbers in the book to get some idea of the value of the coin in the chests, when I heard a floorboard creak. To the right or the left? I dodged to my right. A musket shot cleared my head so close that I could feel the ball move my hair as it passed. A pirate, who was no lad this time, thrust the barrel of his musket toward me as he unsheathed his sword with his free hand.

Steel clanged against steel, and he sliced my lower arm. My blood was seeping into my sayling shirt. I ignored the pain and kept fighting. The quarters we were in were small, but it still gave both of us the opportunity for a good workout. Lunge to the left, parry to the right, hop up onto the quartermaster's table, jump down to avoid the other's sword. We repeated the cycle several times before I knocked him against a wall and stabbed him in the heart. I'll give him this much, as I removed my blade from his heart, he laughed at me.

But as he fell, so did I. His descent was to death; mine was from the loss of blood. I didn't know what to do, but I did know that I needed to return to my ship. I struggled to my feet, and using the walls for support, managed to make in on deck. I hobbled over the plank and collapsed onto the deck of our ship.

Bart called to me, but with both of his thighs bleeding, one severely, he was in no position to physically come to my aid. He yelled to the crew to get me below deck and to come back for him.

Gimp came to me first and took me to where Doc was treating the wounded. He wrapped my arm so I wouldn't bleed to death and patched my leg, and when Bart was brought in, he did the same for his legs.

Shaken more than ever before in my life, I asked Bart, 'Can we sink that godforsaken ship?'

Both Gimp and Git were near us, and they could hear Bart tell me that I could give the order.

I instructed Gimp to take Fatboy and two more men to get the coin chests. I also told him to order the cannon room to open fire as soon as they were ready. I wanted to be on deck to watch every last plank of that ship sink, so with my arm in a sling, I left Bart.

I was topside for several minutes before I spotted Gimp and Fatboy dragging the heavy chests across the deck. The other saylors were having an easier time with the chest they were lugging, as Gimp was only so agile and Fatboy only so strong. Both teams stopped to rest before balancing on the plank between both ships, with the chests in tow. I had a sinking feeling: What if our men didn't clear the boat before the cannons sank it?

To compound matters, I saw Git trip over some rope and twist an ankle. I hollered to have the cannon fire held up. On deck, it was bustling and noisy, but a crewman saluted me, and I saw his lips move to repeat my order so it could be passed down to the cannon area.

Gimp was now pulling the chest onto the plank by himself, obviously having too much pride to let either of the other crewman help him. The other men followed behind with their chest as Gimp hauled his aboard. Gimp then went back for Git. He put his arm underneath his friend's shoulder and picked him up so he wouldn't put pressure on the bad ankle. I saw both of them step onto the plank and get halfway across when five cannons exploded and hit the other ship at what amounted to pointblank range.

Ten seconds later, a great explosion ripped through the other boat. It took the top deck with it. Miraculously, I saw both Gimp and Git jump for our deck and make it. How Gimp could leap that far on his pitiful excuse for legs still confounds me. However, all was not well. A board from the pirate ship flew across our deck and hit a crewman right above the shoulders, decapitating the man. I have always felt responsible for that man's death, as all I had to do was wait until we were a safe distance away before issuing the order to sink the ship. I continue to send his family money. It's the least I could do, but it makes me ill each time I think about his needless death.

Crow later came to Bart and said when he was throwing the dead into the water he saw two pirates in a small sayling craft on a heading toward the Seychelles. One person in the boat appeared badly injured, while the other was definitely no saylor. I asked why he thought that, and he replied, "Oye, 'cause he had on this gentleman's jacket and a hat pulled down over one eye." I shook my head. It had to be a silly coincidence.

After our ship's "doctor" made his way from the most serious injuries to ours, which indicates just how bad some of the crew were hurt, he came to Bart and me. A set of cloth strips were soaked in a poultice that included garlic juice and applied to my gaping wound, which he then closed with needle and thread. The process was long and painful, and I bit through a piece of leather he'd stuck in my mouth. Bart had to endure the same thing, but on both legs and not just on one arm and leg like me. I couldn't speak for Bart, but my wound felt better without being cleansed and closed. Both of us were then given strong drink to put us to sleep.

But I couldn't. It's one thing to kill another in battle. But Lord, please explain to me why it had to be children I had to kill. They should have had their whole lives to do Your bidding. Why strike them down?"

– I, Walter –

I began to weep, and Maria wept next to me. My fever was growing, and I never felt so weak and feeble. Maria held both my hands in hers. Her tears were for the young boys, no doubt, but I could tell they were also for the anguish I've endured and kept inside me for so long. She wanted me to go to bed, but I told her there was more. And now that she'd set my demons free, she'd have to hear the rest.

– Mike Hartner –

Chapter 12

Maria wiped my brow with a cold damp cloth and stroked my head. She kissed my forehead. "Mi amor, I know I've badgered you for years to tell me everything, but you don't have to go any further. I wish I'd never been so selfishly persistent."

"Now that I've started, I must finish. If I succumb now, these bastardly demons will kill me in my sleep."

"What demons? There aren't any demons." She applied another compress to my face. "Do you want me to leave?"

I really didn't want her to go. The war raged on within me while I closed my eyes and felt the cool cloth on my face. With her by my side, I felt much calmer, safer. But my heart told me it would be better to do the rest of it alone. I held her hand and said, "You're right, there aren't any demons. I'll be all right. You go."

But my fever was starting to come back, and more powerful than ever. This meant my demons were indeed getting closer. I wanted to defeat them one last time, knowing that if I didn't, the only alternative was to surrender to them forever. I fought to open my eyes and keep them open. Shakily, I picked up the quill and dipped it into the inkwell. For some reason, this renewed my energy. I blotted the tip and put it to parchment.

In addition to the coin in the two large chests, one of them had a panel underneath stuffed with tobacco leaf, and a few small coins from a country I'd never heard of. The tobacco piqued my interest again, and I was back to thinking about how to sell the leaves so that people would buy it like salt or spices, and then either chew or smoke it. If I could figure out a way to do this, it would demonstrate my abilities as a trader to Maria's father, because I'd decided this would be my last trip at sea. I would take the money I had in the bank, and any more that Marek might have deposited for me, and sayle to northern Spain on the fastest ship I could find. I'd propose to Maria, show Don Castabel the money I had amassed, and tell him of my success with sugar, and my ideas for tobacco.

***

A few days after our battle, the sun set to light breezes and clear skies. We'd passed the equator, and while we'd been warned that this portion of the ocean was known for its volatile weather, we'd already experienced what I thought was the worst of it when we were blown out to sea earlier. I chuckled like a madman. Isn't it terribly ironic how we often get more than we ask for? The local pastor once said, "What doesn't kill you makes you stronger." By that logic, after I finished this voyage, I should have been damned near invincible.

Bart and I were in quarters with other saylors recovering from their wounds. Doc wanted us all in one place. I was sleeping fitfully and awoke with a start. I saw Bart sitting up. I was in severe pain and needed water, but could feel the boat's being tossed harshly back and forth. Both Bart and I needed to get up. The death of Captain Thomas had left Bart in charge, and he had unofficially promoted me to his second. Not one crewmember made a disparaging comment when he made the announcement, and this helped my spirits, if only temporarily, as the pain in my arm was intense and had spread to my entire upper body.

We both struggled on deck. Bart limped badly, and I thought he'd pass out at any moment. The stitches in his thighs hadn't held, and he'd had to endure Doc's sewing up both legs again. Each of his wounds was twice the length of the single one on my arm, and just as deep. I'll never forget his screams, as Bart was not the sort of man to wince about anything. I thought about this and forgot about my pain, which had to be trivial by comparison.

What faced us was quite a sight to behold. Two foremasts were down, and only one mast to the stern was without damage.

The riggings on the mainmast looked like human arms going crazy in the wind. Waves were hitting the boat from all directions, and there was so much water I feared it had made its way to the hold. What I dreaded was soon confirmed by Crab, who called some men off the deck to help set up a bucket line to bail water. Then the worst thing happened that could have, as the hold was breached. The hole had to be plugged or our ship would sink.

To add to our problems, as if we didn't have enough to contend with, it started to rain. Not a light mist, but pounding sheets containing heavy drops that wouldn't allow us to see for more than a foot on any side of where we stood. I held my hand up to my face and had trouble seeing my fingers.

Crow came back with a report of the situation down below. "Oye, it looks pretty bad. We're gonna have a hard time makin' it through this one."

Bart shook him. "Get whoever is still alive on his feet. I don't care what shape he's in, have him help you fix that hole."

"That be eight men. Five midshipmen, and two ensigns, myself included," Crow said.

Bart said, "I don't care about their ranks or their condition. Carry them down to that hole in the side if you have to. Every man. Get the bailing started and the water up to Walt and me. We'll get it over the side. Patching the hole in these seas is goin' to be damn hard, but if we don't do it, we're all shark bait."

Crow ran down the stairs and I heard him holler to start moving the men.

Bart took over the wheel, which was being held by Hambone, and sent him below. Somehow, Bart managed to turn the boat so that it was riding the waves. And ride them we did. Up and down in the swells, with water pouring over the masthead spike at the front as we went down and then nearly washing both of us out to sea as we pitched back. The second time we pitched so violently I was thrown backwards and caught the riggings on the back of the mainmast before being pitched forward again and timing my release. Strangely, perhaps due to fear or the excitement of being so close to death at any moment, I no longer felt the pain from my wound.

The first bucket made it on deck, and I threw the seawater over the side and handed it back. I did have to use my good arm for this, however. After a half-hour of tossing seawater into the sea, Cat came up with a bucket and I asked what was happening below.

He said, "E'ry time we pull two buckets a water up, two more come in. The good news is we're nary losin' too much agin' it. We're just not gainin' much neither. We got some large pieces of wood from under the cannons, and the men are pluggin' the hole with it now."

The work was slow, since hitting spikes with hammers in fierce seas is not easy. I began feeling pain again and I had an intense headache and fever, when Cat hollered that the first piece of wood was secured, and the breach was now half. He also said there was only about a fourth the water coming in, which I knew from experience was what happened when a hole was patched.

The battle against the elements was by no means over, though, as the boat pitched hard again and again. Her hull also creaked repeatedly. I watched as water pitched onto the bow ran to the stern, with some of it running into the open stairwell we'd been passing buckets through, and adding to the water we'd just bailed from down below.

Out of the corner of my eye, I saw Bart venturing from the wheel to the captain's office. It looked like he was trying to tie a sayle line to a notch above the door, when CRACK!

Lightning struck the mainsayle mast, and it fell forward, smashing through the area Bart had just vacated, just missing the ship's wheel. Part of the wood rigging pinned him to the floor. He was thrashing his arms, and I ran toward him. The ship pitched hard, and I saw the mast shudder. I grabbed onto a step up the wheelhouse, and held onto it with all my might.

On the next reverse pitch, I lost my grip and slid down the deck, all the way to the stairwell. As it turned out, this was where I needed to be. I yelled below for someone to come topside, that Bart was badly hurt. Frog came running up the steps.

I said, "Bart is pinned down by part of the mast the lightning just hit. You have to go to the wheel and first get it steady and then steer the ship so we're facing into the waves and riding them. Otherwise, this ship could capsize."

He appeared dazed by my request. "Sir, I never done it before. 'Ow will I know I'm doin' it right?"

"It's either you do it or we all die. I've got to get Bart from under that mast before it moves and he gets crushed to death."

He saluted. "Aye, sir, I'll do me best."

I was lying on my back, along three stairs going up to where Bart was face down with the rigging covering most of his body. He could talk to me, but he wasn't making much sense, so I thought he might be in so much pain that he was delirious.

I was uncomfortable in the position I found myself in, and made even more so because I had to tuck my knees against my chest, and the pain in my arm and upper body was back in full force. I dug my feet into the heavy mast support, praying I could move it off Bart. I winced with each thrust of my legs, but the rigging didn't budge and I was exhausted.

The rain was not letting up. Water pelted my face, and the wind was pitching our vessel back and forth against the waves with such force that I thought the hull would snap in two.

I couldn't ask Frog to help me. He was doing a decent job of holding the wheel steady, even though he didn't have the ship riding into the waves, when it struck me that this might work to my advantage. I'd wait for just the right time, and the boat's motion could assist me.

The boat pitched forward, and the water rushed onto deck in what was now its usual pattern. Then the boat swelled backwards, and as it did, I pushed my legs to try to get them straight and get the mast crossbeam to move up and flip over. The first time, there was no movement.

Every time the boat started to pitch backwards, I pushed with my legs. After fighting the waves and the water until I was on the brink of passing out from fatigue, there was a violent crash and the ship pitched forward at the highest angle yet.

I waited, and just as the boat was beginning to pitch back, I put all my strength into one last shove. I heard a pop as the mast heaved and then rolled to the side, taking the rigging with it and freeing Bart.

The pop came from my knee, and as I moved up to Bart with as much speed as I could muster, I now had another searing pain to contend with. It almost caused me to buckle over, as it was as severe as what I was feeling from the injury to my arm.

But I steeled myself and ignored everything that was hurting me, when one of the spars on the side of the mast gashed my right calf. I hobbled over to Bart, gritting my teeth to try to forget this latest sharp pain. He was on the deck, his face partly in water. He coughed when I pulled his head up, and I was able to get under him, and with his help walk him back to the captain's quarters, where I laid him on the captain's bed and prayed for his recovery. And mine too.

Cat came into the room. "Frog told me where you was. 'Tweren't waterproofed, but by God's grace, no more water is spillin' in," he said.

Bart and I both drank enough brandy so we could sleep. I left him in the bed and crawled atop the captain's huge desk, resting my head on some parchment I rolled up. I dreamt about things even more horrible than what had happened to us. We were fighting with the pirates, and one of them sliced off my right arm. I saw myself falling to the deck, and then waking to find a pirate standing in front of me, his sword at my chest. I could feel the pain as he plunged the steel tip into my heart.

I awoke with a start. The storm had passed, and as I looked through the window I could see the stars twinkling. I closed my eyes, wrapped in pain and not knowing which part of my body hurt worst, and managed somehow to fall asleep again.

I had another dream. I was back in the battle. This time, just after I'd slain the children, I spied a pirate getting the better of Bart. I threw a knife at the pirate, and it missed him. I threw another and it missed too, by a wider mark than the first one. The pirate plunged his sword into Bart. I screamed and woke up.

The sky was gray, and the sun would soon be up. I tried to return to sleep but couldn't. I pushed myself to my feet and hobbled to check on Bart. I felt something on my ankle, and when I focused my eyes, Doc had placed a bandage on that wound.

He'd also changed the dressing on my arm, yet not once was I aware he was in the cabin.

Bart was asleep. I struggled on deck. Hambone was back at the helm, and as he saluted me I nodded to him, because I couldn't raise my right arm. The deck was strewn with buckets. I dipped one into the ocean. The water was cool and refreshing, so I took a bucketful of it to Bart. I ripped a sleeve from my shirt to create a cool press, and laid it on him.

Several minutes later, I heard him mumble, "Walt?"

"I'm right here."

"I think, my friend, if ye and I make it home, our saylin' days are done."

"I couldn't agree more, sir."

Bart's back was cut and horribly bruised, but he didn't have any broken bones. Doc splinted my knee and sewed my calf. I was still not immune to the pain of his stitches. I hoped that someday there would be a way to keep this from hurting so much.

The crew worked to repair the beams and sayles, but we needed to be docked and have plenty of time to get the ship genuinely seaworthy. And for us to heal and rest as much as to fix the ship. In a week, with the aid of clear skies and the quadrant, we drifted as much as sayled into the harbor at Mauritius.

The morning we dropped anchor, Doc had Bart and me take off our bandages. I had a wide scar that ran nearly a third of my forearm. I also had a three-inch scar on my right calf, and a very sore left knee that wouldn't allow me to place any pressure on it. I assumed I would be joining Gimp and have a limp for life, and I would be right. But I was alive, and I would forever mourn the saylors who died saving me.

At a market in Mauritius, I found some large flat squares of tin and traded salt for them. I wanted to try to repair the masts with them. Some laborers were willing to help us for spirits, and we wrapped rope around the main and started pulling it backwards where it split. We matched up the wood as best we could and took a piece of tin and hammered it to both sections. We flipped over the mast and repeated the process. The work was slow and we had to take many breaks. The deck where the mast had been originally fitted also had to be repaired, but at the end of the day the first mast was hanging again.

We spent the next two weeks refitting the remaining masts and sewing sayles. Under Gimp's direction, the crew did a proper job of repairing the hull breach and tarring it to make it waterproof. Our final function before loading food was to climb the masts and repair the rigging, of which there were many issues. Some were so tangled they had to be cut away and new ones assembled. Bart gave all of us a day of rest before we loaded food and water and set sayle in our "new" boat.

Chapter 13

We had good, steady winds for most of our trip home, but it still seemed to take forever. We stopped in several ports along the way, but just long enough to get food and fresh water. Every time we got under sayle, I prayed that nothing else would happen to us. I think if we had been attacked by another pirate ship, we would waved a white flag of surrender immediately. My heart wasn't in another fight, and I could sense that neither was Bart's.

While we continued to convalesce together, we talked about everything imaginable. He discussed his wife and children at length, and especially about what his kids were like when they were younger. And then he told me stories of his wife when they were courting. What he went through wasn't necessarily comparable with what I was having to deal with, but in some ways it was the same, particularly with his often being away and wondering if she'd continue to be there for him when he returned.

"Do ye plan to go to ask Maria to marry when we get back?" Bart asked me during one of our conversations.

"As fast as I can get to her. I'd ask to get off the ship if we dock in northern Spain for supplies, but I want to heal more and have my money together to show Don Castabel when I ask his permission to marry her. I'm worried, though. I'm only a common man. A saylor. How could he possibly give his daughter to me? It's also been another year since I saw her last. Maybe he's found a different suitor for her, or she loves someone else she's met on her own? I hate thinking about this, but I have no choice."

"Ye have nothing to worry about, lad. Don Castabel is an honorable man, and I'm sure he recognizes the same in you."

Bart tried several times over the next few days to ease my fears. I'd love to say I was a friend and listened intently, but that would be a lie. I was too wrapped up in thinking about Maria and what could go wrong with our relationship. I so wanted to get back to her, and as we approached northern Spain, everywhere I looked I could see her face and her hair and her smile, and hear her voice. For more times than I could count, I decided to go ashore, certain Bart would give me a small boat, a pair of oars, and his blessing. But I stayed aboard. I would go to her only when I was at my best.

Bart's wounds were mending, as were mine. Doc's stitches had long since rotted away on both of us, and while I once thought blood poisoning was the reason my whole upper body was in such pain, I was now without the agonizing discomfort that plagued my every breath for days at a time. My calf was healed, but the scar was wide, as the stitches had come out and I wouldn't let Doc sew me up again. I'd tossed away the sling and could move my arm freely and pick up heavy objects again, but my knee hurt whenever I leaned on it, and I was forced to walk with a limp because I had to shift my weight with each step to keep as much pressure off it as possible. I didn't realize I'd have to deal with this for the rest of my life. I'm proud to report we didn't lose one injured crewman during the return trip, and Gimp and Git were almost fully recovered by the time we reached Portsmouth.

We made port at night. Bart immediately hired a carriage and left, without explanation. The next morning, I went to a real physician and he ordered me to bed for at least a week. I made it three days. My first task was to go to the bank and see if Marek had made another deposit in my account. He hadn't, and there was no letter from him at the tavern. But my bank account was huge, and this didn't include my share of the spoils from our encounters with the pirates. I called it blood money, but I wasn't going to refuse it. I'd find a way to put it to good use, maybe give it to the families of the crewmen we lost.

I figured I'd need another few weeks before I'd be able to leave to see Maria and the Don, and make arrangements for safe passage. The bank would give me an official ledger to show Maria's father, but I wanted to take many gold coin so he could see for himself that I really had money to give to his daughter. The banker sent a letter I wrote to Maria to tell her I'd soon be coming to the hacienda, and I figured it would get to her at about the time I would be leaving England.

I rented a room and spent most of my time getting used to being on dry land again, and buying gifts for Maria. I took most of my meals at The Drenched Seaman.

I hadn't seen Bart for two weeks, when just after I ordered my evening meal at the pub, he walked in with the aid of not one but two canes. He sat with me, talked about how glad he was to be back and see his family, and ordered a meal for himself.

"I been to see a number of people higher in the chain of command than me, Walter." he said after we'd finished eating. "I recommended ye for a jump of several levels in rank. I figured ye earned at least two on the water. For more than half the trip, ye acted as the second on our ship, even though you didn't have the rank for it. But the Officer's Board must review the promotion I asked for, not tests by a group of proctors. Aye, I can tell ye, I got harder questions from them than ye got."

"But I want to quit sayling, and you said the same."

"Lad, there's a reason for all this. But for now, we need to get ye to the tailor for a new uniform. You bein' a lieutenant colonel and all."

"What!"

"It won't be official until ye meet with one very special person, and that will be a little while from now, but ye will be very pleased when this is all over."

"I don't want another promotion, I want to go to Maria." My voice was louder than I would've liked.

"You're gonna need the promotion. Trust me on this. And don't worry, Maria will still be there for ye. She's not marryin' anybody else."

"How can you be sure?"

"Just know I'm statin' the facts."

Uncomfortable as I was in having to remain in England longer than I'd planned, I wasn't going to let the news ruin my time with Bart. I trusted him, and after a few mugs of ale, believed he was looking after my best interests--somehow.

***

Bart and I were sitting on a park bench the next day when a man walked up to us. He limped and had a patch over one eye, and I immediately respected him, as was my custom now for anyone with a disability. He stopped in front of our bench and in a gravelly voice addressed me: "Your name is Walter Crofter, sir?" I nodded.

"I was told by the owner of the Seaman I'd find you here with another man. Guess ye both just left. My ship's cap'n asked me to bring this to ye, as a favor for someone he knows at a bank." He reached in his coat pocket and pulled out an envelope.

I thanked him and handed him a guinea.

I recognized Maria's handwriting, and my hands shook as I opened the letter:

"My Dearest Walter,

I have not seen or heard from you in such a long time, and I am terribly worried. Did I do something to make you stay away?

In my heart, I hope you are safe and will be with me soon. A few men have come to see my father about me. He knows how I feel, however, and he is willing to give me a little more time before he makes a decision about my future. But I can tell he is getting impatient.

I hope you will come soon.
Maria."

I showed the letter to Bart. "I guess that clears up most of your worries, doesn't it now, lad?" he said.

"If Don Castabel is interviewing suitors for Maria, I can only imagine the wealth they are offering him." My whole body was shaking, not just my hands. "Now, I'm more worried than ever."

"Let's go back to the boat."

"Why leave now? It's a beautiful day other than the news I was just brought."

We came aboard and went to Bart's old quarters, which was now my room. Two chests were placed in front of what had been his desk. I recognized them as the ones from the pirate ship with the children. "What are these in here for? I hoped to never see them again. They make me think of those…children."

"Aye, but they both hold a lot of coin, and tobacco leaves."

"I know. I opened them before they were brought on board."

"They are yours, lad. Everything inside is yours."

With as much money I now had, I was positive no one could offer more for Maria. However, I felt guilty.

"Shouldn't the men have a share in this? And what about you, since you're now the cap'n."

"I'm glad you recognize me as the captain, and that's why I can make this decision and none of ye can argue with me about it." He put his hand on my shoulder. "Ye were responsible for bringing these chests on board. And for saving the ship once, and me twice, along the way back. These are yours. Use them to help ye win Maria, if this is what ye think ye'll have to do. Me, I don't think ye have a problem. And so ye know, there was plenty of booty, and with what ye gave the crew earlier, each man and his family will live a comfortable life, forever."

With such a great fortune now at my disposal, and Maria's letter safely tucked in my pea coat, I went back to my room in town and lay awake well into the night, thinking about all of the things I could do for this woman I wanted to be my wife.

***

I'd been putting off getting the new uniform, as I hadn't decided to accept the promotion Bart had arranged for me. However, first thing the next day, I went to the tailor's shop and had a jacket made for me with the designation of a lieutenant colonel on its sleeves. I also went to a cobbler for new pair of boots and a belt.

I would be ready, but I had no idea for what.

Chapter 14

I was passing by The Drenched Seaman on the way back to the ship when I was accosted by an old saylor and literally thrown into the pub. My bad leg didn't allow me to put up much of an argument, but as I turned to take a swing at the man, I saw my business partner from the past five years sitting at an empty table. Marek looked at me with a smile on his ruddy face, which I assumed was even redder because he'd been drinking all day. "I see my mate found ye. Sit down, Walter."

I sat.

"I look for you for ev'ry time I come to port. But we seem to keep missing each other of late."

"A lot, of late," I said.

"Hell, don't let it worry ye none. Tell me what ye been up to."

He ordered me a pint and I went over everything except killing the child pirates. In two hours, and many more drinks, I was as drunk as he was, yet he never seemed to get any drunker than when I'd first sat down.

Apparently I'd told the story well, as he seldom interrupted me except to order more mead. Several other people sitting near us seemed equally intrigued by what I'd had to say. When I finished, one of the men listening to my adventures brought me another pint, which I didn't need. He patted me on the shoulder as he was leaving and said, "It's good ye got back safely." A comment like this from a man I didn't know made me feel especially good.

Marek took a drink from his personal flagon, which he said he'd brought with him. "I almost called you 'boy,' which would a been wrong. Ye definitely are a man now. But ye got very lucky." He made the sign of the cross.

I nodded my agreement and asked him about what was happening with our trading business during the time he hadn't been in contact with me, which was considerable, and why there hadn't been a deposit made in my account since the first one.

He belched and cast me the look of a hopeless drunk. "You, sir," he said as he pointed directly at me with a fat index finger, "are a true rogue. Do ye know that, Walter Crofter?"

I didn't know what to say to that, and when Bart hobbled into the bar, I motioned for him to sit with us.

Marek and I were both quiet and Bart asked, "Did I interrupt somethin'?"

Marek said, "I was telling Walter what a rogue he really is."

"And how is that?" Bart asked as a bar wench brought him a pint.

Marek took some papers from his coat pocket and shook them in front of both of us. He fixed his eyes on mine. "I got to admit, when ye came up with this poppycock idea about sugar, I thought ye'd lost ye mind. I mean, it had been staring me and many other traders in the face for at least 15 years that I know of, yet none of us ever done anythin' about it. All of a sudden, here comes a kid with more money than most men make in ten year, and he's willin' to bet it all on a fancy idea." He took a gulp of mead, which produced a loud belch. "Sorry 'bout that. Now, lemme go on. In my own mind, it could never a been that simple. I only took the money from ye 'cause I knew it wouldn't work and I'd make a big profit for doin' nothin'. Turns out, I was wrong. Wrong by a lot. These here papers is the final accounting since ye and me started business five year ago." He thrust everything at me as if he were angry.

I couldn't understand anything but the ending tally for each year.

I handed the papers to Bart. "Do you know what these numbers mean?"

His eyes got big and he chuckled but said nothing.

– I, Walter –

"Walter, Bart knows just how big those numbers are, and because ye got me into this, I've added at least one boat every year. Last year, three of the biggest cargo ships I could find. Each of them laden with sugar going to England and other ports in Europe as fast as we can get them loaded and back again for more. We have orders for more sugar than I could bring in if I had ten more ships. And I'm not searchin' for business, mind ye, it's searchin' for me. Ye have made both of us very rich men. So much so that I bought an estate, and me wife has formed an association to help others improve their lot in life."

Dumbfounded, I asked the only thing to come to mind: "So why am I a rogue?"

"Because, with all the boats to keep saylin', I've had to work more than ever."

I laughed.

He glared at me and said, "Don't laugh at me, boy. I worked harder for ye in the last five years than I worked for meself in all me life. And the only reason was to prove ye wrong." He finished his flagon and asked the wench to have it refilled.

"And now, I'm here this evening to tell you, I'm quittin'. I'm out of this company. I don't want to work no more for you, me, or nobody else." He sighed, and I saw tears form in his eyes until he turned up his flagon and began a swig that lasted until he drained it. "Ye got to know, Walter, I spent the last few months at sea telling ye off. Now, I have to give ye this." He pulled a crumpled receipt from his pocket and handed it to me.

I looked at the piece of paper, and saw the imprint of the Mercantile bank. I also saw a very large number below it.

"What's this?" I asked.

"A statement from the Mercantile Bank, givin' a balance."

The number was staggering. "This is a very, very wealthy person's account." I said.

"It is, indeed."

"Why you showing this to me?"

"'Cause it's ye account. Since the first deposit, I been keepin' ye money in another bank that give me better terms when I needed to borrow money. I transferred ye share to the Mercantile Bank two day ago."

I dropped the ceramic mug that contained my ale, and it shattered on the floor.

Marek's eyes seemed to be dancing around. Maybe he was playing with me. I was too drunk to worry about what I might say that could make him mad. "Teasing me like this is not fair, sir. I've done nothing to deserve this."

"I'm not teasin'. If I was, I'd never be doin' it this way, I can assure ye. That money is ye's. An it's 'xactly half the profit from the business since we started it. Ne'er kept as much as a pence that weren't mine."

I don't remember ever being as overwhelmed by anything, except perhaps the revelation that I'd killed children. Stunned, I sat at the table and stared at the spot on the floor where I'd just dropped the mug that the wench was now sweeping up.

Bart slapped my back and brought me out of my dreamy state. "What do ye think now, Walter?"

"That I need to give half of it to you."

"No, it's ye money. It was ye idea from the start, and ye were the one who suggested we talk to this here sea captain."

I shook Marek's hand and said, "I half expected you to run, regardless of whether you ended up successful or not. Why didn't you?"

"If it had been just ye, I might of. Or cheated ye blind. Ye word against mine, and nobody would know the difference." He took a long pull from still another flagon of mead.

"Why didn't you?" I had to ask him.

"I'll tell ye the truth. It was never just ye, it was 'bout that man sittin' next to ye. I heard a lot about 'im. He's got high connections in London." I glanced at Bart. His eyes seemed to be pleading with Marek not to say anything more, which I found odd.

I become strangely sober, as if I'd never had the first drink of ale. "What will it take to keep you trading, at least for a few more years?" I asked Marek.

"It won't happen." The old captain shook his head and slobbered on his beard.

"How about if I give up half my profits? I'll only get one-fourth instead of half?

And instead of just sugar, what about buying more ships and going to Africa and bringing in tobacco? I'm sure it can make the money from sugar look like a pittance."

I've heard the French talk about tobacco. They crave the stuff. Ye have a reliable source for it?

I made a lot of contacts in Africa. I'm positive we can trade cloth for tobacco, and we'll get ten times more for the leaf than sugar. And cloth costs us very little."

Marek thought for a long time, staring at his flagon but not drinking a drop. He gave his beard a tug. "It could take most of a year to get around the Horn and back with a sample. I don't know if I want to wait that long, regardless of the possibilities."

"We've got some of the leaf in a trunk on our ship. It came from that last pirate battle, and one of that crew told us where they got it, along with who the cap'n traded with."

Marek stared at his flagon again for several minutes before looking up and asking, "And ye be willin' to settle for a fourth and not half this time?" I nodded, and he went back to contemplating his flagon.

"Ye know, I was was goin' to try to get ye to buy out my half of the business, and now I'm bein' roped into another enterprise with ye. But I'll do it."

We quickly shook hands, and I said, "Let's not make it so many years until we meet again."

Marek chuckled and assured me that wouldn't be the case. We agreed to meet on our ship so I could give him the trading contacts and the tobacco and he could get an idea of interest, and what it really might bring in money. My ten times sugar was something I just threw out. Little did I know that some of the better tobacco would bring in 15 times my estimate.

We departed The Drenched Seaman together. Marek left with his man who had "guided" me into the pub, Bart took a carriage back to the dock, and I walked to the inn where I rented a room whenever I stayed in town.

Something in the shadows caught my eye as I ambled down the cobblestone street. A tall, thin man ducked into an alley just as I turned my head his way. I couldn't make out his face, but he was wearing a hat with the brim pulled down.

– Mike Hartner –

Chapter 15

"Nay, no way, lad!"

I don't remember when I'd heard Bart so demonstrative. I'd just put on my new jacket with the lieutenant colonel stripes, and a pair of pants I'd bought to go with it. According to him, my breeches came up three inches too high. I was used to what I wore on the ship, and this is the way I had the tailor make the pants. I remember the man'sm smiling at me when he asked me where I wanted the pants legs to end, and I guess I should have figured that a lieutenant colonel's dress would be different from a common saylor's.

Bart rushed me to the tailor and insisted the man do the alterations immediately. We waited for two hours while he and his two assistants cut and sewed a new pair of pants for me. Bart acted genuinely peeved that the tailor hadn't educated me to the proper length for a high-ranking officer's pants. I on the other hand found it humorous, and couldn't understand why the length of my pants legs was so important. After all, I was leaving the Navy, as was Bart. I wanted to be done with it right away, lofty rank or not, but he said the process required time for everything to go through the proper channels and this is why we couldn't just walk away.

When he was satisfied with the way my outfit looked, he walked me to a store and bought me some more clothes, but of a normal variety, and a bag to put them in. He did the same for himself. I had no idea what was going on, but I also knew better

– I, Walter –

than to ask questions. A coachman I recognized from when Bart had hired him a few days earlier picked us up in a large carriage, and I sat in uncomfortable silence as we were whisked out of town. Our trip took five days, and it ended in London.

After a night at an inn and a good meal, with Bart still not giving me any reason for this trip--even after I finally asked--following breakfast the next morning, the same carriage driver took us to a building with a sign that read "Royal Guard." We were in such a rush that I didn't notice until we were sitting in the carriage that Bart hadn't brought even one of his canes with him today.

I was wearing my new uniform, and Bart was greeted by a friend, based on the greeting, smiles, and warm handshakes they gave each other. We entered a great room filled with a number of soldiers milling about who I assumed be "Royal Guards," since all of them wore colorful capes and elegant uniforms with swords that glimmered at even a hint of light.

Soon the entire group of men stopped and looked at me in silence. Not one man paid the slightest attention to Bart. I felt as though I shrank a foot. I couldn't figure out why they were staring at me. Bart allayed my paranoia by putting his arm on my shoulder and guiding me down a long hall. Frankly, I think he wanted to brace himself as much as anything. At the end of the hall, he walked me into another room with just a table and two benches in the middle.

On the far wall hung chains with handcuffs and leg irons bolted to them. Bart sat me on a bench and turned away, leaving me in this awful place. Then I heard the bolt on the door slamming into its catch, which filled me with terror. I sat in the room, wondering why I'd been brought here, and contemplated my fate. I had no idea what I could have done, only that it had to be something very bad, and I started to sweat.

I didn't know how long I'd been sitting there when I heard the bolt thrown back and the door pushed open. A massive, burly man of at least 6 feet in height, with muscles larger than my whole arm and legs that looked like tree trunks, walked into the room. He was carrying a red, fur-lined robe on one arm, and he placed the garment gently on the bench across the table from me.

I could see that it was red velvet, and I knew he had to be important, because very few people wore fabric anywhere near that plush. He rolled up the long sleeves of his shirt, and held a look that said he was attending to some distasteful work. And that he carried no badge or markings on his clothes to identify himself as sheriff or deputy made me worry even more. I don't remember ever being more scared of one man.

The only thing that kept me from panicking was that Bart had brought me here, and I didn't think he'd want to do me harm. Still, this man might be mistaking me for someone else and kill me with his bare hands. I was very strong for my size, and I was quick. But against this giant, I wouldn't stand a chance.

He stared at me for what seemed to be several minutes but was probably more like 20 seconds. And that he was obviously sizing me up didn't help my disposition either.

"You're Walter, right?" I nodded, and swallowed deep.

"Son of Geoff, who's been trying to curry favor in the courts for more than ten years while waiting for Sir Walter to gain support again, and who may find his wait will continue for a time still?"

I nodded again and gulped once more. This didn't feel right.

"Son of Mildred, a fine woman?"

"And brother of Gerald, a criminal of the worst sort, who's to be hanged and quartered for theft on the high seas, kidnapping, and murder?"

I didn't know that Gerald's crimes were this horrific. I nodded again, not sure what I was getting into by agreeing.

"You're the fine lad who's been sayling with Bart for these past five plus years?"

Finally, other than the question about my mother, one I could easily answer with confidence, yet I squeaked, "Yes, sir."

"Calm down, son. Nobody's here to harm you."

Not realizing that I'd been holding my breath, I let out a huge sigh of relief.

"Bart is my cousin, and when I heard what you did for him, I needed to meet you." He smiled "Let me shake your hand." His hand dwarfed mine, and he shook it warmly and clapped me on the back. "Thank you, Walter, for keeping Bart safe."

"That's what friends are for," I said, something I'd told Bart quite often.

He laughed heartily and said, "Modest, too. I like that."

He stopped laughing and looked at me seriously. "My cousin can spend the rest of his days with his family because of what you have done. Nothing is more important to me than family. So, from all of us, thank you."

I felt my face flush and I nodded.

"The second reason you're here is because Bart tells me you will not be going back out on the water. He also informs me he will be quitting the sea too, but he won't give me the reason why."

"He said that to me, too, sir, but I don't know his reasons. It could be his leg wounds." That was a big white lie. I knew exactly why he wanted to quit being a saylor, and while it was partly family, he knew how lucky he was to have survived that last voyage, and this had nothing to do with my saving his life on two occasions.

This giant of a man waited for me to continue. When I didn't, he stared at me, almost as if he was figuring out an angle to use on me. He let out a heavy sigh and said, "I was really hoping you could tell me why he made that decision. Imagine my surprise when my cousin, a saylor all his life, comes back to England and tells me his sayling days are over. I asked him to explain it to me, and he said, 'I'm finished. It's time to stay home and watch my children grow and be with my wife.' That sentiment is all well and good, but it's not Bart's way. Would you care to explain? Or at least tell me why his voice cracked when he was talking to me?"

"Sir, I'm not going to make up a story. I'm sure Bart will tell you when he feels it's time. But I can't betray his confidence." I rubbed my right arm and the scar on it rather harshly, as it had started to pain me, as if it was listening to my discomfort and trying to tell me something.

"Well, that leaves me with two problems. The first is that I have a ship without a commander I trust. Would you be interested in that job?"

"I assure you, under any other circumstances, I would honored and jump at the chance. But my mind's made up."

"All right, then. That leaves one more thing that has come up. We have received a request from a powerful man in northern Spain, a man whom you know, and from what I understand, the father of the woman you want to marry. It seems he requires help with some shipping problems. He needs someone at the port in San Sebastian, on the ground, and a request came in for you. At the same time, we need an emissary from England in northern Spain. But the problem is, for our country to agree to this, by law the person would have to be at least of a certain military rank, I believe a lieutenant colonel or above. Oh, I see by your sleeves, Walter, you've attained that rank."

I was trying to figure out what to say. I cleared my throat so that I could reply but nothing came out.

He waved me off. "I'm asking if you want this assignment. It would be a two-year appointment, to finish at the end of your eighth year in total service to the King. At that time you will given the option of retiring or continuing to serve the Crown. Are you interested?"

My throat was so dry that I was hoarse when I said, "Yes, sir. More interested than you could know, sir."

"Bart will bring you to this building tomorrow morning at 9 o'clock, and you will be officially sworn in as a lieutenant colonel in the Royal Guards. This is the rank with which you must go to Spain; wear it proudly. Don Castabel is a very important political ally, but people in his country will look at you as representing England and not as his son-in-law. You must never forget that."

"I won't, sire." I was a fool, as I just figured out that I was talking to the King of England. I got down on one knee in front of him and kissed the ring on his hand.

"Rise up, Walter, and I will see you tomorrow morning."

***

That day, I sought out my parents. They were living in the London Commons on the bottom floor in a rat-infested "flat," as this sort of apartment was called. The walls were drafty, and on this particular day the wind could be heard and felt howling through them. My mum was thin and pale, and my father was a shell of the man he once was, even when times had been at their worst. They had both aged badly since I left. He was literally fading away into nothingness with waiting for Sir Walter Raleigh to get back in the good graces of the King. I could now tell him what I had just learned from a pretty good source-- that it wasn't going to happen.

I vowed to change their lives forever, but knowing my father's ways, when times were good he always spent whatever he had as fast as he could, so I needed to come up with a plan and let it work gradually. I gave him three gold coins, told them to buy some warm clothes and bedding, and that they would be moving. But this could take a little while, so I went to the building manager to see if I could at least get them into better living quarters for the time being.

"Is there a way to get the Crofters a better place?" I asked a man with a curmudgeonly look who had an attitude to match.

"Crofter? Ye must be mad, boy. Why should I give them a better anythin' when they's always behin' on his rent by at least a month or two."

"How much do they owe? How much to get them a better apartment right now so that they don't freeze to death?"

"Right now, he's owin' a bit more than a crown."

"Do you have a good apartment they could move into right away?"

"Not for what they're payin' me."

I put a sovereign in the man's hand. "Now, let's see the very best apartment you've got."

I returned to my parents and helped them move three stories up to a flat in the rear of the building. Not great, but the wind couldn't get to it, and it was clean and there was no indication of rats. I took them for a large meal, and I bought them as much food as they could store in the cupboard before it spoiled. I gave Mum another gold coin and told her to treat herself. I assured them I'd have someone find them a nice house, and they'd never have to worry about the cold or starving again.

In honesty, I felt horribly guilty. I hadn't checked on them in years and had no idea things had gotten so bad with my father chasing his dream of tagging along on Sir Walter Raleigh's coattails.

That night, just before I had to leave my parents, I asked them what had happened years ago that caused Gerald to leave.

My father said, "Gerald left because he said I was doin' everything for you and nothin' for him. I kept tellin' him I could barely feed the family, but when Sir Walter comes back, things will be good again. He said I'd still give everythin' to you, so what did it matter? I told him you was workin' with me every day and earnin' your keep more than him. He stormed off and turned to a life a crime. It's killin' your mother, but there's nothin' to be done. She knows he's goin' to end up hangin' at Newcastle, and she says it will kill her too when it happens." He grabbed Mildred's thin hands and she cried. "Walter, I ne'er thought it would end up like this. I know now I done it all wrong."

I placed my hand on theirs. "You won't have to worry anymore. Just take care of Mum. I'm going to Spain to marry the woman of my dreams. Later, I might even send for both of you. But for now, one thing at a time. I'm going to open a bank account in your names, and each month the manager will give you more than enough money to live comfortably. Just take care of yourselves and eat hearty and get some meat on your bones." I smiled at Mum.

Her tears came faster and my father held her. They both were happy now, for what I was certain was the first time in a long while, but I had to ask more about Gerald.

"Did either of you ever have any contact with Gerald after he left?"

"I'm not goin' to lie," my father said. "With no warnin' at all, he come by one night, all dressed up like a gentleman. He says he's heard of your good fortune with the sugar and the boats. I guess that made him angry or jealous or somethin', 'cause he left right after he tells us this. A sheriff was killed in the city a few days later, and your mum told me the authorities was sure Gerald did it." My mum let out a wail that had no tears attached to it. I was ready for the conversation to end, but my father went on. "He keeps disappearing for stretches of time though, and the authorities think he goes to sea. Then he comes back and there's burned-out families, thievery, and murders. Whether these crimes are all caused by him or not, whenever he's seen in London and somethin' happens, they say it's him. Problem is, some of it prob'ly is his doin's."

Listening to my father's description of Gerald's despicable life didn't allow me to leave my parents as I would've liked, but I know they felt good that they'd now be taken care of for the rest of their lives. However, while riding in a hired carriage on my way back to the inn, something concerned me more than anything else my father had said about Gerald. How was it that my brother knew anything about the sugar business and Marek and me?

Chapter 16

The next morning, in front of all his men, the commander of the Royal Guard swore me to secrecy and confirmed me with the rank of lieutenant colonel. I could see Bart smiling as I was sworn in. Dare I say he even looked proud?

When I left the room, I was in a daze. Bart directed me to a large garden and sat me at a bench. He told me he'd be back in a while. I don't think I even responded to him as he walked away, though I could hear his chuckle.

My thoughts, as always of late, turned to Maria. I now had money. I had rank in the service of the King. And I was being positioned to work in the area where Maria lived. Everything was falling into place, and I dreamt of the things I could say to both Maria and her father when I arrived.

Bart came back and broke me out of my reverie by asking if I was hungry. I'd been too nervous to eat breakfast and now I was starved. He took me to where the Royal Guard ate their meals, and then to meet his family. Bart said he'd been anticipating some of them arriving at the time of my swearing-in ceremony, and this was why he had left me in the garden.

Bart's family was throwing him a retirement party, and all of the immediate members were present as well as some distant relatives. Bart's wife, Lady Ellen, was so gracious to me that I was embarrassed. His two oldest children, both girls, introduced themselves while their four siblings, who were much younger, played with another. The gap in ages indicated that Bart had endured a very extended voyage just a couple of years before we'd met. I made a mental note to ask him about this, as a long trip away from home was never discussed in all of our time together.

Bart's oldest brother Sir John thanked me for my service to the Crown and for everything else I'd done. Bart told me he had a lot to do with my promotion and its expediency. When I expressed my appreciation, Sir John said, "Nothing you haven't earned, my boy," and slapped me on the back.

Bart had such a large and congenial family that my hand was sore from shaking theirs. Later that day, his cousin even stepped into the room, which immediately became hushed. The smallest children quieted down too, as if by magic. The King stayed just long enough to make an elegant toast to Bart, and while his attendance was brief, I could see in Bart's eyes that he was grateful for his cousin's recognition of his service.

When the party finally broke up, it was late and Lady Ellen invited me to sleep in her home. The following morning, after many tears on all our parts, Bart gave me a packet and said, "These are ye orders, and ye introduction, even though ye don't need one a those to Don Castabel. Go, Walter, chase Maria down and marry her. She'll be good to ye. I know my Ellen has been for me."

I wanted to leave England immediately, but I had some things I had to do first, including getting my parents settled in a home and accounts set up for them at the bank. I soon learned that I had a myriad of other banking issues needing my attention. Wealth has its own set of problems, which I had to learn about and deal with before I could leave.

***

I put down the quill and went to my bed. That night, my fever broke and I felt good for the first time in what seemed like months. Maria brought me a compress and was happy when I told her I didn't need it. I wanted to get back to writing.

"What are you going to write about today?" she asked.

"I've got some ideas, but won't know for sure until I dip my quill."

"Why not tell what happened in France?"

I sighed. "Something else I'd like to forget altogether."

"But it's a part of you. And if you don't want to write about it, maybe I should."

"I just went through one horrible memory. I don't know if I can deal with another. At least not so soon." I grabbed the compress I'd refused and wiped my forehead with it. Maria came over to me.

"Then why don't you write about what happened at The Salty Dog."

"Because the wedding and what happened afterwards are more important to me."

A hug and kiss and she said, "Tell about those two years first."

"And how we had to postpone our wedding for that entire time?"

"Walter, tell the story. It will make you feel better. You'll see."

Later, when I picked up my quill and dipped it in the inkwell, Maria stood over my shoulder. I checked where I'd left off and wrote:

After my return to England, it was three months before I set foot on Spanish soil and went to Maria. A lot happened during those 90 days, not the least of which was my education into what my assignment for the King really entailed. During a series of meetings with the King's staff, I learn that mine was a full-time job and not the laze in the park I had assumed.

The port in San Sebastian was a mess politically, and the sheriff I'd come to know from my prior visits had his hands full with smugglers seeking refuge and other criminals entering the country with impunity because of some corrupt local officials. At the same time, England was harmed because many of its ships were being captured at sea and the goods sold in Spain. My job would be to set up a system to patrol the seas in the area and to secure the port. If illicit cargo and criminals couldn't get in through the port, many of the other problems would take care of themselves. The King of course had failed to mention any of this to me before I jumped at the job. But he got to be King for a reason, and it wasn't for being stupid.

— I, Walter —

I didn't know what I was going to do about the port, even after a lot of advice from the King's staff, but the lone issue I was certain of was that I couldn't give Maria the life she deserved and perform my duties at the same time. So I reached the awful conclusion that I'd have to postpone marrying her until my term was over. Two more years!

But things weren't as bad as I thought they might be, and the biggest reason was the support Don Castabel gave me. He said was unaware of the issues with the port. When I explained them, he got the local officials who were honest behind me, and the programs I put in place came together quickly and smoothly.

I soon was able to spend considerable time with Maria. But I couldn't stay at the hacienda and give the port the attention it required, and Maria couldn't stay with me in the town even if we were married, since people would know she was my wife and she would be ripe for being kidnapped. She said that the kidnapping she'd had to live through was something that preyed on her mind every day. She made it clear she'd die before letting that happen again, so we never even had a discussion about her living in the town of San Sebastian.

Maria and I did however settle into a comfortable life with each other, and in less than a year the port was as secure as any in Europe. The sheriff had rooted most of the criminal elements from the city, or hanged them, and Maria and I could have gotten married at any time, but she still didn't want to leave the hacienda and live in town, and I couldn't much blame her, since it was a typical, dingy seaport, with all that comes with it.

It didn't take me long to cultivate a taste for the local food, and with Maria's help I learned passable Spanish. Conversely, her English was now as good as mine, although she spoke it with a distinctive accent. I'd rented a modest apartment in the town, because if the truth be known, there wasn't anything beyond it available unless I wanted to have something built, which I didn't desire. I ate most of my meals at a tavern near my office, but on occasion I'd go to a pub called The Salty Dog. Known for its "hospitality," which I wasn't remotely interested in, the food was more what I was accustomed to, since, as with the pub in

Hispaniola, an Englishman also owned this one. So, when I yearned for an English meal, I went to The Dog.

My first visit was one of the luckiest things I'd ever done, even though I'd gotten in a fight.

Maria had been reading as I was writing, and she said, "You were more than lucky."

"I know," I said, and continued:

Two pairs of long tables spanned the pub's main room, and these were flanked by a series of benches and smaller tables. I was passing one of the smaller tables when a well-known ruffian, whom I'd had thrown off the dock many times, held a rather skinny fellow by the arms while another thug I also recognized hit him in the jaw.

Not liking the poor man's odds, I grabbed an empty flagon from the bar and hit the fellow over the head with it before he could take another swing. It didn't faze him. So, if that wasn't going to work, I'd use a cask that had been rolled against the bar, and try to hit him in the head with the section with a metal strap wrapped around it.

Considering the weight of what I'd had to lift aboard ship, I felt no small amount of pride when I hoisted the full cask above my shoulders and came down on his neck and back, forcing him to his knees. He turned, and I planted my boot in his face. His head hit the wood floor and bounced. To my amazement, he got up. But he took one wobbly step and fell again, this time to stay down for good.

While this evened the fight, the thin fellow was now getting pummeled by the man who'd been holding him, and I could see he was woozy. I had to act fast, so I kicked the back of the thug's knees, and they buckled and he fell forward. This gave the gaunt man an opportunity to hit him in the face several times without retaliation. The blows were enough to stun the brute, and this provided the thin man with enough time to catch his second wind. He took a deep breath and wound up and hit the man with a series of hard punches. His assailant soon tumbled to the floor, unconscious.

– I, Walter –

The sheriff and two deputies came and took them to jail. These men would be placed in the hold on the first ship out the next morning, and warned never to return.

The man I had helped was an English saylor named George Willingham. His face was plain but tanned, and he wore long breeches with a blue striped shirt, the latter now bloodied. His face carried the look of youth, but he had a couple of scars that were much too deep to come from play when he was a youngster. He would have been good-looking if not for the scars, but they hadn't made him ugly, either. Except for being skinny as a pike, he was just a plain, normal person who would have blended into the population almost anywhere.

A wench led him to the back and to some water so he could clean himself up as best he could. When he returned, I could see he was going to be sporting a black eye and a fat lip for a while, but those were the only injuries that were noticeable. I was certain there were more, as he'd been hit repeatedly in the stomach and ribs, but since he said nothing I could tell he wasn't a complainer.

He insisted on buying my dinner and as many pints as I could drink. So we ate and drank and talked.

He was looking to captain his own crew, and he had a little less than a year to go before his enlistment obligation in the Merchant Navy was fulfilled. He was the first mate on his current ship and due to be promoted to second in command. By his youthful face and thin frame, I thought he was several years younger than me, and I was surprised to learn he was two years my senior and had already served seven years in service to the Crown. I told him to come and see me when his enlistment was fulfilled.

***

I stopped and said to Maria, "A lot happened in that year before Marek made his surprise visit. Shouldn't I bring this into the story now?"

She said, "Since you're discussing what went on at The Salty Dog, you should keep all of this together. The other can be told later."

So, I continue to write about what went on at The Dog.

A year passed, and I was craving an English meal one day, so this meant another trip to The Dog, and just my third visit to that tavern since I'd been on my assignment for the King. Upon entering the pub, I saw Marek sitting at a table with what I assumed were some of his crew. He got up and smiled as I rushed over to him as rapidly as my bad knee would allow. Shaking my hand, he said, "I was told ye'd be here. And ye see, ye rogue, it's not been three years this time since I'm meetin' with ye."

He sat down, motioning for me to join him. "I asked about ye at the sheriff's office and he told me where ye office was, but I missed ye there, and one of ye mates said he thought ye'd be here." My "mate" had to be Cortez, a local who spoke decent-enough English that I'd hired him to translate Spanish documents. I'd told him I was going to be gone all afternoon, but he if he needed me I was going to The Dog for dinner.

Marek asked his crew to leave so we could have some privacy. Considering what The Dog was famous for, they didn't need any encouragement.

We talked about many things, but mostly my appointment in northern Spain. He knew about Maria from Bart, and we discussed our current situation, and that we had decided to postpone our marriage until my commission was completed. Marek listened attentively, but so many things were wrong. He wasn't drinking. Nor was he boasting or annoyingly loud. He had one glass of ale with his meal, and that was all.

After the wench cleared our plates, Marek gave me a quizzical look. "Prepared?" he asked.

"For what?" I answered

"To look at the papers."

"What papers?"

"These papers." He reached into his jacket and pulled out several sheets that were folded over.

They consisted of ledgers that began a year and a half earlier, when we'd begun our tobacco enterprise, including a report that showed what had happened with the tobacco runs. He'd started with three boats following one another to ward off pirates and stand a better chance of at least one or two making it through in bad weather. On the maiden voyage, all three ships returned.

– I, Walter –

Even after taking a hefty profit, he had enough left over to outfit three more ships with crews.

Mixed in with the ledgers was an envelope. "What is this for?" I asked.

"That's ye portion from the tobacco so far. And I'm goin' to double the fleet again. Soon we'll have 12 ship haulin' tobacco. I plan to be comin' and goin' year round. Ye sugar numbers are on the back sheet, but ye'll see the money earned from what totaled nine boatloads of tobacco was greater than what we'd made during all the time we been trading in sugar. It's damn amazin'. In real money, ye fourth is greater than ye half."

I closed my mouth, not realizing it was wide open until the bar wench gave me a funny look and asked if I'd seen a naked woman running around. Marek started laughing. So did I. When we couldn't laugh any more, he said. "If ye are wonderin', I quit drinkin' large amounts. And quit me boasting too. The last heavy drink I had, I was robbed when I went outside the pub. Pocket change, but it wised me up."

"That's good to hear," I said. "I don't want to lose you."

"Aye, I sought ye out for that reason. I'm here to warn ye that I'll only be on the water for another year, and that be all. It's time I return to me family and be the father I wanted to be when I started doing this. Thank ye, Walter. Thank ye very much for all ye done. But I'm goin' to have to bring this to a close."

Hardly what I was expecting. But as I thought about it, hadn't I also quit the sea? I said, "I don't want you to start drinking any heavier, but I want to propose a toast to you." I ordered a dram of The Dog's best spirits for everyone in the tavern. Along with me, they all stood as I toasted Marek, who sat like a fat friar in all his glory. Few of the patrons likely understood one word of what I'd spoken. But when I finished, everyone said their form of salute to this odd man who was a loyal partner and now just as loyal a friend.

I sat again and we were talking about England, over some very strong Spanish coffee, when Marek said, "There's somethin' else. If I be tellin' the truth, it's what I really come here to see ye about. Walter, would ye be interested in buyin' out me shares in the company?"

I sat silently for several minutes. Marek left me to my thoughts as I ran numbers around in my head until I felt dizzy. "Have you figured out what I would need to pay you for your half share of the sugar ships and three-fourth share of the tobacco ships?"

Marek handed me a slip of paper he'd already made out. It would cost me half of everything in my account, but some quick arithmetic on my part showed me I'd make it back double in one year, barring great difficulty.

I did some more figuring and said, "I agree to what you're asking for, but on one condition. Shortly after I first came here, I helped out a saylor in the King's Merchant Navy in a fight. His name is George Willingham, and at that time his commission was up in a year. He was being promoted to second, and he said he wanted his own ship when he was discharged. I told him to look me up as soon as he had his papers. A ship he's supposed to be on is to drop anchor here in the next few days. I'd like you to stay here until he arrives and meet with him and me."

"I wasn't goin' anywhere that fast."

"Good. I'll send a letter with you to take to the manager of the Mercantile Bank. He knows my handwriting, and he gave me a seal that I've never used before but will now."

"I don't want to be negative, but what if this George chap don't work out? Is our deal off?"

"He'll work out." I paid the bill, and we both left for the night.

George's ship encountered calm seas and was three days late. Marek said he didn't mind, but he was acting jittery and I was certain I could get his shares for less money, but that wasn't me. I had too much respect for what he'd done to deprive him of what he was asking. And even if I lost every ship, I'd be insured and would be able to start over I was also positive that Don Castabel would approve of my business sense, and I was no longer worried, regardless of the amount of money in my account, about his accepting me as Maria's husband. However, other problems arose during this year that affected this immensely.

I paused again to ask Maria, "Shouldn't I write about this now? After all, it almost prevented us from ever getting married."

– I, Walter –

"If you do, your story will be too jumbled. So please finish this part first."

Again, I did as she asked.

I met with George Willingham in my office, without Marek present. With the excitement right after the fight, I really hadn't had the chance to learn much about him. After a casual morning together, I found out that he was a lot like me. He'd gone straight into being a saylor, sure that he'd come back with some money and be able to present himself as respectable. From this perspective, his aspirations had been a success.

He brought a letter from the captain of his last ship, and the message was glowing in every regard. He wrote that George could handle the quadrant, he could figure stores with the best of them, and indicated his Second in Command George Willingham was ready for his own ship.

We talked about places we'd sayled and docked, and though they were often the same, he'd never been around the Cape, and that meant he'd never experienced the Indian Ocean. But I wasn't worried, as I thought he'd be as good under pressure as anyone, except maybe Bart.

The more I was listening to George, the more I was working out an idea, and it was time to bring it all together. We finished and ate an afternoon meal at The Dog, which is where I'd asked Marek to meet us at 3 o'clock.

He was prompt, and after the introductions I said to Marek, "George here is the merchant saylor I told you about. He's just discharged and wants to sayle for a living, but I've already told you that. I think the answer is to put George on the water to ship tobacco. Let him answer to you for the next year, and when he's proven himself, then he can take over and manage things while you retire to be with your family."

Marek looked at me like I'd sprouted horns. "George, here, is goin' to go from a sea captain to managin' a shippin' operation, all in the same year?"

George came up in his seat. "Tobacco? Sir, I don't know nothin' about the stuff."

"What do you know about sugar?"

He thought a moment. "Nothin', sir."

"We sell sugar and tobacco. If you want to work for us, you have to pick one. But being I'm one of the owners, and soon to be the sole owner, I'm picking one for you. And it's tobacco. I'm going to have Cap'n Marek start selling more in France. Jean Nicot brought it to the French 60-odd years ago, and there's never been enough to satisfy the demand. In my free time, I've been studying this while I've been stationed here, and I believe France would be the perfect place for you to start. Cap'n Marek can put a man with you who knows the trading ropes in Africa. Cap'n Marek will also find someone who speaks French and English. That man will be left in France until you get there with a boatload of tobacco leaves. All the sales will be made ahead of time, and all you'll have to do if offload the ship. You'll be paid a captain's wage from the first day you sign on with us."

George sprang forward in his seat. "Where do I sign?"

"I was going to ask you if you want to think about it, but I guess you answered." We all shook hands. "I'll draw up some papers, and Cap'n Marek can get everything formalized in Portsmouth. Now, if you'll excuse us, the cap'n and I have some things we need to discuss."

When George left, Marek said, "Ye sure is puttin' a lot a faith in the lad." I showed him the letter from his ship's captain. "Aye, he's got the marks, that's for sure. I'll give 'im all I know. But ye really thin' he can sayle a ship and learn the whole operation? When's he gonna have time to learn the land part?"

"I was thinking, since you're no longer going to be at sea, you might want to stop by and check on him now and again. I've been reading about stock, too, and I'm going to give you some stock in the company, even though you won't be a partner. This way, you'll always have an interest in seeing it succeed."

"I was right all along, Walter."

"How's that?"

"Ye are a rogue. A real big rogue."

We both laughed and hugged each other.

– I, Walter –

Chapter 17

I set down my quill and Maria kissed me on my cheek. "I liked that," she said. "Now you can tell about the trip to France."
"Do I have to?"
"Only if you want everything out in the open."
I once again reached for my quill, and Maria left the room.

A few months before my commission was to expire, I was sitting with Maria on the porch at the hacienda when Don Castabel approached us. "As soon as you two can tear yourselves apart for a minute, I need to ask Walter about a transportation issue."
Maria and I laughed at his opening remark, and I followed him into the living room. We sat and he had a man bring in some wine, which both of us began drinking.
I said, "This wine is very good. It comes from grapes raised on your land?"
"Grapes are about the only things that grow well in this climate. This wine is from an aged vintage, just opened." He held his glass up to the light coming through a window. "For a long time, growing grapes and making wine has been a hobby for me, and I have always experimented with creating new varieties. Over these past ten years, I have increased the size of the vineyards for the best of what I have grafted, to the point that I now make several distinct wines, and even a few highly regarded grappa. A few years ago, I began selling my wines in limited quantities in

France and England. Shipping to England was never a problem, and it used to be easy to go cross-country to the French border, but it's no longer safe. It seems the criminals we took off the sea are now robbing shipments on land."

We talked and drank the wine. A lot of the wine. Whether it was the result of too much of it or not, I said, "Don Castabel, I will work out a plan to get your wine to France."

I remember those fateful words as if I had just said them, and as I sat at my desk my eyes became flushed with tears. Throughout the years, I continued to not only have painful memories from the Indian Ocean voyage, but from the trip to France as well.

After rinsing my face in a basin of cool water Maria had placed in a corner of the room, I returned to my desk. While struggling hard against writing any further, I lost the battle with my conscience and dipped my quill in the ink once again and poured more memories onto the parchment.

The day after I'd committed to help Don Castabel, I realized I shouldn't have been so quick to offer my services. But I said I would help him, so I started planning. I spent much of the next week going over maps and reports from robberies and other mishaps along the only route wide enough to allow a convoy of wagons through the mountain pass that led into France from Don Castabel's hacienda in northern Spain.

At the start of the second week, I was feeling smothered by the large number of problems I wasn't getting anywhere near solving. And not only for this shipment, but for others that followed so they wouldn't face a good chance of getting hijacked or lost along the way. To add to my misery, when I fell asleep that night, I had a series of vivid nightmares. They dealt with everything from horrible disasters while transporting wine through the mountain pass to reliving the terrors on the Indian Ocean. I woke up in a sweat and skipped breakfast and went for a brisk walk instead. I was going by the entrance to The Dog, when who did I see coming at me in the opposite direction but Marek, carrying a folio filled with papers. A couple of crewmen I recognized from his previous visit were with him.

"Looks like I always know where to fine ye now," he said as we shook hands.

"Not really. I was heading back to my office and just came by this way. What are you doing back so soon?" I had an awful thought. "Didn't George work out?"

"Nothing like that. Let's go in The Dog. I need to set this stuff down and get a pint. Not drinkin' heavy again, mind ye, but I need to get somethin' down my throat other than seawater."

We settled in at a table. Marek excused his men and said, "George and me had a fine time goin' back together, and I got him on a ship right away. I thin' he'll be a good one, and ye made a fine choice, it seems. But I went to the bank with the letter ye' gave me, and the manager spent a week making up papers for me to sign. Then he said ye had to sign 'em too, and I was to bring 'em back. I told him ye was in Spain. Chap said ye still had to sign them to finish up the sale. That's what all this is. I about had enough time to change me drawers before I got on one of our boats and was back here."

"I'm glad you're here. I'll get everything signed, but I need to spend some time with this to make sure the manager got it the way you and I agreed." Marek gave me a cross look. "I don't have the slightest fear you didn't ask him to do this exactly as we agreed, but I want to be sure."

Marek settled back in his chair, as far as his big body would allow. "Aye, I'd do the same."

I had an appetite now, so we ate and I told him I'd take him out to Don Castabel's hacienda the next day. Even though Marek's expertise was on the water and at trading, I wanted him to look at the maps and reports to see if he had any ideas that could help me with the French venture, and I thought he and Maria's father might enjoy meeting one another, as I'd told Don Castabel a lot about the chubby captain and how he'd never cheated me out of a pence. I also thought this would be an ideal opportunity to send a shipment of wine to England on Marek's return trip, since he'd said that my signing the papers was the only reason for his visit and the boat he came in on was empty.

When we arrived at the hacienda the next morning, I noticed several horses tied out front, and a fancy carriage I'd never seen before. Maria came out to greet us. I introduced Marek, whom she, like her father, knew from my many conversations about him. She said, "How wonderful that you are here, Señor. My cousin, Carlos, is here with his father Pedro, and the young man wants to be a sea captain. Maybe you can take him with you and train him. Si?"

"Aye, I've heard a lot about ye from Walter. Ye are a beauty, and if ye says ye cousin wants to be a seaman, ye already charmed me into takin' him under me sayle."

While Marek was just trying to be nice to Maria, I was pleased her exuberance hadn't offended him. She playfully ushered us inside, where we both met Carlos and Pedro.

Carlos was a strapping boy, I guessed 15 or maybe a little older. Thin but muscular, the strong family resemblance was undeniable, and he was quite tall, standing nearly two inches above everyone else, including his father. To my surprise, he spoke some English, and Maria told me he'd had the benefit of studying with the same priest who'd taught her, only he hadn't visited Carlos nearly as often. I chuckled to myself at that.

Carlos and Marek talked and, from what I could pick up of their conversation, Carlos had been studying a book about seamanship. His father had taken him on some trips on the ocean, and the family owned a saylboat on which the boy had learned basic sayling techniques. In reality, Carlos knew a hundred times more than I'd known when I signed on with Bart, and he was obviously stronger than I was at the time. He also already loved the sea, something I don't think I ever could say, although I'd certainly learned to tolerate it, and then some.

Don Castabel put out a lavish meal. It became instantly clear that Marek was not going to insult his host by not trying everything in abundant portions. I'd seen Marek eat many times, but nothing like this. Undoubtedly, every inch of his large girth was earned, not heredity.

Uncle Pedro also spoke English, but nowhere near enough to carry on a fluent conversation. He was eager to know what Marek thought of Carlos' prospects as a seaman, not knowing that it would be my decision. In English, Carlos spoke for his father, although I now understood Spanish well enough to know he was really speaking for himself. Of course, no one knew it was now my decision, not even Maria or her father.

Marek glanced at me and I nodded. He said, "If the boy works out, maybe in three or four years, he can stay on and run a ship." That short time frame almost forced a gut laugh, but I held my composure and smiled.

We had a fine afternoon and evening, and it was decided that Marek and I would stay over, which I thought was a good idea, as this would give the old captain a chance to clear his head--and his body. He wasn't drunk, but he'd had so much to eat he could barely move. I was positive he'd be in much better shape to look at the maps and reports after a good sleep, which had already come to him, as I heard him snoring loudly in a chair on the porch when Maria and I walked outside.

The next morning, I presented Marek with the map and the paperwork on the robberies and natural disasters that had plagued travelers and shipments passing along the route to Spain from Don Castabel's hacienda.

To my dismay, after a couple of hours of poring over everything, Marek said he'd forget the land route and bring the wine in by sea. When I told him there were too many problems getting it to central and eastern France from the ports, and this was the reason a land route had to be used, he threw up his hands and said, "I wish I could help ye, Walter, and ye know I would, but other than tellin' ye to bring a big crew and many cannon, I don't know what else."

I didn't even want to think about the cannon part of it. After an afternoon meal, Don Castabel, Pedro, and Carlos joined us. The two brothers had talked at length about the terrain and transport problems from the past, and Pedro was interested in what I'd come up with thus far as a plan.

Rather than stumble around with a reply, I said, "The first solution is still the water. Cap'n Marek has agreed to transport a boatload to market in England on the ship he came here in. If Carlos wants to go back with him, he can help out on the ship and get some training right away." As I was speaking, a bell rang in my head. "And we just put on a new cap'n, name is George, and by the time he gets back from his first trip around the Horn, Carlos will be ready to go out with him on the next voyage."

Carlos starting whooping and hollering, so loud that Maria and two of the house staff rushed into the room, thinking the boy was hurt. He hugged Marek, which was no easy chore, then me and his father and Don Castabel. I arched an eyebrow to Maria, and she took Carlos to the stables to go on a ride so we could continue without distraction.

Unquestionably, any caravan making this trek was most vulnerable when turning into the numerous blind narrow alleyways where bandits could lie in waiting. These sections were impossible to avoid, so I decided we'd send out a scout before proceeding into any of these areas. Others had done this before, but had been tripped up by not protecting the rear, and I thought about Marek's cannon remark.

"Have you any cannons on the schooner you came on?" I asked Marek.

"Small, but ye can take some if ye want."

"Only one. We'll stick its barrel out the back of our last wagon. Might be enough to scare anyone from attacking us from the rear."

November was upon us, and although the weather had been mild to this point, some snow was expected to fall in the mountains, especially in higher elevations we couldn't avoid, and the nights would range from chilly to freezing. Our horses would need to be hardy, and we would require plenty of heavy clothes and food, as well as hay for the horses when they couldn't graze.

If we made it through the mountain passes unscathed, two more problem issues I foresaw involved a heavily forested area in southern France that the reports said was notorious for highwaymen because of the protection offered by the trees, and the inevitable down time for the horses, something I knew nothing about until I read that more than half the attacks occurred when horses were hobbled while resting and eating.

Peppered with questions from Don Castabel and Pedro, who had both made the trip on this exact route, I answered what they asked to the best of my abilities. They both liked the idea of the

— I, Walter —

cannon in the rear wagon, for which I was quick to give Marek full credit.

Pedro and I would take the lead carriage, followed by flatbed wagons loaded with barrels of wine. A covered wagon at the rear would hold supplies--and the cannon. Another horse would be tethered to a wagon, and this would be ridden to scout the blind alleys and the forest later in the trip. Two farm hands would ride alongside on their own horses to take any urgent messages back to Don Castabel.

Each wagon would be pulled by two horses, with the wagons tethered by a rope, Each man would need to be a light sleeper, capable of spelling the others at odd hours. And of greatest importance, one of the men had to speak French. The more I discussed what was needed to get this wine to France, the more I was trying to talk myself out of the whole thing.

I was not, however, given the chance. I didn't need an interpreter when Pedro said, "I will be one of the hombres in the wagon to kill banditos. And, I know French." He smiled and blabbered a few words, none of which I knew the meaning of, but Don Castabel nodded. So that took care of that, which now meant there was no turning back.

***

Four days later, Marek's boat, a schooner he'd used only for fast trips, was loaded. Carlos had come on board two days earlier to get a head start on learning his way around the deck. Marek agreed with me that he couldn't be faulted for his enthusiasm. I met with the sheriff to make certain all was quiet. He assured me that my leaving for five to six weeks would not cause any hardship, since crime on the dock was nothing compared to the past. When I returned, I'd have about a month to finish up with everything and send my final report to the King. Then my commission would be over and Maria and I would marry.

Don Castabel asked me to dine with him the evening before I was to leave. I was more interested in spending my time with Maria, but I accepted, and did so graciously. I arrived to find Maria in the front yard, looking as spectacular as always. Tonight, she was wearing a lavender dress, and had a scarf tied around her hair to keep it out of the way.

She wrapped her arms around me and gave me one of her special kisses. She then whispered in a throaty voice, "Thank you for helping my father. He told me this is his best wine ever, and he wants the French to know that Spanish wine can be just as good as theirs. It's a matter of pride with him. So, darling, thank you, thank you, thank you." Every inch of my body tingled when she gave me another of her kisses and hugs. Moments like this one made me realize just how much I adored Maria.

Chapter 18

At dawn the next morning, Pedro and I walked over to the caravan. We would ride in the lead carriage. One man would handle the horses pulling the flatbeds loaded with wine, and one man would hold the reins in a covered wagon in the rear that carried supplies and the cannon. The two farm hands would ride on each side to help keep the horses in line. Either or both would be sent back to Don Casabel if we ran into trouble or to provide a report on our progress if all went well.

Even with four muskets and the usual items that couldn't be tied to the top or placed in the trunk in back, Pedro and I fit comfortably inside our carriage. Just before leaving, Don Castabel came up and put even greater emphasis on what Maria had told me the prior evening. This shipment was to make an impact on the Royal Court of France. I shook hands with him and embraced Maria, promising I'd be back soon, and hoping that the more I repeated this to her, the more I might actually believe it myself.

Three hours later we reached the entrance to the trail into the mountains. The ride through the pass took us seven hours. It might have taken us a few hours less, but high winds and rain made the travel difficult, but the way the reports had read and Don Castabel and Pedro talked, I expected much worse. After what I'd endured aboard ship for six years, this was child's play.

At noon the next day, Pedro said to me, "Señor, this is the border between my country and France. It is where our property ends." This shocked me. We were a day's ride from the house on horseback, and we were just now leaving the family land.

So far, we had been very lucky. We encountered little snow on the trip through the pass, and no banditos. We had sent the farm hands ahead to check the blind alleys, and all was clear, except for some mountain sheep. We came upon a creek on the other side of the pass, which Pedro said would be there. We stopped to refresh and feed the horses. The weather looked as if it was going to turn bad, so we tied the horses up for the night, and then made a schedule for four to sleep and two to guard our camp, one in the rear and one in the front. I and a farm hand took the first watch. I found it exciting, like when I first went aboard ship and everything was new to me.

Oh, how I would rue those words, but they were exactly what I'd felt at the time. That sort of naiveté is something a person never forgets. Many years after Don Castabel died, Maria gave me a diary her father kept. I guess she believed it would give me solace, and to some degree it did. I opened my desk drawer and pulled out the thick leather-covered book and opened it. It took me a while, but I found the section I was looking for:

November 2

They have been gone for three days now. My farm hand Diego returned today to tell me they had crossed the mountains safely.

November 14

They have been gone 12 days now. My farm hand Manuel returned to tell me that they were almost to Versayleles. I wished he had stayed with them. I should have sent Diego back to stop Manuel and keep them both for the return trip.

November 27

Maria is worried. I am trying not to show my concern, but she saw me pacing the room, something I never do. I am very nervous about Walter. He is a good man, a good amigo to me, and will be so good for my Maria. I will never forgive myself if he comes to some harm because of my vanity. I only want Spain to look good, but it was a stupid idea.

November 28

Maria and I keep staring out the window to where the only trail from the hacienda leads to the foothills. I keep staring, hoping I will see Walter and Pedro and our men.

December 1

The sun set on another day, and as my daughter and I finished our evening repast, we would not speak about what was dwelt in our minds. We headed to our bedrooms with tears in our eyes. I hate to see her cry, but this day passed and still no news. I wanted to be positive, but I could not shake the feeling that something had happened. And that it was not good.

I put away Don Castabel's diary and wiped the tears from my eyes. I always had problems remembering some things about this time in my life. I had entered the trip with more luck than anyone could dream of having, and then it crumbled around me. My heart was in anguish as I remembered the events that overtook our carriages on the way back. I'm glad Maria wasn't in the room to see me so sad. My hand shook, and I had a hard time holding the quill steady enough to dip it in the ink. But I succeeded.

The trip through France and on to Paris was special. Although most of the trees had shed their leaves, the beautiful reminders of what they had just looked like covered the ground. Along the way we came to several groves of fir and evergreen trees that could have hidden gangs of highwaymen, but we checked them out in advance and passed through each without incident. Days earlier, I had send the farm hand Diego back to Don Castabel to tell him we made it through the mountain pass. Today, I am sending Manuel, the other farm hand, back to the hacienda to let Don Castabel know we are on the outskirts of Versayleles. And since we are now near a city, we are taking the cannon barrel inside the wagon so we do not appear dangerous.

After sampling it, tavern owners and innkeepers in Versayleles wanted to buy our wine. Pedro sold one wagonload and could have sold much more, but Don Castabel had told him he wanted it presented in Paris. That would be the true test.

As we came closer, we saw several manor houses surrounding a large castle. Just before dusk we entered the city of Paris. Pedro told me the population was estimated at 450,000. I didn't know how he knew this, but it would make it twice the size of London and four times that of Cairo. In all the places I had traveled, nothing matched Paris in size or, as I would learn, splendor.

We slept well that night in a pleasant inn with a hot bath. Pedro hired a security detail to guard our wine, but one of our men still stood watch throughout the night. Pedro took one man and went out for the morning to seek the best prospects for our wine. When he returned, he and I went to the castle with one wagon.

Along a wall before we reached the moat and drawbridge was Le Vin Boutique. We stopped and went in. In a visit earlier that day, Pedro had discovered that the proprietor spoke English.

I had to step back and chuckle when a skinny man with nubs for teeth said, "'Bout time ye got here. King is down to 'is last keg and the party is s'posed to go on till t'morrow."

Pedro collected payment in gold coin, as he had in Versayleles. I could see he was a good businessman, since he charged this man substantially more for the same number of kegs we sold in Versayleles.

The fellow was so eager to get the wine inside that he even called on the guards in a watchtower to help unload our wagon. We'd sold the other flatbed and horses in Versayleles, but this man didn't want these, so we drove them back to the inn.

The inn was a long large building with several rooms facing the river, and a room for eating facing the heart of the city. Across the road was a fort, marked with wooden poles sharpened on the top, and two-story guard towers every hundred feet. We saw several people wearing long shining swords and dressed in capes that had the fleur-de-lis patterned into them.

Pedro gestured their way. "Here in France, those are the King's most-trusted guards, called Musketeers." Just as he finished, a couple of burly brutes came toward us from across the street. Their clothes were tattered, their faces scarred, and their heads were a crisscross of missing hair and ragged scalp. They were holding knives and headed our way. I looked at Pedro, and we both prepared to defend ourselves.

We didn't have to. Three of the Musketeers we had seen ran up before the thugs could reach us. One hoodlum was slashed in the wrist and howled as he dropped his knife, while the other one threw his knife into the air and got on his knees. He placed his head down as if he expected to be beheaded. Instead, a Musketeer hit him on the noggin with the massive handle of his sword, knocking him out and adding to the disfigurement that already adorned the top of his head.

The following day, we went to the Paris market. Outdoors and open, it was much the same as others in that respect. The fruits and vegetables were placed on the outer edges of the market, which was what I was also used to. But this is where the similarities ended.

Once inside, there were rows and rows of meats, breads and pastries, the likes of which I'd never seen or tasted before. Some of the pastries were works of art, and so good to eat, especially those filled with jelly and a cream like cheese.

In another section, merchants displayed hats and dresses, perfumes, leathers, and jewelry, and lace finer than any I'd ever seen. Some soaps smelled like lilacs, which I purchased with some silver I carried with me. I thought Maria would like them, and then I went back for some of the lace and some cotton fabric. I used a gold crown and got smaller gold coin in exchange. Pedro nodded, so I assumed I got the right change.

I also found a dainty shawl, woven in a variety of light colors, that I was certain would look fantastic around Maria's shoulders. We had planned to sell the flatbeds, but if I kept going, I would have them loaded and need to bring them back too, so I quit my buying for Maria and took back only what Pedro and I could carry. He bought several things for his wife too, and I got the impression he had given her a great many fineries from his previous trips to Paris.

Early the next morning, a courier came from the King. We had told the man in the wine store that we had five more wagonloads, and Pedro was handed a formal letter that said to come to the castle with the kegs we had left. Before the day was done, all of our wine was unloaded at the castle, and Pedro was paid in gold at the exact rate of the first wagonload.

Nothing could speak more highly for Don Castabel's wine than to essentially have all of it purchased by the King of France. Pedro had mentioned his brother's name to the proprietor of the wine store, and the note on the King's personal stationery mentioned Don Castabel. I couldn't understand the letter, but the King's message, according to Pedro, was that his brother's wine would have no problem being accepted in the taverns and inns in France.

The next day we sold the wagons and the horses that had pulled them, and the following morning we started down the same road we had arrived on, quite happy with our efforts. We had been fortunate not to encounter anything untoward, and now we just had to pray we could get back safely. Storms were in our future though, as dark clouds were building on the horizon and we were heading in their direction. The chilling thought kept running through my mind that these clouds were as much a warning as they were a precursor of bad weather.

The wind picked up and we slept in our carriages in a forest that night. Thunder came early the next morning, spooking the horses. It took a while to calm the animals and harness them to the carriages. Although we were traveling much faster now with just the carriages, it would still require nine or ten days to make the mountain pass.

A few days into our return trip, while in the throes of a heavy, unrelenting rain, we met a wagon along the way. The drivers told Pedro they had just come from Spain. Some fresh snow had fallen in the pass, but they had not much trouble getting through.

– I, Walter –

However, with the rain we were experiencing on the ground, it was obvious there would now be more snow in the mountains. We would either have to try it or stay in France for many months. The decision was easy. All of us wanted to get back to Spain, and I'm positive no one more than me.

***

I was better at predicting weather at sea than on land. Two days after we'd met the wagon coming from Spain, the heavy rains quit and the sun came out and stayed that way. The route was sloppy and the travel slow, but we were ahead of the schedule we were on when transporting the wagonloads of wine.

I remarked to Pedro that we had not needed to pick up our muskets one time during the entire trip. Yet while I was not overconfident and continued to keep them loaded and primed, I secured them to straps overhead so we'd have more room in the carriage. I was also more lax with our guard at night. I agreed to using one man and not two, not as concerned if our "watch" occasionally fell asleep, which often happened in a long trip like ours, as fatigue was always an issue.

The next day, we approached a small village I remembered well from coming through the first time. The town had one inn, and a sign on its door that Pedro told me said it was the location of the first campfire in France. I'm glad I didn't speak French, because I would have had a hard time listening to that claim without arguing.

That night we all slept in a bed, but I remember falling asleep in the bath and waking up in cold water and thinking I was at sea and the hull was breached.

The past ten days had been hard travel, and I would not have minded staying another day to rest, but then I thought about Maria and quickly changed my mind. I could see that everyone else was eager to get home too, so we started out, and in the early afternoon came the first of the dangerous forests we would encounter in reverse order.

We were moving along at a slow but steady pace, and I could see a clearing through the trees at the end of the trail, which I guessed to be a half mile away. I checked the extensive log I kept from the moment we had entered France, and once we exited this last section of trees, my notes indicated we would be in relatively open spaces for the rest of the day.

Pedro was engaging me in a lengthy conversation about the university he'd attended in Salamanca, which he proudly told me was the first school ever to be granted university status, and that the school's status was even confirmed by the Pope in 1255. Pedro had a penchant for dates, often keeping me amused with his memory. Of course, I had no idea if he was right about any of this, but it broke the monotony. I had quit worrying as much about being attacked, as it seemed much more likely coming into France and not leaving the country, and believed our greatest challenge would be getting through the pass if snow came down in any quantity.

We had been traveling for two days in and out of the forests, and saw nothing sinister but some bears. We had one more woods to make it through, and then we'd be a half-day from the mountain pass. Our carriage was in the customary lead position. Pedro and I were talking, and I hadn't been paying attention to the covered wagon lagging behind. When I did realize that the distance between the wagon and our carriage was too great, I asked Pedro, who had the reins, to slow our horses so the wagon could catch up. When we were almost to a halt, I heard two loud crashes, one after the other, hit the top of our carriage. Two men began yelling as one of them jumped down and pulled the reins from Pedro.

I scrambled to untie the muskets. One discharged inadvertently as I was picking it up and shot a hole in the roof. By pure luck, the load hit the man who was atop our carriage, and he fell headfirst to the ground. Pedro grabbed a musket and shot the man who had taken the reins from him in the chest. All of this happened so fast that I didn't see what was going on behind us with the covered wagon, only hearing the reports from two muskets. It would take too long to turn the carriage around, so I took one of the other loaded muskets and rushed to the covered wagon as fast as I could, expecting to find both our men holding their spare muskets, since they also carried four and I'd only heard two shots, which I assumed they had fired.

One highwayman was on the ground, but two of our men were slumped over on the bench that was their seat. The driver had a dagger in his neck, and our other man had been run through with a sword, the blade coming out his back. I assumed there were two assailants, since I'd heard only two shots, and I tried to figure out where the other one could be hiding, when I was rushed from the side. I had just enough time to swing the heavy musket at him and pull the trigger, a shot hitting him full force in the chest and knocking him backward as if he were hooked to a huge spring. The cannon had proved worthless. With the barrel of it pointing straight out the rear of the wagon, lugging it in a fixed position was not nearly the brilliant idea I had thought. It needed to be on a swivel to have any chance of being effective. How could I have been so stupid?

I hoped that the man I'd shot was last member of the crew of bandits. But with no way to be certain, I did not have time to grieve for the men we lost, only to get back to Pedro to help protect him if there were still more robbers on horseback or on foot lurking in the woods.

I limped with as much speed as I could muster, and as I got closer to our carriage I could see Pedro trying the wrest the reins from the man he'd shot. But he couldn't pull them loose, as the dead man was wedged between the wagon yoke and the harness, with the reins wrapped around both hands.

Pedro climbed onto the yoke and got the reins free. He pushed the bandit off the harness apparatus with his foot and got back in the driver's seat. I thought I'd noticed a slight movement coming from the body, but when I went over to check, I couldn't see or hear him breathing; all I saw was his chest and face covered in blood. Still, I aimed the musket at the body. I was going to make sure the robber was dead. But then I uncocked the musket. I might need the weapon at ready in case there was another bandit. I gestured to Pedro."We should get to the pass as fast as we can. Let's load what food and supplies we can into the carriage and forget the rest."For whatever crazy reason, I thought about the shawl I'd bought Maria.

"Si," was all Pedro said. I could tell by his eyes that the fineries he'd gotten for his wife were the last thing he cared about at that moment.

We would not even have time to give our men a decent burial, but the ground was soft and we dug one grave as fast as we could that was large enough for all three. We covered it with nearby rocksand said a short prayer and climbed aboard the carriage.

Just as Pedro went to flick the switch he used to get the horses moving, a loud gunshot rang out. The man I'd thought was dead had risen and walked 100 yards. And he was holding a pistol. All I could think was that he must have fallen on it, and that's why I hadn't seen it. He let the gun drop from his hand and pulled a knife from his belt. He brought his arm back to throw it at me, and I blew off half his head.

I felt the horses jerk hard. They started galloping. Blood was running down Pedro's neck, and he was trying hard to hang on to the reins, intentionally leaning into me and using me as a prop so he wouldn't fall over. His face ashen, he was in no condition to control our runaway carriage, and the only choice was for me to pry the reins from him. But his hands were steeled to them. It took what seemed like minutes before I had the leather straps in my hands. And what seemed like hours before I was able to slow the horses.

I got the carriage stopped and beheld a cold, lifeless expression on Pedro's face, with all the color drained from him. My complacency had killed him. I'd let my guard down and Pedro was dead. And I'd lost two other good men because I wasn't paying attention and had let our carriage get too far ahead of their wagon. I closed Pedro's eyes and prayed that his soul would at least have peace.

And now I was on my own, traveling back the way I came. I was responsible for the deaths of three people, and one the uncle of my beloved Maria and brother of her father. Now I was truly on my own. No matter what else happened I was certain that there was no way that I would ever be able to marry Maria now. I could never show my face in front of her father and ask him for his daughter. How could I? *Yes, sir, remember me? I'm the one responsible for the deaths of three of your most trusted employees. Oh, and your brother. Better planning might have saved all of them, and certainly your brother, but now I'm going to ask you to give me your daughter to protect too?*

No sane, rational man would ever say yes to that. At the port, I would have to attend to the administrative responsibilities I had left, which would mainly involve writing a final report for the King, without seeing Maria or her father again, and then pray that I could go home and forget about the woman who has captivated my heart for the last seven years. Tears were streaming down my face as I stopped the carriage for the night.

I didn't sleep very much that night. What sleep I did get was punctuated by nightmares reproaching me for ever planning this trip or for being the only one to live through it.

The next day, I made it to the mountain pass, where it was cold. But this was good, since the cold helped preserve Pedro's body, which I had bound in linen he had brought from the wagon. He said he'd wanted to bring this one thing back for his wife. I couldn't argue, since I'd retrieved the scarf for Maria.

The people we had met along the way had not lied to us. as there was little snow. However, to my surprise considering the temperature, it began to rain. I had hoped to make it through the pass in eight hours or less, but now the rain was pouring, and with it thunder and lightning.

Yet even with the rain, I was making good progress, and when I was at the halfway point in the pass, I analyzed the weather. The rain was cleansing me, trying to help me forget the deaths and my responsibility for them, and ultimately washing the slate clean. But I came to my senses; the rains can't do that. A phrase from the Bible kept coming to mind: *Yea, though I walk through the valley of the shadow of death, I shall fear no evil.* Then I remember what an old salt aboard ship yelled to Bart and me when we were under attack and all seemed lost: *For I am the meanest sonofabitch in the valley.*

I drove the carriage like a madman, with the rain coming stronger and then turning to sleet. I couldn't see 25 feet in front of me, and I prayed the horses wouldn't trip and topple the carriage and I'd be crushed.

Without the sun, I had no way to judge the time, but I felt the steady uphill section of the pass. As the horses adjusted to the incline, the sleet turned to snow, and the wind increased, creating a blizzard of fantastic proportions. Visibility was sometimes at zero, and as we wound our way through the highest elevation in the pass, it often felt as though we were pushing forward at a snail's pace. I was freezing but I couldn't stop the horses. So, the animals and I shivered our way through the altitude for several more hours of painstakingly slow movement.

What should have required two hours took four before I sensed the pass begin its decline on the Spanish side. The blizzard turned to light snow, and a short while later, as the trail straightened out, the snow stopped altogether. Two hours later, and with the hacienda an hour away, I had a decision to make. I had no intention of meeting Don Castabel and Maria, with Pedro dead and draped in linen in the trunk in the back of the carriage. On my many rides with Maria, I had learned the trails that ran beyond sight or sound of the ranch. She had made certain we would have places to go that assured our privacy.

***

I approached the sheriff's office in the carriage. A deputy I knew greeted me, and I asked him to feed and water the horses. I also told him to find someone to wash them down and make certain they were provided with the best shelter available. I tossed him a gold coin, which was 100 times more than the cost for this service, but I didn't care. The deputy tripped over himself catching the coin said he would do it himself.

Soaked, shivering, and starved, since I hadn't eaten anything but hardtack in the past 16 hours, I told the sheriff everything that had happened, including that I felt responsible for the deaths of four people. I told him that Pedro was in a "burial cloth" in the trunk, and I convinced him that I couldn't take the carriage back to Juan and his family. I said that the money from the French King and the letter praising the wine and agreeing to accept it into the country was in a pouch under the rear seat inside the carriage.

He was reluctant, saying that I was just tired and full of anxiety because of all that had happened, and I would feel better after a good night's sleep. But when I raised my voice, something I never did with him, he agreed to my request.

Instead of going to my small apartment, I went to the Salty Dog. I needed a drink, if not to steel my conscience, certainly to warm my belly. By the time I staggered out of there, I had put down three mugs of ale and seven fingers of the most disgusting, most vile, drinks I could have ordered. The ones, incidentally, with the highest alcohol content. And all without one morsel of food.

I missed my apartment that night. I awoke the next morning to a brisk wind and clear, cold skies. I was on the ground, sandwiched between several bushes. My head hurt, my clothes were torn, and I felt just as bad as when I'd been hurt so severely in the final pirate attack. Emotionally, however, I was worse off, something I would not have thought possible.

I got up and walked with the limp of a drunken saylor, not with what was now my normal gait, and turned the corner when I saw Juan and Maria both pounding frantically on the door to the stairs that led up to my apartment. I turned and staggered the other way, toward the water, praying that I could get clear of the port at San Sebastian and forget all about it and them as soon as possible.

I did not want to risk their finding me at my office, so I slept under one of the main piers. The wood overhead and corner pilings broke the wind and also hid me from view. It was cold though, and even though the water generated a certain amount of warmth, it did very little good when even the sand on the shore around it was frozen.

In the very early hours of the morning, I made my way, shivering, to my apartment, and quickly built a fire and got out of my wet and now disgusting clothes. I heated water for a bath and when I bathed myself I began to cry. And when I settled in to bed, every time I closed my eyes, I cried some more. I cried for the loss of Pedro, who was a fine man. He didn't deserve to get killed just because he was helping his brother. I cried for the loss of the three men, who had families of their own and were very good at what they did. Seven people had left for Paris. Two came back with reports of the trip, telling Don Castabel all was well. But all was not well, and now only one has returned. Me. Why, God? Why spare me with not so much as a scrape and kill the other four?

I cried for the loss of Don Castabel and his friendship, and for the many ways I could see he was thinking of me as a son. And now it was over. Yes, we got his wine to Paris. And the King liked it. But even I knew what a Pyrrhic victory was, and this certainly was one. I had gotten four people killed in the process, including Don Castabel's brother.

It would have been better if I had died with the rest. Nobody would ever miss me. I had spent the past eight years privately pursuing my interests. I had no dependents, except my parents, and they were now taken care of for life. But nobody really wanted me--especially now. I might have been able to make a case for Maria wanting me before this happened. But what good would it be for her to continue to want me if her father would forever be saddened whenever he looked at me? What good would it be to want her if there was no possible way to get him to accept me? The battle was over, and even though I was the one who had lived, I definitely lost the war. I had traded my future with the woman I love, and her fine father, for foolhardy adventure, and in the offing caused the deaths of three good men.

Chapter 19

Maria came into my study with some bread and cheese and a glass of wine. She set down the tray carrying this meal and slipped a piece of faded parchment next to my writing. Since she didn't say anything, I waited until she left to pick up what was one of Don Castabel's journal entries that had been removed from his diary. I ignored the meal and read:

I sat in the living room with my eyes affixed on the trail. The December chill was upon us, and I would have to receive a message soon or send men to search for my brother, Walter, and the men.

I had not been able to sleep and began watching the trail heading into the mountains at six o'clock in the morning. Now, ten hours later, after returning to this dismal task, my head hurt and my eyes were sore and glazed over. I was ready for a meal when I heard some noise and glanced in the opposite direction. I could not believe what I was seeing. The carriage I had provided for Pedro and Walter was coming from town--and not from the mountains. I hollered to a servant who was cleaning in the living room to get Maria. Together, we ran outside and waited for the carriage to be brought to a halt in the courtyard. Maria held my hand as it came to a complete stop.

But when the door opened, instead of Pedro or Walter, the sheriff, Juarez, stepped down. He started talking before I could ask anything.

"Don Castabel, three hours ago, Walter stopped this carriage in front of my office and implored me to bring it to you. He said he could not do it himself."

"Why?" I asked. Maria was now grasping my hand so hard that it hurt.

"Señor, he said he would not be welcome here ever again."

That made both Maria and me gasp. How could Walter say something so preposterous?

Sheriff Juarez related what Walter had told him. He repeated himself often, and it required an hour before he was done. I was certain he was relating everything exactly as he'd heard it, and he finished by saying, "Walter said to tell both of you he is very sorry." He turned to Maria and his voice cracked. "Señorita, I have never seen a man in such pain as when he said how much he loved you and now knew you would never want him. I am a strong man, but I was almost in tears when he left the jail."

The sheriff explained where I'd find the money with the letter from the King of France, but I would have burned the carriage and all that was in it if my brother was not inside. I and one of my men pulled Pedro's body from the trunk. Much of the wrapping had come undone, and I tried shield Maria's view but she saw her uncle's face. Her wailing brought the same from me, and I had the body placed in a root cellar beside the barn and sent men to tell my sister-in-law what had happened. It would require four days to ride to his hacienda and bring his wife and children back. I would bury Pedro in the family graveyard on my land, and I hoped the cold would preserve his body so he could be viewed with dignity before he was placed in he ground.

I loaned the sheriff a horse so he could get back to town. I had my two fastest horses saddled, and Maria and I galloped off ahead of him. I was furious with Walter and wanted to get to him as soon as possible.

***

Reading this page from Don Castabel's diary distressed me greatly. I needed to eat something, so I quickly devoured what Maria had brought for me and kept writing. For if I stopped now, I feared it would be forever.

– I, Walter –

Two days later, at the start of the second week in December, I watched Marek's schooner "The Bahama Sugar" approach the dock. Through my ocular, I could clearly see Carlos on deck, working the sayles. I made a thorough search of the area and didn't notice Don Castabel or Maria anywhere, so I walked out on the dock.

Carlos came off the boat first with a grin on his face so wide that nobody could mistake his joy with being on the sea. He shook my hand and said, "Gracias, gracias." I couldn't bring myself to smile, but I shook his hand. He asked how my trip had gone, and I turned from him and walked away. How could I possibly tell him that I had killed his father? With my guilt killing me, I waved him on and walked up the plank and found Marek in his cabin.

He beckoned me to sit and handed me a folio, with all the documents and their proper seals, that showed me as the sole owner of the company. I looked over everything, told Marek he didn't need to have done this so quickly, and asked about Carlos.

"That lad is as close to a natural saylor as we ever are goin' to find."

"Then keep him on the water for four or five years, and maybe he really can have his own ship in that short a time."

"Ye think his parents will really want him at sea that long?"

"I don't know. You can tell Don Castabel what you think about Carlos. You'll need him to direct you. Or at least send a message to Carlos' mother, and she can tell you what she wants for the boy."

"Ye are not mentionin' the father."

"And I won't be. Before you ask, I don't want to discuss it. You can go out to the ranch with Carlos and find out everything from Don Castabel."

"If ye want me to go out there, can't ye take me?"

"Let's just say that I'm not in the good graces of Don Castabel or Maria, and leave it at that." I got up. "Let me know what I owe you for this trip."

"Walter, we're in this together. There be no payment for this trip. With all ye have done for me o'er the last five year, saylin' here was a drop in the bucket." Marek patted his round belly and loosened his belt a notch. "I want to say somethin' more about Carlos. The boy is intelligent an' he plans ahead. He can sense what needs to be done, and he gets it done. But better for me, he made this trip goin' and comin' fun. I never thought I would say somethin' like that this late in the game."

"Good. You can tell that to Don Castabel when you see him."

Marek sat silently for a moment, and I left him with his thoughts. "The time for the King is more than done with now," he said. "Ye want to come back to England with me?"

"I've still got loose ends around here, then I'm going to go somewhere for a while. I'll find some way of contacting you with where I'll be. And, yes, I'm going to want you to keep running the company, but do it all on land. Bring George or someone you like better and train him on the whole operation. I'm going to double the stock I gave you. Will you do it?"

Marek shook his head at first but then nodded. It must have been the dejection on my face that convinced him the company would fall apart if left in my hands now.

"Safe travels, my friend," I said and turned to leave.

Marek called to me. "It can't be that bad, Walter. Do you want to talk about it over a drink?"

In a voice rife with self-pity, I said, "You need to find a better class of drinking partner. With me sitting next to you at The Dog, you'd probably get shot or knifed."

Carlos rode up to the dock on a horse I assumed he'd borrowed from the sheriff. I asked Marek to have Carlos request another horse for him, and I'd stay on board until the two of them were on their way. I couldn't face Carlos again, because if I had to look into his eager eyes, I was certain I would have grabbed the knife Marek always carried and stabbed myself with it.

***

My commission had ended, and I'd been able to do my job in the shadows during that final week. I didn't even say goodbye to Marek, but I did send a courier with a note for him to give to the banker to set up a fund for Carlos, and that it should compare to what I'd done for my parents. Carlos didn't need the money, but it was the least I could do for the boy.

– I, Walter –

I officially relinquished my office at the port by giving the key to the sheriff. I thanked this fine man for his invaluable help and honesty, and made my way down the main street for what I decided would be the last time. At least I had the satisfaction of getting the dock cleaned up in the two years I'd been on the job, and in setting up an organized patrol of the harbor the sheriff would now administer. The King had not lost one ship anywhere near our port. I would have heard about this if he had, and no such message ever came.

With every struggling step down the wide thoroughfare, I believed people were watching me closely. Even the wench at The Dog, who had carried on a playful banter with me from the first time I'd gone in the tavern, gave me long stares as I went by. Or so it seemed. Some people offered a look of what I felt was genuine concern, but most had either a sneer of disgust or a superior mien that denoted pity. Bah! What did they know, anyway? Nobody else could possibly be aware of how horribly I had ruined my life. Nor, I dare say, would anyone care.

I'd not been in contact with Maria since I'd returned, and other than that night when I'd seen her and Don Castabel at my door, she hadn't tried to reach me that I knew of. Overall, this was the best thing. The longer we were apart, the quicker we would forget each other. I hoped she was doing better at this than I, as my stomach was a constant mess and I was having a horrible time holding down much of anything.

I kept chanting out loud, or saying over and over in my mind, how much I needed to forget her, to get over her. My mind wanted to believe it but my heart wasn't close to accepting this.

But I didn't leave San Sebastian, and I remained in the same state for the next two weeks in December. I always enjoyed Christmas, whether at home as a child or at sea or in some foreign port where I didn't know a soul. I could commune with God in my own simple way, and I felt something special, especially on Christmas Eve. But as this Christmas neared, I was so depressed that there was no way for me to have any cheer. I was in a strange land, without any friends, and with no hope for the rest of my life.

Each hour leading up to Christmas was more painful than the one that preceded it. I cursed my decisions and swore at myself for letting a woman capture my heart so completely and then losing her. Even the waters of the Indian Ocean, which had caused me such mental anguish and left me with physical injuries that would stay with me forever, didn't hold as much distaste as I held for myself.

Before dipping my quill in the inkwell again, I had to pause to look at the portrait of my beautiful wife, which hangs in my study on the wall in front of me. Even now, so many years later, my heart still aches for the pain I caused her. But since I've written so much about what I never thought I would, I now must finish all of it.

Late at night, I slipped through a window into a church I had attended, and after lighting a torch to get my bearings, I found the stairway to the basement and got as comfortable as I could in a corner next to the wine cellar. The priest and altar boys would come down during the next day for sacramental wines for the mass on Christmas Eve, but I would find a way to hide quietly in the shadows so no one would discover me.

And while no human found me that evening, my dreams had, forcing me to relive the Indian Ocean and the forest. I had a nightmare about the child pirates I remembered so vividly that I heard myself scream myself awake. When I was able to fall asleep again, I saw Pedro's ashen face and I woke up sobbing. Terrible dreams continued throughout the night, when I heard footfalls above me and saw light coming through the foundation of the church. I spotted some loose fabric, so I brought it under the stairwell to hide behind, but this was not necessary, since not one person who came down to the wine cellar throughout the day looked my way. In addition to the wine, there was a supply of cheese, so I had plenty to eat and drink, and even a latrine in another corner of the basement.

On Christmas Eve, with the exception of the altar boys who came for the wine, I was left alone. The priest started the evening service, and the echo of his voice could be heard in the basement with such clarity it was as though I was sitting right in front of him. I could hear him when he proclaimed the birth of our Lord

Jesus Christ as though he was speaking only to me. And no voice was unheard, including mine, when he started singing O Come All Ye Faithful. I made it just past the first verse before my voice cracked and I burst into tears. I prayed for forgiveness. I prayed for a chance. If I had to leave Spain a beaten man, robbed of my love and hopes and desires, then so be it.

But I needed to apologize in person, to tell Don Castabel and Maria I was sorry about what had happened to those four men.

I stayed in the church all through Christmas Day. The next morning, I got up to find the church closed up tight and everyone gone, which is what I expected. *Hard work is good for the soul* they say, so on this day I cleaned the church.

For the first time in over a month, I was able to ignore all of my problems. I focused on the inside of the church, committed to give it a sheen like a shiny boot before I was through. I oiled the pews and cleaned the brass on the pipe organ. I swept the floors and found a compost bin for some food scraps from the floor in the church kitchen. I spent a few minutes in front of the altar, looking up and praying that He would forgive all of my failures, in spite of their severity.

I remained until dark, and left through the same window I had entered days earlier. For the first time in more than a month, I had a peace in my own mind and heart.

I was still very much broken, but for now I was able to ignore the pain. I didn't encounter anyone as I went through the village on the way to my apartment. It had been three days since I'd last been there, and I needed to change clothes and give my face and body a good washing.

I glanced around as I fumbled with the lock to the stairway up to my apartment. I saw no one, and now all I wanted was to heat some water for a sponge bath and then some sound sleep in a real bed.

Maria had come in my study, but I was so intent on writing that I didn't notice her reading over my shoulder until I felt her warm breath on my neck. She always does this in a way that sets my pulse racing the same as if we were young again. But when I turned up to her face, it was somber and not passionate, and she looked at me and said, "It is interesting the things you have remembered after all these years, and the things you have conveniently forgotten."

"I promise not to leave anything out. And I'm getting to the part I think concerns you the most at this point of the story." Maria felt my forehead.

"You seem much better today."

I said, "I am, dear, much better," and went back to my story.

***

I walked up to the apartment, and in the dark went straight to the bedroom. I lighted a candle but did not go back through the living area that also contained a small kitchen and eating area. I stood in the doorway to my bedroom and sensed movement, but didn't know where it came from and was too tired and dirty to worry about a mouse. I threw my coat onto the bed and stripped off my shirt. But I slowly returned to the living area, my mind nagging me that there was something there that wasn't supposed to be in that room.

In the candlelight, I found Maria asleep in the big stuffed chair in my living room.

Chapter 20

I'd bought the chair off the dock, and it was the only luxury I'd allowed myself at the apartment. For a moment I considered I might be dreaming. I went to the kitchen and pumped some cold water into a basin and sponged myself down. None of this woke her, and I returned to the bedroom and changed into clean clothes and tried very hard to forget that I had seen her.

I heard a creak in the living room floor. I stood with my back to the bedroom door, praying that by standing still she would not hear me, and if she was moving around, she would be leaving. Of course I'd forgotten I'd lighted a candle. But I couldn't deal with seeing her right now. These weren't my terms.

A minute after I heard the floor creak, I could sense she was right behind me. And then she said, "Look at me, damn it."

I began to shake, and it took me awhile before I could turn and look at her. When I did, there she was in the faint light, hair disheveled, dressed in her finest Christmas attire, and not at all happy. I ached at seeing her so sad. And then I fell to my knees, my body heaving, my lungs gasping for air, and my heart broken more than ever.

She knelt and held me as I cried. In a few minutes I could weep no more, and she led me to the chair in the living room, carrying the candle in her other hand. We both sat in the chair together, and she placed her legs across my lap.

"Why are you here?" I asked in a whisper, overwhelmed by her legs touching mine and the warmth of her body so close to me, something I never held any hope of ever experiencing again.

"I came here after church ended yesterday."

"Why, Maria? Why would you do that? And you know how dangerous it is for you to be in town on your own." She peered into my eyes with such sorrow in hers that I prayed she would never, ever have cause to look at anything that way again, let alone me.

"Walter, I can take care of myself. It's you I'm worried about. Tell me what happened. And I want to hear all of it."

I was physically and emotionally exhausted, but I told her everything exactly as it had taken place. I mentioned the things in Paris I had bought for her, thinking about how much she would like them, and how the shawl was the only thing that made it back. And then I told her how I had let down my guard first by letting the carriage get too far ahead of the wagon, and then not making certain the one bandit was dead. For these reasons, her uncle and three other good men were dead. I spared nothing, telling her every gory detail, even our burying the men in the single shallow grave right before Pedro was killed.

"So, Uncle Pedro was murdered while trying to save everyone. He died most honorably, yet you wouldn't tell us. How could you not do that, Walter?"

"How was I supposed to tell Don Castabel that his wine made it to market in Paris, but I not only got three of his best men killed while doing this, but also his brother died too, and all because I fell down on my watch. Then, to top it off, I'm supposed to tell your father that I want him to give me his daughter's hand in marriage."

"You're blaming yourself for everything that happened?"

"Who am I supposed to blame? Whose poor planning cost four people their lives? On a ship, that would get a man hanged from the yardarm."

"You caused the attack? How did you set it up?"

"I didn't say that. You're twisting my words." She moved in the chair. Her body heat was driving me crazy, and I was wide awake and alert now.

"And you're staying away from me and my father? What is the reason for that?"

"Because of what I did, or I should say what I didn't do, your uncle is gone. Any time I spend in your father's presence, I would remind him of that." I couldn't sit any longer, so I stood and paced the floor. Watching Maria sit seductively in the chair didn't help my resolution never to see her again.

"Now you're answering for my father too? What about me? What did you think of about my feelings."

"All I've thought about is your feelings. I still do. But, after what happened, I've ruined any chance I ever had with you."

"Let me understand you clearly, Walter. You caused the attack. You are the reason for Uncle Pedro's death. You already answered for my father. Which means you have the ability to read minds, too." Her voice dripping with sarcasm, she added, "Oh, Walter, please go and touch my dead uncle. You obviously have the ability to raise him out of the grave."

"You're twisting my words."

"I'm not laughing. Do you hear me laughing?" I said nothing.

"Tell me, Walter, Son of God, martyr of all mankind, before these delusions, was there ever any love for me?"

Horrified that she would ever question my love, I began shaking with anger. "How can you possibly ask that? I've loved you since the first time I set my eyes on you in that ship on the Atlantic. I've defended you against other saylors, and even proctors who questioned my loyalty to you over my King and my country. If anything, my love has grown so great that the pain I'm in at this moment is more than I can bear, realizing now that my chances with you are gone forever." I began to sob. "Yes, yes, damn it, it's killing me, but I do love you, and I always have and always will. Question anything you want about me, but don't ever question my love for you. Don't ever."

From behind me, a deep voice said, "Good. Now that we have that point settled, sit down again, Walter." I turned to see Don Castabel standing at the top of the steps to my apartment. He was dressed in dark riding breeches and a suit jacket with his family crest on the left breast. He looked fresh, and was probably at the sheriff's office before coming here to look for his daughter.

Sheriff Juarez had several keys to my apartment, as his men were always leaving things for me here rather than at my office, since my building was right around the corner. He must have given one to Don Castabel as well as to Maria. I was so overwrought that I never heard Maria's father coming up the stairs. I wondered how long he'd been listening to us, and in horror I considered his power in the province and the many ways he could extract revenge.

Don Castabel drew his sword from its sheath. He took a handkerchief from his coat and started polishing the blade while idly walking back and forth in front of the chair I was now sitting on. His eyes seldom left mine, and even then only to look at his daughter. He was polishing the sword to use on me, I was certain of it. But I would be getting what I deserved, and I would not try to escape. I lowered my head, just as the hoodlum had done when confronted by the Musketeer. However, instead of getting hit with the hasp, I heard Don Castabel clear his throat.

"This has been my family's worst Christmas for a very long time. Yes, this had a lot to do with my brother's death. Carlos telling me that he would rather live on the water than in my home, which I offered, hurt me too. But what bothered me the most was that my beautiful daughter, the most precious person to me on this earth, was not happy. And there was nothing I could do to help her." He swung the sword in front of my face.

"How could this happen? I am her father. I have been there for her for all of her life, kissing the scratches on her arms and the scrapes on her knees to make them better when she was little, and easing her fears and doubts when she became a young woman. But now, Walter, when she is an adult and I am no longer the person who fixes everything, it is heartbreaking. Only the father of a daughter who is an only child can understand this sort of thing."

He waved the sword in front of me a few times, seeming to take great pleasure in seeing the blade glimmer in the candlelight. He stopped and placed the tip on my chest, right in front of my heart.

"Son, you are not God! There will never be a time when you will ever speak for me! I will never let you become a martyr! Do you understand all of this!"

"Yes, sir," I said after the moment I needed to allow the words to form in my throat. I could feel my heart pounding against his sword, which was cutting into my shirt.

"From what the sheriff told me you said to him, my brother died fighting to save the others. He died a noble death."

"Yes, sir. He shot one of the bandits." I couldn't tell him that it was the same man who then came back and killed his brother.

"You, Pedro, and my men got the wine to Paris. This will be very important to future commerce between the two countries, and will extend much further than just wine. You do not know this, but there was a witness to what you endured. A young boy in the woods saw the bandits setting up for the attack. He went for help, but was on foot and got to the town where he lived well afterwards. When the sheriff and his men found the bodies of the dead bandits, they were identified as some of the most wanted criminals in all of France. A courier was sent from the King to my hacienda. He arrived three days ago. The letter he brought to me said that the King wants to give you a medal in a special ceremony in honor of ridding France of what was referred to as the worst kind of miscreants."

"What?" How things had turned in just a few minutes. I let my head clear. "I don't deserve a medal."

"You have proven otherwise."

"But what about Pedro and the men?" I hung my head.

"He knew the risks. He listened to your plan, the same as I. He thought your idea was sound, and that anyone seeing the cannon would be scared out of attacking you."

"The cannon was a dumb idea. The wagon could never be turned in a position so it could be used."

"Now we know. But the idea was not dumb. It just didn't work as planned." Don Castabel took a deep breath. "Carlos wants to stay at sea. I'm not pleased. I'd like to see him care for his mother and run the hacienda, since he's the oldest son, and then follow his destiny. But his mind is made up, and as a prince, he can do as he pleases."

I gasped when he said "prince" and smiled for the first time since I'd come back to the apartment. "Marek says he's the best natural saylor he's ever met."

"Then the sea will be good for him. But it leaves so much for me to have to deal with." He sighed and looked deeply into my eyes and smiled. "Confession is good for the soul. I've got a few of my own to make to you, but before I do, I want to hear yours. Let's start with Marek. What exactly is your arrangement with him? I pulled him aside and asked him about it, but all he said was he was just a trader and you and he had a small business arrangement. He's not a good liar."

Maria was now sitting in the chair with me, and I told Don Castabel how Marek and I had met, and with Bart's help was able to convince him to let us provide protection for his trip back across the Atlantic. I described what had happened after that, and what I'd asked from him. I explained how I got the chest of gold coin from the pirate booty to fund the first sugar venture, and that I gave Marek all the money I had in my account to begin trading in tobacco as well.

"Why did you do this?"

"I wanted to have enough money to prove to you I was worthy of Maria." I got up and went to a dresser drawer and pulled out several sheets of paper and handed them to Don Castabel. Then I retook my seat.

"What is this?" he asked, holding up a ledger page.

"It's what I have in my bank account in England, and this is after buying out Marek. The only difference is that I'm giving him 20 percent stock in the new company so he will keep running the operational side of things, instead of the 10 percent I'd originally planned to give him."

"And what about this promissory note from a George Willingham?"

"He was in the British Merchant Navy, same as I was, and I decided he was a lot like me before I got off the water. So, when Marek said that his days at sea were coming to a close, I sent him George with a little money I'd lent him so he would have a financial stake in the ship he'd be sayling to bring tobacco from the Congo to trade with Monsieur Nicot in Le Havre. He'll learn the sugar side of the business from Marek, but shipping tobacco will be his primary role. My hope is that he can someday take over the entire operation. I'll just have see what he makes of the opportunity."

Don Castabel leafed through the ledger sheets. "What were you planning to use all this money for?"

"To show you that I am worthy of Maria. To persuade you to support my asking for her hand." I couldn't believe what I'd just said. I was no longer on edge as I had been, but with that statement my heart started to race again.

"Let me understand this. While securing my port for both my country's benefit and that of the Crown, as a sideline you are a merchant, trading in both sugar and tobacco, and now helping me trade wine?"

I didn't answer. Even in the dim light, I could see a twinkle in his eyes and that he was very close to laughing.

"You tell me you still love my daughter." He stepped over to Maria. "Do you still love him."

"Yes, father. More than ever."

I sat there, numb and stunned. How could she possibly love me after what I'd done? I was swept away by the emotion of the moment.

She took my hands in hers and said, "I think I understand how you feel, and much more so than you might think. My mother died giving birth to me, and it hurts every waking morning to know that my mother died to bring me into this world. I can only imagine how it pained my father when he looked at me right after I was born. When I grew up, he always said I resembled my mother in so many ways, yet all I have is a painting of her, with nothing I can truly identify with. But while this has bothered me at times, and if I'm to be honest, it still does on occasion, I know that my mother lived to make my father happy and to put me on this Earth. So even though I could never know my mother, I still love her dearly for giving me life. Some days, when I see her face in the painting, I imagine her talking to me. And while I might become sad because she died for me, I have learned not to let this destroy me, which it would have, had my father not sat me down and told me what happened was not my fault, but God's decision.

And even though His choice might not make any sense, it was still His to make, and His alone."

Maria had always carried herself with a level of dignity I'd found indescribable, and now she had lighted a spark in my mind that said to me maybe, just maybe, if Maria can handle her grief with such character, perhaps I can too.

"You've taken the weight of the world off my shoulders, but I'm still horribly sorry," I said and hugged her and didn't want to let go.

"You have nothing to be sorry about," she said after gently pushing me away. "Walter, if you have been listening to me, you need to accept what I have been saying. From the beginning, you and I were two people very much in love with one another. Now, we are two people who are also very much alike in that both of us believe we have caused a tragedy that each of us has survived. The only thing to do is to show you can overcome your guilt, as I have mine, and marry me and claim your title."

I moved uneasily. "Title? What title?"

Don Castabel held up his hand to stop Maria from answering me. "I guess it's my turn to confess," he said, sheathing his sword. "Walter, the Bay of Biscayne to the coastline of the Mediterranean near Barcelona, and everything in between, belonged to one of Spain's only kings. When the last of his immediate family died about thirty years ago, his honor and title fell upon Pedro and me, since we were his nephews. Pedro was the oldest, even though he looked younger than me, and thereby inherited everything. But he was not a greedy man, so he parceled out the land so that the southern and eastern half was his to rule and the northern and western half mine to govern under *his* rule. That meant, however, that everything from Santander to Vitoria to Saragossa, as well as Sabadell to Andorra, belonged to me. Even the village of San Sebastian is mine.

I learned early on as the Don of this vast territory that the economy was always going to be an issue. And unless our people had marketable goods to sell outside Spain, we would never truly prosper as a nation. I will now tell you the truth about the grapes, and it is that Pedro was to approach the King of France as the

– I, Walter –

King of Spain, with the grapes as a means to open up trade to both our countries for many other products."

I said, "I remembered Pedro leaving when we were in Versayleles, but that was the only time." I was more than a little confused. "So all of that was a ruse to fool me so Pedro's meeting with the King would be a secret. And the King came to Versayleles to meet him?"

"This is what was worked out ahead of time."

"The party at the King's residence, and all the rest, was a ploy, too, as well as the sale of the wine to the inn in Versayleles?"

Don Castabel gave me a sheepish grin. "I know nothing about any of that, only that many plans were in place so the trip with the wine could not be found out to be an official visit from the King of Spain."

If I could feel any worse, now I was responsible for the death of the King of Spain. "Don't the people know their King is dead?"

"Don Pedro's body was placed in ice and shipped to Barcelona, where a funeral was held. Word spreads slowly, and it will be a month or two or even three before news of Don Pedro's death will reach the people."

"And they won't know how he died?" I asked.

"They can't. Something like this could cause a war between Spain and France. Pedro knew the risks. And we had planned, if he should die for some reason, that it would not become an international incident. When his death was found out, the story would be that he was on a private trip to buy Christmas presents for his wife in France, and attacked by highwaymen from Spain on the way back."

Nothing was humorous about the way Don Castable had put this, but what happened was ironic. Also not funny, I was the one who was taken advantage of, because had word of King Pedro's trip to France gotten out beforehand, I would have been in much greater danger than attack by a few highwaymen.

"I see that I'm not as wise as I thought I was. The King of England sneaks in a few things at the end, after I've accepted the assignment to clean up the port, and I end up taking one King to meet another, without my knowledge of what was happening." I groaned.

"Would you have done it otherwise?" Don Castabel asked.

"I don't know, but I would like to have made a decision *after* knowing all the facts."

Don Castabel placed his hand on my shoulder. "Now you know my guilt. I put my country over your safety, my brother's, and my men." In the flickering candlelight, I could see how watery his eyes had become.

"I have another confession. I've had someone watching you ever since you came back. Once the sheriff told me the story of what happened to my brother, two people have followed your every movement. Even to the church and the basement, and your cleaning the pews and the organ. What I didn't know was that Maria had her own spies, and they had decided you would eventually be coming to your apartment, so she left to wait for you here."

I have never had such a range of feelings at one time: elation, anger, humiliation, betrayal. But at least I knew now that I wasn't crazy in thinking people were watching me when I walked around town. Don Castabel's men were.

I asked Maria, "Where do we go from here?" She looked at her father.

"I don't know where you ever got the idea that you needed money to impress me," Don Castabel said. "You have more noble character in you than any member of European nobility I know. I never wanted a prince for my little girl. She's too special. She cost me my wife, my best friend, and my lover. And while I regularly mourn for her mother, I would not give up my daughter to someone just because that person had royal blood."

He smiled at her, then turned back to me. "When I first met you, you were respectful and responsible, and you had saved my little girl. I hoped beyond all hope that my Maria saw the same things I did. Soon, it was clear she did. And by helping to get the wine to market while knowing the risk, I realized you were even more special."

I had to stand. "I never thought of myself as doing something another person wouldn't have done under similar circumstances."

"You helped Marek, and now he is willing to serve you again. You helped Bart, who I know better than you are aware of, and he thinks of you as a son. You are helping George, and he admires you tremendously."

"You're able to keep track of George, too?" I asked, shaking my head in disbelief.

"Marek has let me place two of my men on George's boat to make certain nothing out of the ordinary happens to Carlos. We discussed this when he came to the hacienda. This was important, because if I died without a rightful heir, Carlos would be the King of Spain. But I don't plan on dying anytime soon, and Spain needs someone older than 15 to run the country if I did." Don Castabel laughed, something I hadn't heard from him in so long that I was glad he still knew how.

– Mike Hartner –

Chapter 21

The wick on the candle was almost spent, but not Don Castabel's oration. I replaced the candle so he wouldn't be talking in the dark. What he'd said so far had just started to register in my mind. I had rescued the daughter of the future King of Spain, and I, a commoner, was now asking for her hand in marriage.

"Was Maria captured by the pirates and then intended to be ransomed to Spain?"

"You ask a very good question," Don Castabel said as he tapped the hilt of his sword. "She was coming back from her first visit to England when her ship was attacked. She was traveling in a way that would not bring attention to herself, and after much investigation, I was certain she was a victim of a pirate's evil personal intentions and nothing else. You saved her from anything happening to her in this way, and for this I am grateful beyond words."

"You never told me much about the time on the pirate ship, and now I understand why." I smiled at her. "You might have slipped up and I would have figured out more about you and your family."

I could see Maria's eyes come alive in the dark. "My father has not wanted to let people know just who he is. He prefers to be thought of as the Don of northern Spain, and its what you'd call benefactor, not as King."

"Pedro conducted himself in the same way," Don Castabel said. "Spain has functioned without a monarchy for 30 years,

– I, Walter –

letting each province and city operate its own government. Pedro and I were simply the two people to whom most of the country belongs to."

"But in reality, you are now Spain's king," I said. "And now I'm responsible for killing the brother of the King of Spain." I buried my face in my hands, as my grief returned, stronger than ever.

"My brother died with honor and dignity in living the life he wanted. He knew the risks, and he saw your plan and thought it was good. He particularly liked the idea of the cannon protruding from the wagon, since it would warn criminals that they could be in for a lot more than a sword fight if the caravan was attacked. When we were boys, we were sent to England and put into a military school, which is where we learned to speak English. I was better at language than Pedro, but he came through with better grades in Tactics. I should say the best grades, as he graduated at the top of the class. So he should know a good plan when he sees it. And good character. Walter, we discussed his safety at length, and he told me he had complete confidence in you. That's high praise from my brother."

I had kept my face covered as Don Castabel spoke. Now he said, "Take your hands away from your face. Why is it, Walter, martyr of all the world and direct Son of God, that you can't see the goodness in your own self? Why is it that everyone else sees you for the honorable person that you are, but you cannot? Look hard, Walter. Look very hard. Few young boys the ages of you and Carlos have the maturity to go aboard a ship and deal with the crew and then do a man's job working right alongside them. An even smaller number respect honor and practice chivalry like you. An even smaller number than this display your modesty and show such courtesy for others. Why can't you stop running away from yourself and just admit to being a good person?"

I didn't have to think about an answer. "Because I've always been running. My parents tried to do the best they could, but I never fit in with what they wanted out of life. So I ran away. My father has always curried favor and friendship yet has never received it. When my brother left home, he changed and became even more spineless. Nobody respected him, and I found this impossible to accept. I ran away from home so I could be my own man and find my place in this world." I put my hands up to my face again.

"You only did what you had to. You can't live your life with guilt. Get these thoughts of guilt out of your mind, and I'm sure you'll have a long and happy life. If not, you will be fighting yourself, and I would not want that for Maria. So think about it."

"It's just not easy, sir."

"I'm sure it's not." He walked toward the stairs, but stopped before opening the door. "My giving Maria's hand to you was never about money. I offered you wealth when you were earning a saylor's pay, and if you had ever asked me, and if Maria wanted you for her husband, I would have gladly given my approval even then. You are more honorable than anyone else I've ever met, and everyone who knows you thinks the same. You just need to start believing in yourself rather than living under a dark cloud that is not justified. You have nothing to hang your head about, ever." He walked away, closing the door behind him.

Maria kissed me and again placed her legs atop mine. Exhausted from the late hour, but excited by what had transpired, I still needed to find out some things I had to know, and if I didn't ask now, I was concerned I might never have all the answers.

"I'm amazed your father could keep his true identity a secret."

"A few people know." She smiled coyly.

"I would wager that Sheriff Juarez is one of them."

"And you would win your bet." She kissed me on the cheek. "He is a second cousin, and my father made sure he became sheriff many years ago. He was very good at things on land but not so good with what happened on the sea. My father petitioned the King of England for help, and he sent you. He could not have made a better choice, could he?" She kissed me again, this time not on the cheek, and she was pressing against me and driving me crazy.

"I suppose you had nothing to do with getting me here?" I managed to ask between heavy breaths.

"My prodding my father might have helped a little," Maria said. She giggled and rose from the chair. I followed her.

***

– I, Walter –

A certain amount of comfort comes from sleeping in one's own bed, even if it is only wood and hay separated by thin layers of linen. But a heavy blanket helps, and so does sleeping beside the woman a man loves. To this day, tears come to my eyes when I think of that night together, and that it meant we would be with each other forever.

I spent the rest of the next day at the hacienda with Maria and Don Castabel. Now having the opportunity to digest everything I'd learned the preceding evening, I clearly understood why the proctors had questioned me so unrelentingly about Maria's potential influence on me. The King of England knew who she really was, and consequently so did those men.

Among the many tasks that day was to start planning for the wedding. Maria and her father wanted the ceremony to take place in a monastery in a town some distance away that I was not familiar with, and there was going to be a huge celebration afterwards. I knew better than to ask questions about this decision, but it seemed odd that the wedding wouldn't take place in San Sebastian, since Don Castabel was well known as a prominent caballero and quite a few people knew me from the work I'd done in cleaning up the port. Why travel a hundred miles to someplace else? However, this was one issue I was going to keep my nose out of.

I went back to San Sebastian the next day. I needed to thank the sheriff and tell him I now knew everything. On my ride to town, Juarez's close family relationship to Don Castabel now made it clear to me why he was so honest, as never once did I have to worry about his being bribed or otherwise corrupted by criminals.

***

By the last weekend of January, our wedding plans were proceeding quite nicely. A seamstress from the town where the wedding was to take place was brought to the hacienda, and she spent the better part of a day measuring every inch of Maria. If she had asked me, I could have saved her the time, as I told Maria when I was certain only she could hear me. I can't write here what she'd said to me in reply.

For all practical purposes, I had moved out to the hacienda. But a few personal items remained at my apartment, so I had to retrieve them. Afterwards, I went to The Dog for what I was fairly certain would be the last time. I entered and was met by a few men who knew me. They shook my hand and wished me well, not knowing I was marrying Maria but that my commission was up and I'd be leaving. I'd known a couple of these people since I first came to San Sebastian, and it was a bittersweet time for me, since they had become friends.

I asked the waitress to bring me a cup of mead, something I seldom drank except when I was thinking about Marek. I was just finishing my mead and a bowl of hearty stew when the proprietor walked over, waving a letter back and forth. "You came in so quiet-like, I didn't know you was here. You haven't been around for a while, but this here letter was left for you last Friday, I think it was. One o' the saylors brought it in after his boat dropped anchor. Said he was told to bring it here if you wasn't in your office. Marked 'urgent,' so I'm sorry I couldn't get it to you sooner."

The handwriting looked familiar. It read:

Walter, I hope this message finds you well. Right now, I'm not in good health, and I don't think I'll be able to continue watching over the company for you. I hope to see you before I pass, and will try to hold on until you get here, but I'm coughing badly right now and have a fever. You need to take control of the company right away. I'm at the infirmary in Portsmouth. Please come soon, I'm told I haven't got long. Marek.

I turned around and left the tavern so quickly that I nearly knocked over two saylors entering the bar. I rode as fast as the horse that Don Castabel lent me would go and showed the letter from Marek to Maria and her father. I was enormously relieved when both told me the wedding could wait and I should go to Marek. I was given another horse to ride back and leave with the sheriff. I scoured the docks and found a cargo boat headed for Portsmouth. The captain was reluctant to take on another

– I, Walter –

passenger until I agreed to pay him handsomely for any inconvenience I might cause.

Chapter 22

My wife came into the study with some fresh ink. After reading what I'd just written, she gave me a long hug and let a kiss linger on my forehead. "What you've written is so profound and so true. It never was about the money. You were always of noble mind and heart." She paused for a minute and I heard a light sniffle. "This is why I have always loved you. Above all, no matter what happened, you never let your principles waver."

The lump in my throat made it difficult to swallow. I was able to hold myself together until just after she left and closed the door, then the tears flowed. "I wonder," I said under my breath, and then I repeated the phrase.

I wiped my eyes and dipped a new quill into the fresh ink.

The ship was leaving the next day, and there were several times that night when I wanted to unpack everything and let the boat go without me. Maria was more important to me than Marek. And since both Maria and her father had told me that the money my trading company was generating was not an issue for them, why should it be for me? But, no matter my justification for staying, as I thought about it longer, I knew what I owed Marek. He had been extremely loyal to me, and I couldn't leave him on his deathbed without saying a final goodbye. So, even after a sleepless night of doing my best to talk myself out of the trip, I kept to my plans and early the next morning climbed aboard *The Lucky Stars* to sayle for Portsmouth.

– I, Walter –

The Lord must have been on my side for this journey, and I got to learn what the word "Godspeed" meant firsthand. The trip from San Sebastian to Portsmouth was unchallenged in any way, and with very strong winds behind us the entire time, we made what I had to believe was record time for a cargo ship, since port to port required less than 48 hours on the water.

I had given the captain enough money that I was allowed the run of the ship. I spent most of my daylight hours standing at the bow and thinking about how much my life had turned around in the past six weeks. I had run the gamut from the worst depression to the greatest joy, and I dreamed of Maria and me growing old together. I dreamed of her having several children, and that they would all be healthy. I dreamed of the different places we might live, from Spain to England to a Greek island where Bart had dropped anchor one time. But every time I though about our bliss together, it was followed by the emptiness of not being around her, much as what I was experiencing at that very moment. I prayed that God would protect her, and me, and bring me safely back to her. That I was sayling again was not lost on me.

The night before we landed in Portsmouth, the clouds were heavy and rain looked and felt imminent. For whatever reason, the thick skies made me think about Marek, and I considered what his death would mean to me. I was on a cot at the time, and I came straight up out of it. I knew nothing about managing a business with a dozen ships. And I couldn't teach George or anyone else what I didn't know myself.

***

Portsmouth hadn't changed much in the last two years. Most of the streets were still full of ruts and large holes, although I was told city workers were starting to use stones to fill in places where the problems were particularly severe.

My first stop was the infirmary, but it had already closed to the public, and even though I pleaded to be let in, I was refused admittance. I went to The Drenched Seaman. I saw a few people I recognized, including a saylor from San Sebastian, nicknamed Shorty. He was at least a foot taller than me, and I went over and said hello.

"What are you doing these days?" I asked, slapping him on the back. "Still plying the same barque?"

"Aye, Walter, still plying the same boat. But she's mine now. The cap'n passed a year ago an' give her to me."

"What are you carrying now?"

"I was s'posed to be gettin' ready to leave soon. New cap'n asked me if I'd like to work for him. Tells me he's got too much work, an' not enough boats. But I ha'nt seen 'im in a few days."

"What's his name, and what you are going to be plying?"

"Big roly-poly chap. Name a Marek, but I'm wonderin' how long I should wait 'round. Been a while already."

I chuckled to myself. Even ill, Marek was drumming up business and crews to take product to market. "Truth be known, I'm looking for Marek myself. Hang around for a little longer, and I'll get word to you on a shipment you can load."

"You always was an honest man, so I'll wait." He glanced around The Seaman and spotted the buxom wench who had been there from the first time I ever walked in the pub. "Aye, for sure not the worst place to be stuck." I grinned and sat down at a table I always liked, which was by the front entrance.

I ordered a pint, and while I was waiting for it, the owner of the tavern motioned me to come over to him. "Ye be Walter Crofter, right?" he asked as I approached.

"You know damn well I am!" I laughed and shook his hand.

He chuckled. "Just tryin' ta 'ave a little fun is all. Got somethin' for ye." He handed me a letter with a seal on it I recognized as Bart's. The message was brief and scared me when I read it: "Marek was moved to Bethlem Hospital in London so that he could be watched closer. Come as soon as you can."

I was hungry, but as I thought about Marek, I lost my appetite. If he was moved to London, his condition must indeed be dire. Yet, he was considered able to travel, so all might not be lost. I turned back to Shorty.

"I just got a note about Marek. He's in London for a while. I'm going to leave to see him as soon as I can get a carriage to take me. So it might be longer than I thought, but if I don't get back in a few days, I'm going to give you a letter to take to the manager at

– I, Walter –

the Mercantile Bank. He'll give you an advance, and information on where I want you to go to pick up a shipment."

"I don't mean it to come out this way, but the man'ger will know you?"

"Yeah, he'll know me." I went the bar and borrowed a quill and ink and wrote a my own note on the back of the paper I'd been handed with Bart's message. I gave it to Shorty and left to scurry around for the first passage I could find to London.

Leaving The Seaman, I had an eerie feeling. In the back of the tavern, against a recess in the wall, I visualized a well-dressed man with a hat pulled down over his face. I spun around so fast my bad knee twisted and I winced in pain, but when I shuffled back inside, I could see that no one stood in the cavity against the wall. I pulled my hands across the sides of my face and left, deciding the ale must have gotten to me on an empty stomach.

I walked down the street and rested against a pole with a "Wanted" poster nailed to it. The brad wasn't rusted, so the criminal and the activity had be current. I almost fell over when I looked at it closer. The sketch was of my brother Gerald. Underneath, it read:

"By Order of the Sheriff of London and the Crown: A reward of 5,000 gold sovereigns is now placed on the return, dead or alive, of the man known as Gerald Crofter. He is wanted on the charges of Robbery, Blackmail, Kidnapping, and Murder. He is recently charged with killing a sheriff in Manchester."

I remember wondering what had caused my brother to go to the bad. I shook my head, and after a few minutes took the poster down and placed it inside my coat.

I could not get a coach to London until the next morning, so I rented a horse that I could leave at a London stable. I could have bought a horse for what I was being charged, but I didn't have time to bicker, so I paid the outlandish fee and left on my mount. Ten miles into the trip and I knew I should have bought a horse, as this one had a mind of its own and would trot a mile and walk two. The 60-mile distance to London was going to be a two-day trip anyhow, so I stopped at an inn halfway to rest my great steed, and arrived at the stable the following afternoon. From there, I took a livery to Bethlem Royal Hospital.

I'd never been to this hospital, but had only heard it was large, which was a lie. It was mammoth. When I found Marek, I had the shock of my life. A man was in the bed, but it was not the same Marek I'd known for more than five years. This fellow was half his size and wore a red beard. The Marek I knew had a long white beard and his teeth weren't as good. A lot of things could change a man's appearance, but his teeth aren't going to get better.

I asked him, "You mind telling your name?"

"Ye see it on the card."

"Why don't you tell me so I can be sure I'm in the right place?"

"Ye know where you are, don't ye?"

"Yeah, I see exactly where I am."

I had no idea what was going on. I needed to see Bart, but he'd retired to the country and it would be another two-day's ride. My most pressing interest was to find out where Marek really was, and then to see Shorty with orders on whom to contact in Hispaniola for sugar, as there would be too many problems sending him around the horn on a maiden voyage with my company. I might not know much about operations, but I knew that wouldn't be a good idea with a new crew.

Since I was in London, I wanted to see my parents. The day was now late, so I got a room at an inn and left for their house the next day. The grounds were not well maintained, which disturbed me since there should have been plenty of money for this sort of thing, and an outer door was hanging on the main entrance.

When I knocked, my father hollered out to ask who it was. When I told him it was me, he said to wait a minute. When he came to the door, he looked as though he'd been drinking for a week straight.

"*What* is going on here?" I asked. "I'd think that mom would have you keeping this place up better."

He glanced away and said, "Walter, you need to come inside."

The living room was filthy, and from what I could see of the rest of the house, it wasn't any better. He told me to sit on a sofa that was soiled and smell awful. I stood.

"Your mum died a year ago," he said and broke down.

I went to him. "How?"

– I, Walter –

"She got something. A doctor said it might a been in the water. She was sick for two weeks after that, and then--then she was gone. She's buried next to her mum and dad."

"Did she suffer?"

"Not that she let on. She just turned a yellow color and died."

"Why have you let this place run down? Is the bank not sending you the money you're supposed to be getting?"

"I've not been touching much of it." He sniffled and blew his nose. "I never knew how much I needed your mum until she was gone."

I didn't want to ask if he knew about Gerald's ascension into the ranks of England's "Most Wanted," so I stayed with him and the state of the house. "I'm going to get you out of here and to Portsmouth. The man I started the shipping company with is not to be found. I don't know what's going on, but I'll give you a job helping out with the inside operations back in Portsmouth." I helped him up from a chair he was sitting in. "For now, let's get you out for a good meal, and then I'll tell what I'd like you to do."

I got my father cleaned up, and the next day had some ladies come in and scrub the house as if it were a dirty child, and I found a crew to tidy up the outside and a man to fix the door. I got in touch with the police, but Marek was not listed as a missing person. I stayed for several days in the house with my father. We visited my mom's grave and talked about many things, but mostly about how her death had affected him. But we also discussed Marek, and the need to find someone who could organize and look after the boats, as well as put the costs together and coordinate orders with the shipping schedules.

My father surprised me, as he started to take a serious interest in what I was discussing about the business. It sounded like he was considering at shipping as a way to acquire the respectability he had never attained on his own. He told me he wanted to try to learn the operation, and the more he talked about it, the more I convinced myself that my father was indeed capable of at least making a good showing for himself.

Days earlier, I'd sent a message to Shorty in Portsmouth, telling him I'd be there in a couple of days. I'd also sent one to Bart but had not received an answer. I desperately wanted to see him, hoping with his contacts he could help in finding Marek, but I had to get with Shorty or lose him and his ship, which I didn't want to happen. So, with considerable disappointment and anxiety, I left London in a hired coach, with my father by my side. He was the one bright spot in the whole mess.

***

The minute we set foot in Portsmouth, the time went quickly. I introduced myself to Marek's right-hand man in "our" local office, and he was delighted to have help and didn't act the least bit concerned when I told him Geoff was my father. He hadn't heard a thing from Marek and didn't even know he was sick, but the bills were being paid, as well as payroll. And money was being allocated for outfitting the ships. I assumed the bank manager was handling this, since I got the impression we were one of his biggest and best customers, but he wasn't going to do this for long, regardless of the size of our account.

***

I'd been in England for ten days, and I needed to get back to Spain and Maria as fast as I could. It appeared that my father would work out, but he was still holding onto his "want-to-please-everybody" attitude, and this worried me. His disposition had been the cause of so many problems at home, I wasn't willing to sacrifice the shipping company so that my father could build character. I thought long and hard about this and told his "boss" to drive him hard to do the right thing for the company and not back down from issues that could cost us money.

The man said he would, but I didn't sense much enthusiasm. With Marek not on the scene, he just wanted help. As busy as we were, I couldn't blame him, so I gave him permission to hire someone if my father couldn't hold up his end, or if he simply needed another person. I gave him a letter to take to the banker with the same information, along with instructions.

I now had everything in order as best I could. But I still had no news on Marek, and I'd checked everywhere and with every mutual acquaintance who might know him.

– I, Walter –

The next morning, I awoke to a chill in the air and the rapid pitter-patter of rain hitting the tin roof and splattering against the windows. It was gray and miserable outside, and I wished once more that I could crawl back into my room and forget about the day.

I'd managed to stall Shorty, and as it was ending up, this was a good thing. I wanted his ship up to Marek's standards, and it needed a great deal of work to accomplish this. I also found our company's strict conditions while at sea didn't sit well with many of his old crewmen, who had threatened to quit. I told Shorty to let them make a decision to follow our policies or leave. Half did, so Shorty had to spend the time to hire their replacements. While all of this was occurring, the itineraries for our ships indicated that George's vessel should be returning any day, and I wanted him and Shorty to meet while we had this opportunity. So I paid him and the crew as if they were at sea, and all they had to do was eat and drink at The Seaman.

The good news was that I had the chance to get to know Shorty. After a long afternoon of drinking at the pub, I asked him, "If this works out, would you want to sayle, or manage the ships? I'm asking because the man we have in the office needs help, and even with my father in there with him, there's too much work. And we need someone to manage the whole operation, because I'm going back to Spain."

He looked up from a just-empty mug he was staring into as if it would miraculously refill itself. "I've always wanted me own boat. But I know a very good person who could work for ye, and it would be good 'cause this one's retired and has nothin' to do now that her husband's dead."

"And who would this miracle woman be?"

"Me mum."

He was so serious that I didn't dare laugh. "Tell me about your mum that you think she'd be right for managing a shipping company."

Shorty went on for an hour. Mrs. Channing had retired from working as an office manager in an insurance company, and before that had managed a women's shop.

When he finished, I smiled. "Go to your mum and see if she's interested. If she is, bring her to the office tomorrow. I'll be there all day."

Mrs. Shirley Channing sat quietly as I explained what we were looking for. A small woman, she had a feisty appearance that I liked, and I noticed my father seemed attracted to her, but I certainly didn't know his reason.

I gave her a test assignment of outfitting *The Bahama Sugar* for the trip to Hispaniola upon its return to England, and told her she could have as much time as she needed. I'd have Marek's man compare what she came up with to my father's work on the same ship and make a decision as who would be best in that position. The "loser" would still have a job, but one that would be more clerical, which deep down I believed would suit my father best.

George arrived in port three days later. I went aboard and met him in the captain's quarters. I expected him to immediately tell me about his trip, and he did in general terms with his stoic British features not changing in the least. However, when I asked about Carlos, his face brightened. He echoed Marek's words about Carlos' natural skills as a saylor, adding that the boy was the quickest learner he'd ever seen. Then he got up and went to a cabinet and took out a bottle of brandy. He handed me a glass and filled it, along for one for himself.

"This was given to me by me father. He asked me to open it only on moments of great significance, and to drink it sparin'ly. Walter, for you, I offer everythin' left in this bottle." He handed it to me and we toasted each other.

For the next several hours he talked about what he'd encountered on his latest voyage, which was his first trip around the Horn of Africa. We talked about the water, and the temperatures of the North versus the South Atlantic, and about the experience of crossing the Equator. After we'd both finished most of what had remained in the bottle, he got around to discussing the particulars of trading. Whether drunk or not, he was as giddy as a youngster.

"I thought you was crazy, but if you was willin' to put up the money to back me, I thought I should carry out your wishes to the letter, least once."

"That was noble of you." I laughed and George even cracked a smile.

"So, we sayled from here. An' I must tell you, we took our time gettin' 'round the bulge of Africa. We found the port you was tellin' us to go to, on the mouth of the Quorra. We had problems, though. See, the locals call it Jeliba, and we thought we was lost. But we anchored and came ashore, 'cause we needed fresh water, and it was then we knowed we was in the right place, since the local leader had already brought some salt on carts to the bank of the river. We traded for a shipload for a very small amount of spirits and fabric, just as you said."

George poured me the last glass of the brandy. "After tradin' for the salt, and some salted fish and other foodstuffs, we set sayle down to the Horn of Africa. We come to a harbor there, and we replenished our food and water. Seven days later, we made it to the islands and then to east Africa. It was here that we was able to get the best trades for the salt, and it was for loads and loads of the tobacco plant we wanted. I couldn't believe they wanted salt instead of gold, but you was right again. We stuffed every open inch of our boat with as many of these leaves as we could, and then a few more. By the time we left east Africa, it was difficult to walk around our boat because we'd taken on so much."

"A week ago we arrived in Le Havre and went to see Nicot like you told me to. He took every leaf of our tobacco and paid ten times more than I got for that load of sugar I brought back from Hispaniola. He even asked if we could send two ships on the next trip. It took me a few days in Le Havre, but I was finally able to outfit a second boat. I'll meet up with it down there, and then we're off for another run to east Africa."

George paused for a minute and rummaged through a desk drawer before hauling out two bags. He began dumping coin from both on his desk. The amount in the first bag was paltry in comparison to what was in the second. He said, "This first bag was your initial investment. This second bag is your share of the profit from this trip."

"What about what you spent to set up the new ship?"

"It was from a split of our profits after I returned your investment."

"No, it's not." I shoved the entirety of the coin to his side of the desk. "I want you take all of my profit and expand our fleet. Have ships built if you have to. Just stop in San Sebastian on each trip as you leave for Africa and provide me with a ledger. I'm going to set up an account, and you are to deposit my share from each trip in that bank. You are also going to be a 20 percent owner in the entire tobacco business. I'll have the documents drawn up tomorrow. Is that satisfactory?"

Once what I'd just said sank in, George staggered over to me, not from the spirits, but from elation over I'd just provided for him. He shook my hand, and I could see in his eyes that he would never want to work in an office and run my operation. He was a seaman, and I was delighted to make him a very rich one as he made his mark as a most respected trader until the day he died, 35 years later.

***

I had the horrible chore of telling Carlos what had happened to his father, and my involvement. I told him I would take him back with me to be with his mother, and he could decide if he wanted to come back to the sea. George seemed more upset than Carlos.

Carlos and I were sitting in The Seaman having an afternoon meal on the day before we were to depart for San Sebastian when a man walked up to me and handed me a letter with Bart's seal on it. After the last such missive, I didn't know what to expect from this one. The message was almost as brief:

Walter,
The King wants you to come to London immediately. Wear your dress uniform if you have it with you. I know you have tried to reach me. All will be explained, but you must hurry.
Bart

I didn't know why I'd packed my dress uniform, but I had, so I'd carry it with me and change when I got to London. I decided to bring Carlos along, and he was happy at not being left alone waiting for me to get back to Portsmouth.

A carriage would not work for this trip, even though Carlos was a prince. I laughed at forgetting to tell George his prize student's heritage as I rented the two best horses I could find, now believing I could definitely have bought them cheaper if I'd had time to bargain.

What this trip held in store for me I didn't know, but I was very worried about Marek and hoped to have Bart help me find him so I could learn the reason for his mysterious disappearance. I also prayed he was still alive.

Chapter 23

Remembering how nervous I was back then, I furrowed my brow. I was doing the same thing now, but I dipped my quill into the ink, and kept writing.

Carlos and I got a room at an inn in London, which was nicer than those I'd stayed in previously, anywhere. Carlos slept in another bed in the same room and said I'd tossed and turned all night long, and my rustling kept waking him. I apologized, but my usually analytical mind had brought me no answers as to why I was summoned to London--only fears. The chambermaid heated water and poured me a hot bath. I was just getting ready to sit in the tub and soak when I was interrupted by a knock at the door. A formally attired courier handed me a message. I gave him a shilling and read the note:

"Walter, your presence is required at Westminster Abbey at noon today. Wear your dress uniform. If you don't have it with you, come an hour early and I'll have something for you to wear. Bart."

Some medals came with my promotions. I cared nothing for them, but since Bart had made me place them on my dress jacket, I left them. One medal was for Valor, another was for Service With Distinction, and several indicated levels of training I'd

– I, Walter –

completed. Stripes denoting the rank of lieutenant colonel finished off the uniform. At several inches above five feet, and weighing some 12 stone, I was not scrawny by any means. And while I now walked with a visible limp and displayed a long deep scar on my right arm, I looked more the soldier than the saylor. But the uniform covered my wounds, and when I stepped in front of the mirror in the room, I saw of man with stature and dignity. Maybe my appearance would lessen the weight of whatever was about to befall me.

Maria came into the study to see if I needed anything. She read what I'd just written and laughed and gave me a hug. "You always did underestimate yourself." She left, and in this instance, looking back on it now, she was right.

I had never been in Westminster Abbey, but my mother had told me of its religious and historical significance, so I was aware of its importance to England. I arrived early and a Royal Guardsman ushered me into a section of the church a sign said was closed to the public. He'd done this so quickly that I barely noticed the large number of people and guards milling about the courtyard. There seemed to be even more of The Royal Guard than when the King had met with me years earlier. The Guardsmen I'd walked by on my way to the entrance either nodded or smiled at me, making me even more nervous.

Once I entered Westminster Abbey, its splendor took my breath away. The nave of this church is a massive area, with columns directly in front of it at least 50 feet apart. Diagonal struts are mounted atop them. But when I entered the vast room and was directed forward, the columns appeared to be soldiers and the struts raised swords. I was under enough stress and didn't need this imagery adding to my anxiety.

Pews, long enough to accommodate 15 people, were situated to each side of a wide aisle. I was taking in all of this as I slowly walked forward, when I saw the beautiful stained glass window above the altar. Before I could concentrate on the intricate design and spectacular colors, I noticed the large number of people seated in the church. This made me wonder if I was supposed to be there. But then I saw Bart, in the first pew, gesturing for me to join him. And right next to him were the colors of the British Royal Monarch.

I paused a moment to take in everything. I looked at Bart. He again motioned me forward, this time more forcefully. As I came toward him, everyone in the pews stood. I found this embarrassing, but now that I was going to be sitting next to Bart, I'd relaxed immeasurably. And while I couldn't figure out what was going on, since it had to be one of Bart's elaborate ruses, I would play along.

When I sat next to Bart and glanced at those near us, I saw my father sitting in the pew down the aisle from me. He was wearing a suit that looked as if it had just come from the tailor, but he looked perplexed, as if enjoying being in the presence of a lot of important people but not knowing why. I knew how he felt. I turned to the aisle across from me and saw Don Castabel. It took a few seconds for this to register. *What? How could this be?* I leaned forward to get a better look. And who was sitting next to him but Maria! I wanted to go to her immediately, and I started to, but Bart was grasped my arm as he cleared his throat.

He was about to say something when a Royal Guardsman blew a trumpet that brought all of us to our feet. Moments later, dressed in his royal garb, the King of England, James, the man I'd known as Bart's cousin, walked toward the two of us.

Even though I had met with him in private before, I stood in awe of his presence.

I looked at Bart, who said, "I'm sorry, my friend, I couldn't tell ye. Now, kneel before the King." I knelt, trembling. So much was happening and I could not have been more confused.

A throne was brought in behind the King and he took his seat. He seemed to be surveying the hall, then he turned his eyes down to me and said, "Rise and come forward, Walter Crofter." He raised and lowered his arms to signal everyone else to become seated.

In a voice that all could hear, the King said. "You have now finished your duty in Spain, and your obligation to the Crown is completed. Will you continue your service or shall I formally end your commission?"

"If it pleases you, I would like to leave the Merchant Navy and pursue other interests." I had barely been able to speak, and I wanted to look at Maria but didn't dare take my eyes from the King.

"So be it. But there is more. You had choices, yet thrice in the last eight years you have saved my cousin from death. So now you will have to make choices. You deserve to be honored, and will be. I am offering you title and position. What say you?"

"Sire, I am honored and humbled. But I did nothing that anyone else would not have done in the same situations. If you want to honor someone, honor the men on our ship who died so that we might live. They are the heroes."

"I am told your humanity is known by all you serve with. For me, this is the second time I have experienced it for myself. I will deal with this in a moment, but for now, I have been informed that you wish to marry Maria Castabel, the daughter of Don Juan Castabel, Sovereign of Spain. What say you?"

I could not help but look toward Maria, who was smiling and starting to sob with what I hoped was joy.

The King motioned me to step back and called forth Don Castabel. "Walter Crofter has asked for your daughter in marriage. Does he have your consent?"

Don Castabel handed me a small gold box. "In this case, Walter, is the ring I gave to Maria's mother when we married 21 years ago. I have kept it these many years to give to my daughter when she married. Now, it is yours to give to her. Do this, please, for me?" I could not believe Don Castabel was pleading with me to marry Maria, but those were his exact words.

Placing myself on one knee in front of her, I opened the box and asked. "Will you be mine, forever?"

She stood and pulled me up by my hands and said, "Forever."

The King gave us one small nod and turned to the crowd. "All ye, rise." Clothes could be heard rustling as everyone in the audience stood.

King James spoke slowly, emphasizing each syllable. "Honor above self is a great gift. Walter Crofter has asked that his only honor be the hand of Maria Castabel, on this day, in matrimony. I will grant that wish, but I will say unto you, it will not be the only honor conferred here today." He gestured to a man in a robe standing to the side of us. "Abbot, marry these two and allow them to live in peace."

The abbot looked at Maria's father and said, "Do ye give this flower away?"

Don Castabel said, "Yes, this honor belongs to me." He took Maria's hand and placed it in mine.

The Abbott looked over those in attendance. "Is there any of ye who believe this wedding should not be?" I don't know why, but I held my breath until the abbot spoke again.

He smiled at Maria. "Maria Rosa, do you take Walter Crofter to be your husband?"

"I do."

"Walter, do you take Maria Rosa to be your wife?"

"I do."

"Then by the power vested in me as the Abbott of Westminster Abbey, may God join ye and keep ye in peace, and may ye live happily ever after. "He smiled to the crowd " I present to all of ye, Walter and Maria Crofter, husband and wife."

The King departed, and the next few minutes were a whirlwind of activity as people congratulated us, most on Maria's side, as Carlos was there, as well as his mother. I wondered if he was in on the trick that was pulled on me, and I learned later then he'd been told of what was going to happen when he'd left for three days after we came to port. The perhaps the biggest surprise of all was Marek. He looked better than I'd ever seen him, and it was obvious he was one of the lead pranksters. George was sitting next to Marek, and when I looked him in the eyes his face got red as a beet. How this many people had managed to fool me was beyond my comprehension, yet they had pulled it off to perfection. And I could not have been happier.

The Royal Trumpeter blew his horn again, and the King presented himself to the crowd once more. He called out, "Arise," and then, "Walter Crofter, stand before me now."

I came forward, and as before knelt in front of the King, once again not knowing the reason.

He glanced at a piece of parchment and placed it inside his robe. "Walter Crofter has been in the service of our country for

– I, Walter –

more than eight years, attaining the rank of lieutenant colonel. He served the Crown as a seaman. Thrice in six years he saved my cousin from certain death, and for that I am more than thankful. He also saved the woman he is now married to from perhaps a fate worse than death, all the while not knowing she was a Spanish princess. The last two years, he's cleaned up a dangerous port that was crucial to English trade with Spain and taken many murderous pirates off the sea."

"One of his duties included helping Spain bring wine to French markets, not knowing that Don Castabel and I have planned this for some time." The King nodded to Don Castabel. "Spain is an ally, and England can only benefit as that country prospers. And Spain in strengthening its relationship with France aids England in kind. But as Walter Crofter returned to Spain, he and his men were attacked by murderous thieves. Don Castabel's brother, Pedro, the dual ruler of Spain with King Juan Castabel, was killed during the raid, and for this our country is most sad. Those criminals were some of the most wanted in all of France, and the King of France asked the French Royal Court to knight Walter Crofter. But I have asked that this be deferred."

I certainly couldn't blame the King, since I'd gotten Pedro killed. But now I was thoroughly befuddled as to why I was asked to once more kneel before his majesty.

"I can't honor France's request to knight you, and for good reason." The King raised his already booming voice. "In honor of your eight years of service, in honor of your saving my cousin's life thrice, in honor of the forthright service you have given to Crown and Country, often placing your life in grave danger.. . ." He paused and passed his sword over both of my shoulders and tapped them lightly. "Arise, Lord Walter Crofter, Baron of Devon and the lands surrounding her. Live in peace, and honor your own life in the manner in which you have honored so many others around you."

I rose in tears. Don Castabel's allowing me to marry Maria had conferred more honor upon me than anything material ever would. After all that had happened, I could find no reason for any of this, other than being true to myself and following the path I believed was right and what I was certain God had set for me.

Those in attendance began to applaud, and with this soon came raucous cheers. My father came up to me and gave me a strong handshake that I felt was from the heart and not obsequious. Shirley Channing, whom I hadn't noticed earlier, was now standing next to him. I took a moment and sought out Shorty and winked at him.

A woman with his mother's personality and business savvy might be the just the sort of person for my father. I wasn't confident he could ever be turned around, but she wasn't the sort to sit by the wayside and let him be pushed around, or play the sycophant, either.

After everything had died down, while Maria was busy with Bart's wife and her aunt, I got Bart aside. "This was all your doing, wasn't it?"

"Aye, lad, I couldn't come close to arrangin' this all by meself." He let out a laugh that was so loud he coughed several times and turned red. "I had lots a help." He grinned. "I could tell ye was surprised. We was all worried that Carlos, being as young as he is and all, might of said somethin' to ye. So, in addition to all his other good qualities, now ye also know the boy can keep a secret too."

Carlos' not holding his father's death against me was something I would never forget, and for all the time I knew him before he died much too young in a war, not once did he ever blame me for what happened to Pedro. I wiped my eyes as I thought about this now.

After a glorious reception held in the royal ballroom, Bart arranged for Maria and me to have a huge apartment at an inn that was even nicer than where Carlos and I had stayed the previous evening.

Here I was, then, lying next to this creature of such beauty, and finding it impossible to sleep. Her skin was so soft and her hair smelled of flowers. But I did finally succumb to all the excitement and awoke to hear her gentle breathing. I was stirred by a knocking at the door. I found a page holding a message.

– I, Walter –

When he handed it to me, he offered an exaggerated bow and left, refusing a coin as a token of my appreciation.

The message read:

"Lord Crofton, a carriage will be waiting outside at ten. It will take you and Lady Crofton to your new manor."

When we were dressed, breakfast was brought to our room, another new experience for me. Afterwards, the same page returned and led us outside, where three carriages displaying the royal seal awaited. The carriage reserved for Maria and me was in the middle. The front carriage contain Bart's family, as well as Marek and George. Don Castabel, along with his sister-in-law and Carlos and the rest of his siblings, rode in the rear. Heavily armed Royal Guardsmen rode on horses on the front, back, and sides of our procession.

I was positive at the time that this was to assure Don Castabel's safety, but it made me uncomfortable because of all the attention this would draw to us. I didn't suggest an escort of this size when we went into France with the wine for this very reason. However, as I've second-guessed myself so many times during the past 40-plus years regarding what I could have done to deter the attack, I'm convinced now that traveling in this manner would have been the best solution.

Our carriage was over-sized and baggage was everywhere, including strapped to both the roof and outside the trunk. Maria told me she had loaded up a ship. She had not exaggerated.

People stared at our carriages as we were driven down the streets of London and later on the narrower lanes from the city. Maria and I started to have fun with everyone. We waved and they waved at us; if they waved, we waved back at them. After a half-hour of this we were experiencing a giddy pleasure. Every village we passed through produced similar results. All of the people wanted to stop whatever they were doing and celebrate that the Royals were passing through. In truth, I felt much like a fraud.

The journey comprised 170 miles of often miserable roads. The Royal Guardsmen had to use their shoulders and wits to get us out of, and keep us out of, more than a few deep ruts, and to change a couple of broken wheels. I made our first family decision, and it was that in the future we would make the trip by boat. And the inns, and in one case a house where we stayed, were a far cry from those of the past two evenings, but on the fifth day we arrived at Ivybridge, where everyone else but the Guards assigned to us would stay while we enjoyed our honeymoon.

When we left Ivybridge, the roads turned to little more than thin, rutted paths, all bordered by marsh. Along with the marsh came the mosquitoes. Tired of swatting the bugs, even Maria asked if it would be possible to make this trip by boat the next time. I assured her it would be the only way.

Through the marshland we traveled, until this gave way to rolling hills and then to plush forests. At the end of a grueling day we reached Bagnor Castle, which would be my official residence in England.

A beautiful old gray stone structure with ivy running down its front and a tower on each of its four corners, it had a magical look that made me wonder if any of it was real, and if I was really a part of it. Bagnor Castle had been in the royal family's possessions since before Elizabeth, but unused by any members of the original family since the last of them died several years earlier. Now it was to be my responsibility, and ultimately my heritage. Along the way we passed through huge groves of oak and walnut trees, along with many varieties that would provide lumber for building houses.

A member of the Kings Guard had ridden ahead to alert the staff that the Baron and Lady Crofton had arrived. A manservant, who we learned was actually Henry the groom, was waiting at attention at the front of the huge oak doors to the castle, along with Robert the main servant in charge of the staff, who Maria told me was called a majordomo in Spain. Robert helped us step down from the carriage and introduced us to his staff, which consisted of Mary, the cook, who was Robert's wife, and Olivia, the maid, who was their daughter. As soon as we'd met everyone, I picked up my new wife and carried her across the first of many thresholds. Somehow, I never minded this task.

Robert began giving us a tour of the castle, starting with the main foyer where we were standing. A curved oak staircase ran up the right wall to the second of the structure's three stories, and to our left was a huge living area, with furniture covered in plush fabrics that appeared to have never been sat on, they were that bright and fluffy.

A large painting of a man and woman, who Robert told us graced this room 70 years earlier, rested on the mantel of a fireplace large enough to drive a carriage into and leave room on both sides. The man was stately looking, and in his early 50s, I was guessing, with thin gray hair and a monocle. He stood next to an elegant woman who also looked to be in her 50s. Her eyes had a look of grace, and they fit her age. His breeches were tucked inside a long pair of black riding boots, and if his countenance was any indication, he was holding his riding crop with the confidence it brought him. Her smile was warm and loving, but as I stared at her face further, I could also sense the discontent the artist had noticed in her and felt compelled to paint. I hoped that Maria and I would have a similar portrait painted someday, but that it wouldn't portray any discontent, regardless of how subtle.

Robert then led us to the kitchen, where a small serving nook was cut into the wall. The centerpiece of the kitchen, however, was a huge pit in the back that allowed many foods to be cooked at the same time. The large cooking utensils and great number of pots of all shapes and sizes that hung in their places indicated that many a great meal had been prepared at the castle in the past. Most of the cups were pewter rather than ceramic, and there was a cabinet with serving pieces made of silver.

Behind the kitchen, Robert lighted a torch and led us down dirt steps to a root cellar. The air was pungent with the smell of decaying vegetables, and I was curious about why he would allow food to spoil. Maria saw some spiders, so we didn't stay long.

We went back to the main floor and were shown to a beautiful oak-walled study lined with bookcases. The writing on the spines of the leather covering the parchment indicated that the previous residents had left what now amounted to tomes of information about the castle, the forests, the villages nearby, and the farmland and its maintenance.

When we returned to the foyer, Robert announced, "Now, we should look at the upstairs." I didn't know why, but I wasn't getting a good feeling being around the man, but I was probably tired and didn't give it another thought.

He showed us a half-dozen bedrooms, each with a large fireplace and a wash basin. These weren't all the bedrooms, but we were now at the sleeping quarters designed for the master and his wife. It ran the length of one entire wall, with not one but two fireplaces. It contained a four-post bed with mosquito netting around it, and a mattress filled with wool and pillows with down in them. Maria had felt them and explained this to me. Blankets and quilts had been placed in an open chest at the front of the bed. Two large dressers, one that stretched floor to ceiling and had 12 drawers, sat against one wall.

Maria and I joked that this bedroom would be good enough for us. We told Robert we'd go by ourselves to see the rest of the rooms on the floor and come downstairs in a few minutes. But really we wanted to be alone. He left us, and after our "few minutes," we hurried through the other rooms we hadn't seen on the floor, which included three smaller bedrooms and a room devoid of furniture except for a small cabinet mounted to a wall, a chest with washcloths and towels, and a large tub.

A pulley hung outside the back window to bring buckets of hot water from the kitchen. We finished our quick tour of the second floor, met Robert on the stairs, and went to the main floor.

Maria and I ate our first meal at the house and then she discussed food and provisions with Mary. After a few pleasantries, we dismissed everyone and returned to the master's bedroom. Closing the door behind us, spent, the two of us enjoyed our marriage for longer than a few minutes.

We fell asleep with our arms wrapped around each other, and I kept looking at her in the candlelight and wondering how anyone could be so beautiful. And to be able to lie next to her and feel the heat from her body was exquisite beyond description. I remember saying out loud, "If you take me now, Lord, please know that I was the happiest man on earth."

– Mike Hartner –

Chapter 24

On the next day we surveyed the land. We found the forest populated by many good stands of trees. Most of the open ground contained lush foliage too, but also very rocky soil. It would require lot of work if we were going to get much of anything to grow here other than mosquitoes and children. I said that to Maria in an attempt to humor her when she was complaining about the insects. She cast me a wide smile and I swear I saw her eyes twinkle just like stars. I didn't think it was the mosquitoes that caused her such pleasant thoughts.

In subsequent trips around the manor, we visited a small village located adjacent to the river that defined one boundary of our property, and this community consisted of a mill, some stables, a store, and a church. We met with as many of the townspeople as we could, but I spent most of my time with a man I liked very much who was sort of the unofficial mayor. He said the people could use more grain, and he wanted to start raising cattle. I agreed to help him on both accounts. I told the Royal Guardsman who was always with us when we traveled that I would give him a letter under my seal to be taken to Marek so he could fill these requests. I also mentioned to the "mayor" that I'd be sending him something called sugar to make foods sweeter, another item called tobacco to be chewed or smoked for relaxation, and some fine Spanish wine in due time.

After we returned to the castle that evening, I pored through the ledgers that pertained to the manor's finances, as Robert had told me before we left in the morning that he was in dire need of funds to keep everything operating as it had been in the past. The ledgers from the most current prior master were more than ten years old, but they had shown considerable profit from the sale of everything from lumber to prize horses the manor was famous for breeding. Robert kept his own ledgers from when the last master had died, and the numbers were consistent until dropping drastically three years later.

I ordered Robert to bring me the receipts from the past three years from every purchase, including the most recent for what he needed once he learned that Maria and

I would be taking up residency. I then looked through the last few months of bills and called in Maria. I showed her the numbers on the ledgers and what I came up with when I totaled the receipts. During the next day, we matched each line with a receipt. Everything equaled what it should have, but I wasn't convinced.

Late that night, after reading and writing down our own numbers until the last candle we could find in the bedroom had burned out, we came to the inevitable conclusion that Robert, along with help of the groom, had been stealing substantial money from what the King was providing to maintain the manor. The proof was in funds allocated for grain for horses we couldn't find anywhere on the property.

When we asked Henry, he said he knew nothing about any horses. But there were also expenses for wagons, for which he'd signed his X for supplies. He admitted he had built the wagons, but sold them and gave the money to Robert. He had even turned in bills of sale for draft horses that weren't anywhere we could find. With the Royal Guardsman standing over him, he admitted that he never used them to till the soil, but had sold them, too, and once again handed the money over to Robert. After lengthy questioning, he explained that Mary had motivated her husband to begin stealing, and her daughter was just as bad. They both felt they were owed it for what they had to do to keep the Lords' and Ladies' chamber pots clean.

I asked the groom, "What did you get out of all of this?"
"Me job."

"I don't understand."

"Me job, Lord Crofton, me job." He started bawling like a baby and wailed, "I got to keep me job."

I told Henry I'd decide what to do with him later, but for now if he wanted to keep what few teeth he had left, not to breathe a word of our conversation to any of the family. I could see he was terrified of the Royal Guardsman and me, but I asked the guard to keep on eye on him so he didn't accidentally bump into Robert or his wife or daughter until I could confront them properly.

I had just put the ledgers and receipts away when I saw a horse and rider coming through the main gate. I smiled, as I'd ridden too many miles with this person not to recognize him. I went outside to greet my guest, who had two Royal Guardsmen of his own following right behind.

"Hello, Carlos, my friend," I said, as I shook his hand. "What brings you to the estate?"

Carlos pulled a few pouches out of his saddlebags, and I could hear the clinking of coin as he handed them to me. "Marek wanted me to bring you this. He said it's his share of the last trip, and he wants you to have it because he felt so guilty about tricking you. He could have put it in your account, but he wanted you to feel the gold coin. Said you might be not so mad at him if you had the real money in your hands. I'm supposed to give this to you and ride back to where we're all staying in Ivybridge."

I broke out laughing. That old salt would need to give me a lot more than money to make up for worrying me half to death. I handed the pouches back to Carlos. "You put that money back in your saddlebags and give it to that guard to watch over. And you tell Marek he doesn't have enough money to buy me off from what I'm going to do to him when I see him again. But for now, come on in and have a meal with us. It's nothing like Don Castabel can put on the table, but your cousin is going to want to see you, so stay for dinner and ride back in the morning. You can send one of the guards back so everyone will know you're all right, and he can ride back in the morning so you'll have both guards going with you later in the day."

"It seems so silly. I go to sea with no one to attend me. I ride 20 miles in England, and I need two guards." I almost slipped up

– I, Walter –

and told him not to be so sure he's alone at sea. It comes with being a prince, but I was happy I caught myself.

While we awaited the evening repast, we showed Carlos the castle and sat him down in private. Maria and I had made a decision, and she said, "Walter and I have been talking, and as much as this is a wonderful place, both of us would prefer to live in Spain and have our own hacienda near my father's and--"

It pained me to say what I was about to, but I interrupted Maria. "Carlos, with what happened, and you know what I'm talking about, will you be coming home? You're the rightful heir and can be the king of half of Spain."

"Walter, I don't want to be the king of anything. Right now, the best thing that could have happened is that my mother and I are together. I've been having long talks with her. I told her I will do whatever she would want me to, even if that means coming home. But I told her I love to be at sea, and I'm hoping to spend a few years running the routes with George, and maybe take over my own ship in a few years. I realize how immature I was to think that before, but now I honestly believe I can do it when I'm 20 or so, and Marek and George both agree. Mother says she can run the hacienda, and Uncle Juan says he'll run Spain." I laughed at how casually Carlos said this, but it was indeed true.

We enjoyed a good meal and put Carlos in the bedroom next to ours. Later, as we thought about it, this might not have been the best idea. But the next morning he wasn't giving either of us any sly looks, so we were thankful the castle walls were thick.

The other guards arrived back at the manor around noon, and Carlos and both Royal Guardsmen left after we fed everyone a hearty lunch.

An hour later, Maria and I called Robert, Mary, and Olivia into the study and sat them down on a couch in front of my desk. Maria was seated in a smaller chair next to mine, and two Royal Guardsmen stood on either side of the door to the room. Ledgers and assorted papers overlapped the desktop.

I wanted to observe each member of this family as I let them sit for a while in silence. Neither so much as blinked for the first few minutes, but then each got restless. Robert tugged on his collar, Mary played with her apron, and Olivia squirmed on her end of the couch. I left them to their personal discomfort and pretended to review some of the material on the desk. Soon, all three were squirming, and that was how I wanted them.

"According to these numbers," I said as I pointed to a pile of ledgers, "the manor should be making money, so much so that its previous three masters not only had enough left over to improve the property, but funds were available to provide a better life for the people in the little community that's actually on manor grounds." All three were now as still as statues.

"Today, however, the manor is barely breaking even. For one thing, Henry has been selling wagons and horses, and the money is not being entered on the manor accounts--"

"I'll fire the lout right away," Robert said, jumping up from his seat.

"Sit down, Robert," I said and gave one of the Guardsmen a subtle nod. He took a step forward and Robert took his seat. "Henry has told me what's been happening. If he didn't do this, and give you the money, he'd lose his job. You essentially forced him to steal for you."

"That's a bloody lie," Mary said.

"Is it?" I glared at her. "According to my wife, you are billing the King for twice as much food as you can use at the castle even if parties were thrown every week. And Olivia should have enough brooms and mops and buckets to outfit everyone in the town several times over. Now what do you have to say for yourselves?"

"It's all Henry, Sir Crofton," Robert said. "He's twisted this all around and--"

"I don't think so. Henry is a simple man you intimidated and took advantage of so he could keep working here. Each of you should be in a prison cell at Newcastle, but if you return the money you stole, you all can leave here without being arrested."

"Where will we go?" Mary asked, crying.

"If you are wise, far away from here. What say you? The decision is yours."

The guards escorted them out of the study, and ten minutes later they came back to my office with two bags of gold coin. I didn't have to ask if this was all they had, because the Royal

Guardsmen had done this for me, Robert sporting a bruised eye and a bloody nose. I had them gather their belongings, and the Guardsmen escorted the trio to the property line opposite from the town and sent them off in a small cart pulled by a donkey.

***

The original plan was for everyone at Ivybridge to give Maria and me a week to ourselves, and then to come for a visit and stay at the castle before sayling back to England from the port at Plymouth. When they arrived, I had a new staff, altogether untrained and just getting to know where everything was located, but Maria and I decided to keep Henry, and he helped in keeping things orderly. He would never become majordomo as Maria called it, but he probably wouldn't be the groom forever, either.

I'd hired the town "mayor" to take Robert's place, and he, like his predecessor, brought in his wife as cook, but in his case he had two sons and a daughter. I was confident that even with five of them living at the castle, the manor would produce substantially more profit for the King.

I made the announcement at dinner the first night that Maria and I would be going back to Spain. Don Castabel was delighted, and Bart said he figured as much and had told his cousin that he doubted I would remain at the castle. Bart said that the King didn't care where I lived, the manor would be mine until the day I died to do with as I pleased.

The long trip from London to Devon had been enough for Maria, and she didn't want another long ride anytime soon in a carriage. Marek made her happy when he said, if he could have a week or so to get things in order, he would accompany us to San Sebastian in George's ship. Don Castabel had used one of his own ships to come to England, so I thought this was a great idea. George would then take Marek's ship on its regular run around the horn, while the old captain would find passage back to Portsmouth on the next freighter stopping there.

Don Castabel had invited Bart and his family to stay at the hacienda and enjoy his hospitality and see northern Spain. Bart and his wife were delighted with the offer, and their coming with

Maria and me to Spain gave this return even more special meaning.

***

Ten days later, Marek and Don Castabel greeted Maria and me on the dock at Bristol. Marek said, "My boat will be right behind Don Castabel's. We're finishin' loadin' supplies on now. I'll be ready to sayle in the morn."

I knew it was going to be a grand trip, and I was so glad to have Bart and his family sailing with us as well.

A surprise was awaiting us on Don Castabel's ship, as it was not decked out like anything I had ever seen, yet I'd been on only trading vessels before and never one outfitted solely for cruising.

The captain's quarters were situated on the main deck, as anyone experienced with ships would expect. But that's where the similarities to a trading vessel ended. Instead of a large section with crew hammocks, two rooms occupied the entire space. One was bigger than the other, but each was furnished with four-post beds and fitted with fine sheets and pillowcases with intricate designs that only families like...well, like royalty could afford. Even after the experience with my own castle, this seemed so far beyond me that I had to throw some water on my face to make certain I was awake.

Don Castabel gave Maria and me the option of choosing which one we wanted. Maria and I took no time to make the decision. We both liked the smaller of the two rooms, which left Maria's father muttering because he said he'd spent a lot of effort making the other room more opulent. And now he'd be sleeping in it himself--not us.

We wanted that particular room because of its huge windowsill, which held memories for us from the time I rescued Maria and slept next to her on one like it and kept her safe. We had slept on the sill every night on the way to Spain, and we planned to do the same now. While an undeniable intimacy was attached to this before, I could tell that Maria wanted to experience this now as a wife with her husband. And that first night she did.

***

– I, Walter –

The following morning, we set sayle. On the port side, it was clear enough that a sliver of the Devon manor was visible with the naked eye. The air was crisp and clean and, as I walked around the deck with Maria, I noticed two flags flying atop our mainmast.

One was the Royal Flag of England. With Bart on board this was understandable, although not something I expected. The second standard was the Royal Flag of Spain. Both were hung side by side, and I thought that would be the last of the flags atop our ship. I would be wrong.

The next morning, as we were passing out of the strait with our sayles filling in the breeze, Don Castabel told the crew to unfurl the stay sayle. It opened with The Seal of the Crown of England embroidered on it. When the flying jib opened next to it, the Spanish Royal Flag was embroidered on it. And attached to the mainmast in the stern was the spanker sayle showing the two royal seals flying in unison. I'd never seen this before and asked Don Castabel about it.

He said, "In normal situations, each flag or seal stands for an independent family. My seal is on here because the three of us are members of our Spain's royal family."

"It's the other seal I can't figure out."

"That is Bart's doing. He told me that his Royal Seal will always fly with you for as long as you live. He said you are as close to him as family, and he is proud to call you both friend and family."

Tears flowed freely down my face. All I could do was look into the skies, open my arms, and say, "Thank you, Lord, but why me?"

Maria was now standing next to me. She said, "Because you are a good and decent man. It would do you good to believe that yourself." She hugged me, and at that moment I did feel better about myself.

The dual flags indicated that this ship was traveling under the authority and protection of two separate royal families. Here I am, a mere commoner, now married into Spanish nobility and escorted by a member of the royal family of England.

We had been on the water for two days, and everything from the weather to the food was excellent. To the latter, anything would be better than the grog and swill I'd been accustomed to from Cookie. But something was definitely nettling me. I wanted to take a long look at the seas around us. I scaled the mainmast until I was at the branch where the top gallant sayle was attached, and I used the ocular. However, after an hour of meticulously searching the water and horizon in every direction, all I had seen were approaching clouds from the east, and nothing else. This should have placed me at ease, but I couldn't shake the feeling that had come over me.

I slept well that night, only to be awakened at first light by a loud blast. I'd had enough experience to know not only that it was from a cannon, but from one capable of expelling a large ball a long distance. At the sound of a second explosion, Maria scooted off the sill. I told her she must go to her father and stay with him.

She started to leave just as Don Castabel entered our room, and she ran into his arms. I said, "Please, sir, take Maria with you and stay in your quarters. I don't want either of you in unnecessary danger."

"Whatever is happening, we will need every man on deck," Don Castabel said as he took us to his room and told her not to open the door for anyone except him or me. He handed me a dagger and a sword from a cabinet and grabbed one of each for himself.

I stepped on deck to the shock of seeing a ship right next to ours. Our crew was priming our cannons, and a few seconds later I heard and felt five go off, one after other. When the smoke cleared, I saw a large hole in the other ship's hull, but it wasn't low enough to the waterline to sink the vessel in the current seas.

I counted a dozen pirates ready to come aboard as soon a plank could be hooked onto the side of our ship. My hope was that Marek was already tacking back and coming to our aid. But when I was able to take my eyes off what was going on between our ship and the pirates ready to board us, I saw Marek's vessel under siege by a larger ship than the one we were having to contend with.

– I, Walter –

To our crew's credit, before the first pirate had set foot on our deck, they had reloaded and fired another salvo into the other ship, and this had opened a much larger hole in the hull. This would be good, except the pirates now had no choice but to come on our boat or go down with theirs, as it was taking on a lot of water and already listing.

Our crew had the knives they always carried, and a couple of the men readied muskets and pistols and handed them out. The pirates started to board our ship, but the crew managed to shoot five of them and then knock the plank from the side, toppling two more into the water.

Another plank was shoved onto our ship and a pirate ran aboard, screaming. One of our men slashed him in the arm. Slowed, he didn't stop, and he killed one of our men before he was stabbed and went down. The four other pirates managed to get aboard, but they were now hopelessly outnumbered, and my goal was to lose no more of our men while sending the others to a watery grave.

I had no idea what was going on with Marek, but I heard two distinctly different sets of cannons go off, and now for the second time, so his battle was also far from over.

Our men didn't have the time needed to prime the muskets or pistols, so it was now hand-to-hand fighting. Two pirates drew swords, and one attacked me and the other Don Castabel. The remaining duo was having its hands full with several of our crew who had swarmed them. The lone disabled man was being ignored, which I would later learn was a bad error in judgment on my part and brought back a horrible memory.

Don Castabel and I were slashed several times and bleeding, but I didn't notice my wound until after I'd run my sword through my foe's chest.

I had no idea that Maria's father was an expert swordsman, but he was already dancing around the last pirate standing, and his footwork and deft use of the blade were a sight to behold. He cut off the pirate's suspenders and belt, and his pants fell around his feet. He flipped him around and ran the tip of his sword down the man's rump, causing the pirate a bad case of bleeding hemorrhoids. After disarming him and putting him to the deck, Don Castabel had him bound and taken to the hold.

While this was happening, the pirate who was wounded at the beginning of the raid tripped one of our men and stabbed him in the heart when he fell. As this was happening, we heard the other boat creak. Its mizzenmast split and knocked down our foremast, and one of the spars that held the sayles impaled the pirate as he tried to raise his sword to kill another member of our crew. Looking back at this years later, the irony of a pirate ship skewering one of its own who had played dead was hard to ignore.

I surveyed the damage to Don Castabel's ship, and although it was considerable, the ship was still seaworthy. But more important at the moment, it was secure.

I have to rest a moment. My fever has returned. Not as powerful as when I began writing this story, but I am now weak once more, and my memory is coming and going. I hope I can hold on long enough to finish everything I started. Lucky for me, Bart told me many times what happened on Marek's ship, and this I could never forget, so at least I can get this much done before. . . . well, before.

Sound didn't carry our way as it had Bart's, as I never heard the cannons fired at Marek's ship that Bart said occurred at the same time the balls hit our craft. Bart said he'd heard four distinct blasts, two close to him and two farther away. Here's Bart's recollection of what happened, just as he told it to me.

"I didn't expect pirates to attack Marek's ship with yours right behind. And certainly not both our boats at the same time. The raids were so well coordinated that someone had to have gained information from a person who was close to us.

Midshipman John Phister was able to put three cannons low into the opposing boat before two of its cannons bounced off our side and one cracked our hull a third the way down. I'd grabbed the wheel to try to keep us away from the other ship, but I was too

– I, Walter –

late and could feel the two boats bump and see the pirates lay down their plank.

Ensign Evan Greene cut down the first pirate that came across. Greene was in turn felled by musket shot fired from the other side, but before he was shot again and killed, he'd managed to toss the end of the plank over the side so no other pirates could make it across that way.

I had a chance to steer our ship clear of the other when a blast from John's cannons brought down the mainmast and pulled the crow's nest with it. Three pirates were carried aboard our ship with the wood and sayles that crashed onto our deck.

The mast itself fell in such a way as to take out three of our sayles. One pirate was crushed by the mast, another had an arm hanging in two, but the third landed on his feet just long enough for George to put a blade through him.

While all this was going on, the boats touched again, and this time the rest of the pirates clambered aboard. I got down from the wheel and pulled my saber. I'd like to say I engaged in a spectacular swordfight, but a pirate rushed me and tripped on a rope and fell into my sword. I turned to see who I could help, but instead I watched a pirate kill one of our crew and go for the stairs to below deck. Carlos had just felled the man he was dueling and also saw the pirate heading down the stairs, where I had my family huddled together in one room, with Marek protecting Carlos' mother and children with a musket and a pistol in another room at the far end of the ship. My wife had never picked up a gun in her life, so I had given both weapons to Marek.

With my legs as they were, I could move only so fast. But I got down the steps in time to watch the pirate pull himself through the deck window into the cabin my wife and I and our children were using, with Carlos following right behind him.

I tried but couldn't knock down the door to get in the room. I was too big to get through the window, and could only try to get one of the women or children to throw the heavy door's iron latch. But they were all on the side of the room that was farthest from the door, with my daughter Melanie standing in front of her mother and little brother to shield them.

Carlos and the pirate danced around each other, with both holding a sword but doing more with their fists than their blades. After several minutes of fisticuffs that had bloodied both men, the pirate lunged at Melanie and grabbed her around the neck and put his sword under her throat.

Melanie screamed and kicked and clawed at the pirate, but the man put more pressure on the blade and she quit yelling and moving. The pirate told Carlos to drop his sword and move back. I feared the worst.

Carlos told me later that he didn't know I was watching, but as the pirate turned toward my wife and younger children for just the briefest time, I could see the rage coursing through him as he jumped up and gripped the sides of the beam above him and swung his body, feet first, into the back of the pirate.

The pirate stumbled and released Melanie. Carlos then pinned him to the floor, face first. The man's head bounced, and Carlos held him up by his hair as he removed his knife and said, "You never, ever should have touched the girl, she's mine," and slit his throat from ear to ear.

I hollered and Carlos let me in, but there was no time for me to even thank him, as we had to get back on deck. What we walked up to was carnage on both sides, but the pirate crew had all been killed, while half our crew was still alive. Carlos left me as I attended to some of the men. Later, when I went below to see how my family was faring, I noticed the way both my sons were holding their mother. I also saw the way Carlos was holding my daughter and she him. She had a smile on her face, and I have to admit that I had one on mine, too."

– I, Walter –

Chapter 25

I put down my quill long enough to mop my face and have something to drink. My forehead was pounding, and it was an effort to keep going. Still, I needed to finish. I'd come to far to quit now. I inked the quill, and put it to parchment once more.

Both ships had different repair issues, but since we weren't more than a day from San Sebastian, we were confident we could lash the vessels together and have enough combined sayles up and catching the wind to keep our now double-size craft going in the direction we desired.

Since my boat was in somewhat better shape than Marek's, we met in my cabin and discussed what had happened. I told them I'd captured a pirate alive, and wanted to have all of us question him about how the captains of these ships managed to know so much about our travel plans.

George had been talking to the pirate, whose hands were bound, and he brought him in to us and threw him into a chair. "Tell all these men what ya just tol' me, ya bum."

The pirate had no teeth, but I swear I heard his gums chattering. "Please, sirs, don't kill me. I'll tell ya's everythin'. Ya see, I was in The Drenched Seaman 'bout a week ago when this here fellow comes up to our cap'n. Tall and skinny guy, he is. Dressed like a real gentlemen, was he though. Had a fancy hat on he always kept pulled down o'er his face. Tells our cap'n he knows a treasure is on two ships leavin' England for San

Sebastian, they is, and they should be easy pickin's. All it's gonna take is two ships workin' together. Then he gives the cap'n some coin, and he gives it to us to lay low till it's time to go. Four day ago he tells us to set sayle and where to hide to wait for ya's ships to come by. Works just like he says, but we didn't 'spect full crews of fightin' men aboard."

I'd heard all I wanted to hear. "Did this man have a name?"

"Said it was Gerald, it was."

I must have turned white as a sheet, because Bart, Marek, Don Castabel, and George asked me if I was ill. I lied and said I was fine, and then I asked George to see that the pirate's wounds were tended to and then have him thrown in the hold so he could be handed over to the sheriff after we docked.

The trip to Spain took longer than we thought it would, and we limped into San Sebastian more like a group of defeated warriors rather than the victors. I also now had a new issue to contend with. What was Gerald doing--and why?

I stopped writing to wet my face down with a towel and some cold water Maria had just brought me. Either my malaria is making me delirious or I'm truly starting to get better, because I feel like a new person since the last time I took some time to rest. One thing is for certain, writing about everything has made things easier on my soul, yet the most horrible part of my life is yet to come. And, oh, how I hate to tell this. But, alas, I must.

***

The evidence that Gerald was behind the attack was circumstantial, at best. My brother's name and his crimes were papered to poles all over England, so the pirate could've pulled his name out of the air to try to keep from hanging.

Don Castabel, Bart, Marek and I went to The Salty Dog. We posted a guard to keep everyone out, and since Don Castabel was there the owner didn't complain.

Don Castabel began our meeting by asking, "If Gerald planned this attack on us, with his own brother in harm's way, how should we deal with a man this treacherous?"

Bart said, "He's wanted in England for murderin' people and many other crimes. He's even killed a sheriff and a deputy in cold blood. My cousin has had his men lookin' for Gerald for years, but he's sly like a fox and scares a lot a simple folk into protectin' him. So gettin' him will prob'ly cost more lives. An' what he's doin' now seems to be aimed at us."

"Or me," I said.

"Ye thin' maybe he's jealous since ye married into royalty, an' all?" Marek asked.

"I don't know, but now I believe that pirate we captured was telling the truth, and I'll tell you why." I took a swig of ale the wench had just put in front of me. "A tall, thin man with a hat pulled down over his face has been stalking me for years. I always thought it was coincidence whenever I'd see him, or that he wasn't really there, since he often appeared at night like a shadow, and I'd tell myself my mind was playing tricks on me or I'd had too much ale."

Don Castabel gave me a look that was as much for my consent as anything. I had an idea of what he wanted to say, so I nodded. "If Gerald ever sets foot on Spanish soil, it will be the last step this hombre will ever take."

Pewter clanged against pewter, and we all said a solemn, "Hear, hear."

***

Maria and I lived at Don Castabel's hacienda until our house could be built on land he gave us that was four miles away. Just far enough to have lives of our own, but close enough so a short ride would allow his grandchildren to visit or for him to come see them.

During the first eight years of our marriage, Maria and I had seven children, of which five survived. Walter was our first; then Michael, who died at six weeks; then James; then Susanna; then Agnes, who died at six months; then Juan; and, finally Pedro.

Six years after their marriage, at Melanie's urging, Carlos came off the sea, because no matter how much he loved the water, he loved his wife more. They settled into a house Don Castabel had built for them a couple of miles from ours. They were blessed with Charles, Bartholomew, and Anna. William died in his tenth week, and Greta labored over her last breath on her third day.

Life was good for both our families. The children were healthy and growing like weeds, and we all led active lives. We even made a couple of trips to Devon, as a group. But Maria never became comfortable with the castle and hated constantly having to battle the mosquitoes. Melanie, however, didn't find the insects as annoying, and Carlos liked the place, so they agreed to look after the manor at times. With a little direction from me, he began managing the forests. In a short time he was selecting the best hardwoods to sell to Bart so he could build boats for the British Navy.

After returning from the last trip I ever made to the manor, I was at my hacienda and going through some of the old papers that pertained to the estate, which I wanted to give to Carlos when he came back to his hacienda. Mixed in with these was one of the logbooks I'd taken from a pirate ship during my sayling days. I'd gone through most of the logs, page by page, but I didn't remember ever going through this one. My curiosity was piqued, so I dusted it off and began reading the entries. Everything was rather routine until I was stopped by a page that read: Gerald Crofter: Expenses for Operations at Sea.

The pages in this section listed the names of pirates, most long dead, who had been under my brother's control, and the boats that had been attacked, looted, and sunk. I became even more incensed at seeing two ships circled that were Don Castabel's, and which sayled only in Spanish waters and without armament. Why Gerald found it necessary to slaughter the crews was incomprehensible. But the documentation was right in front of me, and indisputable. For a fleeting moment, I wanted to believe I was imagining this, but nothing I could do would erase this reality.

And it only got worse, as the pages that followed disgusted me more than anything I could have imagined in my vilest nightmares. In this log were the names of boys Gerald had kidnapped from British aristocracy and traded as slaves for debts he owed. To make this more horrific, I had come to know the parents of some of these children and shared their pain.

– I, Walter –

When I finished reading that list, I remember thinking of my brother not as Gerald but as Aaron in Shakespeare's "Titus Andronicus." How could my parents have begat such evil? And did I encourage this in some way? Regardless, I knew only too well what I had to write next, and it sickened me so much that I made haste to the basin in our bedroom and vomited.

Maria came into our bedroom just as I was stepping away from the sink and made me lie down on our bed. She washed my face as I explained that what I was going through had nothing to do with my malaria.

She said, "Let me read what you wrote. If you left off where I think you did, I can write the section." She took my hand and ran it over the side of her cheek. "Later, you can finish the rest of story, which only you know." My dear wife seated herself at my desk and took up my quill.

I am a positive person, so always find a solution to even the most difficult things without too much drama. For example, I have lived all these years without a mother. My father could not be more adoring, but it is not the same even though I don't know what the same means. Yet I managed to make his love that of two.

I grieved over the loss of my infant children, but the will of the Lord needs to be respected, and I was calmed by this.

Each of these parts of my life, no matter how hard they were for me to accept, had closure. But something happened for which an answer had never been provided to this day, and it has tormented Walter and me.

One day I was looking at some fabric in a store in San Sebastian with a friend when I heard, "Maria, come quick!"

I turned to see Theresa, the schoolmistress for my children, running toward me with her face strained and gasping for air while raising her dress just enough to maintain her modesty and yet allow her legs more freedom of movement. I had left her just two hours earlier as the children were enjoying a birthday party for my son, James, who was now eleven.

"What's wrong?" I asked, putting my arms around her as she fell against me.

"The children...we...we must get the sheriff!"

"What's happened?"

"James has been kidnapped!"

I sent the woman I was shopping with to get Sheriff Juarez and ran with Theresa as fast as I could to the woman's home, which served as the school I took James to twice a week.

I arrived at her house to find the door to the classroom broken down and a dead man in saylor's garb lying just beyond the threshold. His neck had a large hole where his Adam's apple should have been and the back of his head was missing. I heard children crying, and I had no choice but to step through the blood now covering the floor to get to them.

Five boys and four girls were huddled together in the cellar, where they were trained to go if they were in danger for any reason. The primary concern was storms, since crime in San Sebastian for the past few years was minimal, and was the reason I could travel freely in town and felt comfortable leaving my children at the school while I shopped or visited with my friends while they studied.

Young Walter and Susanna, my other children old enough to attend school, rushed up to me, mumbling, both too traumatized to speak. The other children soon joined them, swarming around me, needing to be consoled. I did what any mother would, but seeing and feeling their pain was more than I could handle, and I told Theresa to keep them in the cellar until the sheriff arrived.

I knew this home well, and it had many rooms where someone could hide. I searched through each of them, but my son was nowhere to be found. Now on the verge of madness, I ran into the woods behind the house and began hollering as loud as I could. Theresa came into the backyard.

"You won't find him out here," she said.

In a rage, I screamed, "What do you mean I won't find him. Where is my boy? Where is he, Theresa? Why was it James who was taken?"

"I don't know, ma'am."

I stumbled my way back to the house just as the sheriff arrived. He had a deputy get both of us some water and asked Theresa to tell him exactly what happened.

She said, "I always keep the door locked when I'm teaching the children. About an hour ago, I heard the knob turning. I peeked through the keyhole and saw three men in saylor's clothes trying to get in. I went to the children and told them to go to the cellar. James helped me with this, then ran to the closet and grabbed my musket. I didn't know he knew I had a gun, or where I kept it, or that he could shoot. I wanted to take the musket from him, but he wouldn't let me have it. He had it primed and a ball loaded just as the door came crashing down." Theresa stopped and gulped some water.

"The musket is heavy, and he braced it against the banister and shot the first man who came through the door in the neck. A second man came in and yanked the gun from James' hands. James fought him as hard as he could, and when I tried to help I was pushed to the floor. The man holding James told the third man, "Let's get out of here," and they left.

"Did James continue to put up a fight?" Sheriff Juarez asked.

"He couldn't." Theresa turned her eyes away. "The man had a knife to his neck."

"Can you describe the two men who abducted James?" the sheriff asked.

"The one who did the talking and held James was tall and thin, and he had a cap pulled down over his face." I'd known from Walter that this was the way his brother Gerald always appeared in public, and I burst into tears and cried like I never had in my life.

I felt Walter's hand on my shoulder. I had been so intent on what I was writing that I hadn't heard him come in the room. He read what I'd just written and said, "You don't know how sorry I am." He repeated this several times before taking the quill from my fingers and telling me that he was the only one who could properly finish the story, and I should go now. I didn't want to leave him, but his tone told me I must.

Sheriff Juarez sent a deputy to get me. I had a fresh horse saddled for him, and we rode to town as fast as our animals would carry us. My horror was indescribable when Maria told me she suspected it was Gerald who had kidnapped our son. All of the deputies and every able-bodied man and woman in town combed the buildings and alleys in San Sebastian, as well as the woods. I took a group of men and went through each and every ship docked or anchored in our harbor. We found no sign of James, nor could anyone report a ship leaving the immediate area. But James hadn't vanished into thin air, so I reached the conclusion he must have sayled in a tender of some sort to a ship that was beyond the eyeshot of anyone in our port, even if aided by an ocular.

Regardless of the way I thought the escape was pulled off, my men and I searched the area around San Sebastian for five straight days, looking for remnants of evening fires that might give me hope. I had little appetite during this time and didn't sleep well at all. When I returned home after that sixth day, I had to admit defeat. I simply told Maria and our children and Don Castabel, "I could find no sign of James anywhere."

But I never gave up hope, and a part of my heart would forever be empty until I learned my son's fate. I became obsessed and searched for him every chance I got. I lost some of my lust for life. I kept searching, until that fateful day ten years later when all was revealed to me.

I jerked the quill away, as if the parchment it was touching had sent a fire through it and into my very soul. My next words would be hardest for me to write of anything in my life, since I'd be admitting to something I was certain I would never confess. But now I had to tell it and do so truthfully. I tapped the tip of my quill against the inkwell ever so gently, and I whispered, "Maria, please don't hate me."

While my enthusiasm for finding James never ebbed, after ten years of dead ends and empty leads that produced nothing but saddle sores, I was not nearly as confident each time someone thought he saw a man in the area who might look like James as an adult.

Crime in San Sebastian, which for many years had been reduced to petty theft and domestic disputes, was now more serious and on the rise. Sheriff Juarez had died when a bull on a farm he owned gored him, and the new man, while I believed him to be honest, didn't command the same respect as his predecessor. The port was nowhere near as rough as when the King had sent me clean it up, and while armed robberies weren't commonplace, night crimes were, especially burglaries. And a gang of thugs was routinely causing trouble at The Dog. Some merchants had been forced to pay protection to these men to keep themselves and their businesses free from harm. Much of the most recent criminal activity seemed too well coordinated to be random, and the new sheriff asked me to help him find the person behind it all.

Maria wanted me at our hacienda, but I felt a responsibility to the community, since I was now a respected member of it. The first thing I did was set up a "watch group" of neighbors to look after each other, and I did the same for the businesses in town.

Occasionally this got out of hand, as some folks were too "watchful" and it turned into downright spying, which had occurred at the home of the town baker. Two men affiliated with the watch committee, looking through the man's bedroom window, saw the baker get badly beaten because he wouldn't pay to have his bakery protected. When the thugs left, one man hurried for the doctor while the other followed at a distance to see where the men went who had just assaulted the baker. He saw them get into a tender, row awhile, attach a small mast with a sayle, and the boat quietly disappear into the night.

The baker didn't want to report what had happened to him, but the men who had witnessed the beating told and sheriff and me what they had seen. The sheriff and I were taken to the spot where the tender had been pulled up on the bank, and while the boat wasn't there now, a natural alcove behind some trees provided an excellent place to hide and wait for the next time these criminals came ashore. The only bad part was that it was quite a way from the shoreline.

On the fourth night I was on this duty, the deputy who was with me and I heard the creaking of oars. With the darkness on this particular evening and our distance from the water, if not for the sound, the men could've beached their boat and we would not have known they had come ashore.

We came close enough to see four men dressed like pirates jumping off the tender, and as each man had a rope around his wrist and was pulling the small craft ashore, the deputy and I each shot one of them with our muskets. Now that the odds were even, we both drew our swords and rushed the two remaining men. Unfortunately, one pirate had a pistol and shot the deputy in the chest. He screamed briefly and fell, blood gushing from his chest. He had no chance.

The man who had shot the deputy threw his gun down and reached for his sword, giving me enough time to run him through before he could pull it from its scabbard. But I had exposed myself and the remaining pirate was on me. I could see he was a teenager. I thought I was done for when I heard a holler from inside the tender: "Don't dare touch him, he's all mine."

The voice was one I knew well; the man lighted a torch and stepped down from the boat. If he charged with it, I'd be blinded and wouldn't have a chance.

I said, "Gerald, I should have known you were responsible for all that's been going on here." He said nothing, and I had to act fast or die. "A man with your guile shouldn't need an assistant in a fight, or fire."

"I agree," my brother said dryly. The young pirate was facing me with his sword drawn as Gerald walked behind him and sliced him with his sword from his head to the bottom of his trunk. The boy had the instinct to turn toward Gerald, and when he did, he took a slash to the neck that almost lopped off his head. Gerald tossed the torch into the sand.

"I thought you might like to see yourself die," he said.

I could see him clearly now in spite of the cap pulled down over part of his face.

Amidst the rising tide and the crash of water along the rocks, amidst the growing winds and the light rain that was painting our faces, we began.

I raised my sword, and as the steel of both blades clanged together, I said. "It's you who's been stalking me all these years. It's you who always had your hat pulled over your face. How long have you been doing this?"

"Long enough to watch you kiss the arse of your commander as your ship foundered with mine in the Indian Ocean." He thrust his sword at me and I blocked it. He lost his balance but caught himself and backed up before I could strike. "I really didn't think you would survive that battle. But I overestimated those children. I thought they would be better fighters. After all, anything would be better than coming back to the life I'd found them in. Dying was the best thing for them."

Our swords struck each other's again, and we engaged in a series of thrusts and defensive moves. Gerald was an adept swordsman, but I made a good stab at his left leg and put a sizeable gash in his thigh. He backed up and I saw him totter, almost falling on the torch. But it was a ruse, because as I stepped forward I felt the air from his blade as it flew by my face. The fight went on, and even though he was wounded, I didn't find I'd gained any purchase.

After several minutes of steady assaults, I backed away and asked, "Why did you do it?"

He placed his sword to his side, but I'd been tricked once and wasn't going to let it happen again. He apparently sensed I wouldn't be duped twice, because when I didn't react he raised his blade to me and said, "Ya little git. I hated you. Our father was a sniveling idiot, yet you idolized him--"

"That's not true, I ran away."

"I came back to see him after you'd left. He never excused me for leaving, but your running away was fine, ya git. I heard him telling people he hoped you'd find what you were looking for. Then you get involved with Bart and then Maria, so you did. You were the talk of London. And all he could do was brag about you."

He struck at me, but I dodged the swipe and his blade hit the sand. He caught his breath and said, "Ya git, every time I sent a boat against you, you defeated it. Fair enough. I was ready to forget about you. But then you also did the noble thing. You didn't just defeat the hijackers in France's waters, you took the daughter back to her father in Spain and refused to take credit for what you'd done. Yeah, I heard about that. You little git, you're a legend among saylors." He coughed and spit. "Ten years later, you're back in France and this time going up against some of the orneriest pains in the French arse. But you defeated them too, and with them, me. I wanted to beat you, to show you and everybody else that I was the one who deserved the glory, but you just kept besting me." He laughed, and the sound was full of evil. "One thing where we were even, though, while you kept gaining rank and prestige in the eyes of the nobility, I was gaining rank and prestige in the criminal world. I finally got ahead of you when I took your son and killed him. And, now, ya git, here we are."

I gasped for breath, incensed at his admission that he had killed James. I managed to snag the top of the cap he was wearing with the tip of my sword and pull if off. This time I gasped in horror. Gerald's left eye was missing, and he wore a long scar from his forehead to the middle of his cheek. Covering his face was as much to do with hiding his disfigurement as his identity.

"I suppose I'm also to be blamed for what happened to you?"

"Don't worry about me. Others got a lot worse than what I got, I can assure you." He swung his sword wildly at me, and I blocked it again. He was breathing hard now. "You've become quite good at defending yourself. Too bad you couldn't defend your own son."

Swords passed over our heads and around our backs, almost as if we were playing in the alley at home when we were little kids. Yet each of us knew it wasn't a child's game this time, but a deadly finale for one of us.

"Always the gentlemen, aren't you?" Gerald said. "Always doing other people's bidding? Not me. I do what I want, whenever I want, to whomever I want."

"You misjudge me, brother. I've never done other people's bidding. I've just done what I believed was the right thing to do. And what good are any of us if we can't help others in their moments of need?" Moving in the wet sand was giving my bad knee fits. I could sense my brother getting caught up in the conversation, and I needed him to lose his concentration and drop his guard for only a moment. If not, I'd be a goner, because I wouldn't be able to stand much longer.

"There you go again. Insufferably honorable. You married a princess. Maybe when I'm through with you, I'll take her just like I did James. And when I'm finished taking my pleasures from her, I'll cut our her guts and throw her into the ocean for the sharks, just like I did your boy."

That was all I could take. I reached down and picked up some sand with my free hand and threw it at Gerald's eye. It hit the mark. He swung his sword in a frenzy, and I dropped to the ground and rolled at his legs, forcing him backward and to the ground. I held my boot on the hand that was holding his sword, and with my tip touching his chest, I put all my weight on the hilt and pierced his heart with such force that I could feel the blade enter the sand under him. But after twice in battle thinking someone was dead who wasn't, I stabbed him in the heart again and again.

Exhausted, I knelt down and sobbed deeply. My brother had admitted killing my son and feeding him to the sharks. What did James ever do, Lord, to deserve this? How could anyone kill an innocent child? And especially a relative? I asked these questions over and over until dawn broke, and I faced the miserable task of going to the sheriff and then to Maria to tell her what I had just learned. But I was a coward and couldn't tell her, until all these many years later, that I have always known what had happened to James, and if had I gone after Gerald when I was in England, I might have saved our son.

– Mike Hartner –

Epilogue

They had watched my eldest brother, Walter, get married and have children. They'd watched as my other two brothers and my sister married and had families of their own. They'd watched the death of Don Castabel and Walter's ascending to the throne of the King of Spain by unanimous proclamation. They heard of Bart's death from Melanie. Then they heard of Melanie's death from Carlos. Time marched on.

But not far along in this march of time, and three years ago now, a great surprise astounded King Walter and Queen Maria.

Two days before my 40th birthday, a ship on which I was a passenger anchored in San Sebastian. I was the only person getting off there, and a couple of men from the crew brought me to the dock on the ship's tender.

I walked off the dock and studied the surroundings as I stepped onto the street. It took me a while to believe I was really back home after all these many years. I went by a tavern that had its sign almost worn away by the salt-sea air, appropriately called The Salty Dog. I found some fresh grass growing to the side of the building, and I kneeled down and kissed the soil, not caring in the least that it remained on my lips when I stood. All I cared about was being home again.

I strode to the sheriff's office in San Sebastian. I had long forgotten who was sheriff when I was stolen from my family by my uncle. I asked a deputy, "Where can I find Walter, husband of Maria?"

He scratched his head, and then said, "Walter's wife is not Maria, it's Christine... oh, you must be speaking of King Walter. He still resides and rules from the eastern part of Spain. You have business with the King, señor?"

"He's my father." I expected the deputy's incredulous look. "My name is James, and I was stolen by my uncle from a school here more than 30 years ago."

"Mother of God. So it is true. Everybody knows the story of King Walter and Queen Maria's son being taken. You are really him, señor?"

"I had a brother named after my father, and two other brothers, Juan and Pedro, who were alive when I was taken away. Are either of these people still in the area?" I could only hope.

"Sir, I am very sorry to say that Pedro died a long time ago in a carriage accident, but Juan lives in Don Castabel's old hacienda. The other brother, Walter, I think lives close to the King and Queen."

"Can I borrow a horse to ride out to the hacienda, if I still know how to get there?"

"Señor, if you are who you say you are, I will take you there myself."

I'd been away from the hacienda for so long that I didn't recognize much of it, and Juan was little more than a baby when Gerald took me, so I had a lot of explaining to do to get him to believe me. I don't know what it was, but I said something about our mother that caused Juan to run to me and hug and kiss me. He didn't want to let go. He ran to get his wife and children, and two days later we left for King Walter and Queen Maria's official residence in northeast Spain. Juan explained to me that this was where his Uncle Pedro had lived when he and my grandfather ruled Spain jointly.

During the three-day trip to the royal residence, Juan and I talked about my mother and father more than anything, and he told me, "The only person who was hurt more by your disappearance than our mother was our father. He has always tortured himself wondering what happened to you. Mother let on once to me that he knew, but she said never to ask him about it, only that he was certain you had passed away."

"Then it's time to let him know his information was incorrect." I forced a laugh, trying to make light of this with Juan, but while I couldn't understand exactly what my father had gone through, I'd suffered my own hell because of Gerald.

***

When we arrived at the royal residence, we were stopped by several guards. However, the sergeant-at-arms recognized Juan and we were granted admission onto the grounds.

Juan found the majordomo, and he showed us to my father's office. I stood directly behind Juan as he said, "Hello, Father."

Walter set down some papers he was reading. "Juan, my son, how good to see you. Your mother and I didn't know you were coming. What brings you here?" His face turned serious and he started to rise from his chair. "Is something wrong?"

"Father, nothing is wrong. But you better stay seated, because I have someone with me who I think you'll be surprised to see."

I stepped from behind my brother and walked to the front of my father's desk. I don't know what he thought in the minute or so both of us looked at each other with our mouths open and tears in our eyes. For my part, I saw a small, elegant older man whom the years had treated well. He had wisps of gray hair on his head and temples and an undeniable strength of character that came through his gray eyes even though they were now filled with tears.

We reached for each other and I wouldn't let him get up from his chair. I don't know how long we'd held each other, but I tried to speak several times and couldn't. I guess he was having the same problem, because all I heard were intermittent whispers.

When I was finally able to compose myself, I said, "Father, nothing I'm going to say to you will make any sense, but I promise it's all the tru--"

"Thank you, God, thank you," my father shouted as he got down on his hands and knees. "My boy, James, is alive. Thank you, God, thank you, my boy, James, is alive." I got down on my knees with him, and we both hugged each other again as he kept repeating the phrase.

– I, Walter –

I heard my mother say as she walked in the room, "Walter, Juan is here, and he told me he has...oh, my God, it can't be!" She fainted, but Juan was right next to her and caught her. He got her to a chair and sent for some water, which he poured on his handkerchief and placed on her forehead.

She came around but started crying. My father got up and went to her, and when both of them had calmed down, he asked me to tell him everything.

"Are you sure?"

"Please, son, tell me every last detail."

"Father, the full story would take days, but after I was taken by Uncle Gerald, who couldn't tell me often enough that he was your brother, I was sold by him to a sadistic captain of a slave boat and taken to the country of Oman." My mother started to wail, and if she'd known what was done to me, she'd have every right scream even louder, but I wanted to soothe her, so I lied.

"The captain was a horrible man who I think was the devil's own brother, but many of the crew despised him and befriended me. The boat went back and forth from Goa to the Spice Islands for ten years, when the captain was given orders to pick up a load of some new spices I'd never heard of and take them to England.

We left Goa and entered the Arabian Sea. I remember the first day of this trip being exciting for me. We were headed for England, and I would be that much closer to coming home. I even thought about jumping ship if we were going by northern Spain. The problem was I had no way of knowing where I was on the ocean, so I had to forget that idea. But I was in my 20s now, and bigger and stronger than most of the saylors, as well as the captain.

A week into this voyage, we were at the mercy of a violent storm in the Arabian Sea. The foremast fell and hit the captain. When the storm blew over, those of the crew who were loyal to the captain attended to his wounds and repaired the ship. The rest of us planned our escape.

Six of us took a tender and left in the middle of the night, a lot farther from shore that we thought, and we had brought scant provisions. And instead of the winds taking us to the coastline, we were blown out to sea.

We had no idea of how close we were to land, and soon what little food and drinking water we had was depleted. But we were all free and not one of the six of us who'd escaped made the first complaint. However, after another day at sea, we were desperate for water.

And by the next day, some of the men were delirious. Two jumped into the ocean to try to swim to a shore they couldn't see, and another man took his knife and slit his own throat. I kept thinking, had we escaped to die like this?

The following morning, I was going in and out of consciousness when I heard a loud 'Ahoy.' Certain I was hallucinating, I saw a large ship right next to my tiny craft. A man jumped in, bringing a line over to me, and I was pulled aboard. It took me a couple of days to recover. When I asked about the other men who were with me, I was told the only person in my boat was me.

The ship was trading between India, Africa, and the Arabian Peninsula, so my hope of getting to England anytime soon was gone. Of course I didn't know it would take almost 20 more years before I'd finally get back to Spain.

The ship docked in Arabia, which was overrun with thugs and thieves. This part of the story would take days to tell, but I was lucky, and was able to work and make the money necessary for passage to see both of you. I am married now, and you have grandchildren, indeed, a couple of them are old enough to have children of their own."

My mother said, "There has to be so much more to tell."

"There is, but all that matters is I'm here now." My mother had gotten me talking and I hadn't even hugged and kissed her yet. I made up for it, and then promised I'd tell her the rest of the story later. I lied again. I had told her and my father the parts I wanted them to know, but they would never hear what really happened before I met my wife. Or even after.

***

My brother, Walter, and his family were only a few hours away and came late the next day and stayed for a week. Within a month, every member of my immediate family still living was either visiting me at the residence or had come and gone. My mother constantly asked me in front of the family to tell more about what I'd done while I was away, and I'd toss out bits of information, but never the real facts about what those ten years were like after I was sold into slavery.

My father's knowledge of the sea was so great, his eyes told me he knew I was holding back. But not once did he press me for answers. However, the first couple of months we were together, he kept asking me for forgiveness. I told him he was being silly, yet he'd become teary-eyed and tell me if he had protected me better, none of it would've happened. Happily, as time went by, he quit blaming himself as much, and we really did have the chance to enjoy each other's company without any pressure.

But five months after the joy of my return, while we were all in the main living quarters and laughing at something my mother had said, his face turned ashen and he became ill. Two days later, he was dead.

Prince Walter, my brother, became King, and he would be a good one. Less than one year later, our mother, Maria, died of a broken heart from losing my father. Her last words were, "I'm coming, Walter. I love you."

My father did write one final missive, according to my mother, just before he died, and I produce it here:

"Forgive me, Father, for I have sinned. To not know about your own family is a shame that nobody should ever have to live with. But the ultimate shame is killing your own kin. And now I know I've been responsible for killing Gerald, my brother by blood, by my own hand. I always justified this because of his admission of killing James. Now I find he didn't. Why would he admit to doing something so horrible, when it was false? Something he had to expect would get him killed? I've lead an honorable life. Why, then, was I the one You picked to kill my own brother? Perhaps, when I join You shortly, You will explain it to me."

It is I, James, who now bundles all of these pages together and presents to you the story of my father. In my opinion, he was a great man, and no other I have ever met could hold a candle to him. May he forever rest in peace, and may all remember him with deepest fondness. He gave freely of himself so that others would not have to, and he always honored friendship.

His epitaph reads: "Here lies a man who lived and loved fully. We are all better for his presence in our lives. September 2, 1588- May 24, 1656"

– I, Walter –

– Mike Hartner –